“You have spoke **d.**
“What did he tel

“Nothing.”

“Then you know as much as I.” Suddenly she was tired of the pretense. “I have no idea who my mother or father was. I am accepted in Bath because the Pridhams are rich and claim me as their kin, but I am not considered a suitable match...for anyone. You would be advised to stay away from me.”

“Why? I am responsible to no one for my actions. If I ride beside you it is because I want to do so. I enjoy the company and conversation of an intelligent woman. Many men do, you know, Miss Fairchild.”

She stared straight ahead, blinking away a sudden rush of tears.

“Now, what have I said to make you cry?”

“Why, nothing. I am merely being foolish.”

She forced a smile. Tristan’s words confirmed her fears. She had read of girls being educated to a high standard and given all the accomplishments to amuse a rich and powerful man. Not with the aim of becoming his wife, but his courtesan.

Author Note

Genealogy is very popular at the moment. Many of us are keen to learn more about our history, who we are, where we came from. Today we can even find out most of this information without ever leaving the house. For a small fee we can delve into the records online and even take a DNA test to discover more about our ancestors. For a young lady in Regency England, things were much more difficult.

At the start of this story Natalya, "the mysterious Miss Fairchild," knows nothing about her parents and her questions are met with silence. Growing up, her fertile imagination has imagined all kinds of scenarios, but as she nears her twenty-first birthday, she has no idea if she is the daughter of a countess or a courtesan and it begins to worry her. Because until she knows about her past, she can make no decisions about her future.

I hope you will enjoy Natalya's journey, with its twists and turns. It was a joy to write, and I admit to giving a little sigh of satisfaction when she finally discovers who she is, what she is and, more important, what she wants.

Happy reading!

SARAH MALLORY

The Mysterious Miss Fairchild

If you purchased this book without a cover you should be aware that this book is stolen property. It was reported as "unsold and destroyed" to the publisher, and neither the author nor the publisher has received any payment for this "stripped book."

HARLEQUIN®
HISTORICAL™

ISBN-13: 978-1-335-50548-4

Recycling programs for this product may not exist in your area.

The Mysterious Miss Fairchild

Copyright © 2020 by Sarah Mallory

All rights reserved. No part of this book may be used or reproduced in any manner whatsoever without written permission except in the case of brief quotations embodied in critical articles and reviews.

This is a work of fiction. Names, characters, places and incidents are either the product of the author's imagination or are used fictitiously. Any resemblance to actual persons, living or dead, businesses, companies, events or locales is entirely coincidental.

This edition published by arrangement with Harlequin Books S.A.

For questions and comments about the quality of this book, please contact us at CustomerService@Harlequin.com.

Harlequin Enterprises ULC
22 Adelaide St. West, 40th Floor
Toronto, Ontario M5H 4E3, Canada
www.Harlequin.com

Printed in U.S.A.

Sarah Mallory grew up in the West Country, England, telling stories. She moved to Yorkshire with her young family, but after nearly thirty years living in a farmhouse on the Pennines, she has now moved to live by the sea in Scotland. Sarah is an award-winning novelist with more than twenty books published by Harlequin Historical. She loves to hear from readers; you can reach her via her website at sarahmallory.com.

Books by Sarah Mallory

Harlequin Historical

The Scarlet Gown
Never Trust a Rebel
The Duke's Secret Heir
Pursued for the Viscount's Vengeance
His Countess for a Week
The Mysterious Miss Fairchild

Saved from Disgrace

The Ton's Most Notorious Rake
Beauty and the Brooding Lord
The Highborn Housekeeper

The Infamous Arrandales

The Chaperon's Seduction
Temptation of a Governess
Return of the Runaway
The Outcast's Redemption

Brides of Waterloo

A Lady for Lord Randall

Visit the Author Profile page
at Harlequin.com for more titles.

For my family. All of them.
Wherever they are.

Chapter One

'Tristan, I want to take a wife!'

Tristan Quintrell, Lord Dalmorren, paused a moment before replying to the young man standing on the other side of the desk.

'Well, that has surprised me,' he said at last. 'I knew you wanted *something*, Freddie, but I thought you needed me to bail you out.'

'Good God, no!' Young Mr Erwin looked aggrieved at the suggestion. 'I ain't always in dun territory, you know.'

'Forgive me,' murmured his host drily, 'but it has been the reason for all your other visits to Dalmorren this past year.'

The young man flushed slightly. 'Well, a fellow has to kick up a bit of a dust when he is first on the town, you know. And besides, you told me to come to you rather than Mama if I needed funds. But that's not why I am here, Tristan. I am in love!'

This statement, delivered in ecstatic accents, did not

impress his host. It was on the tip of Tristan's tongue
to retort that, having not yet reached one-and-twenty,
Freddie would fall in and out of love a dozen times before settling down, but he held back. The glowing look
in the young man's eyes and his beatific smile persuaded him that Freddie was well and truly smitten.

A mere eight years separated the two men. Freddie
was the son of Tristan's sister. She was sixteen years
older than he and his only remaining sibling, the others having failed to survive beyond the nursery years.
Her late spouse had taken the precaution of making his
brother-in-law joint guardian of his only child. Tristan
had barely reached his majority when his own father
died and that circumstance, together with the responsibility for his widowed sister and her son three years
later, had weighed heavily upon the young Lord Dalmorren, giving him a maturity well beyond his years.
He therefore did not mock Freddie for his infatuation.
Instead he got up from his desk and walked across his
study to the side table, where he poured two glasses
of Madeira.

'Here.' He handed one to Freddie. 'I think you had
best sit down and tell me all about it.'

The boy needed no second bidding. He pulled a chair
close to the desk and sat down, saying eagerly, 'We met
in Bath, in February. Do you recall I told you I was
going there with Gore Conyer? His family lives there.
I never expected to like the place above half, but then
I saw *Her.*'

'And does the lady have a name?'

Freddie put down his glass and clasped his hands

together. He said ecstatically. 'Miss Fairchild, but she allows me to call her Lya!'

'Leah, the name of Jacob's wife, in the Bible?' Tristan raised an eyebrow and said drily, 'I believe that means weary, in Hebrew.'

Freddie shook his head, saying impatiently, 'No, no, that's not it at all. Quite absurd. Her name is Natalya, but those close to her use the shortened form.' His face relaxed into another blissful smile. 'Lya.'

With a great effort of will Tristan forbore to tease him. 'You had best tell me where it was you first saw the lady.'

'It was just as we were leaving the theatre. Gore's parents had hired a box for us to see *Macbeth*. I am not a lover of Shakespeare, but it would have been churlish not to go. At the end, Gore and I waited in the foyer for Mr and Mrs Conyer to join us. They know everyone in Bath, you see, and it took them an age to make their way to the door. But that's by the bye! I happened to look round and there she was, making her way out of the theatre with an old lady wearing the most outmoded fashions!'

He noted Tristan's look of surprise and laughed. 'No, it wasn't *Natalya* in the odd clothes. She was looking very elegant in cream muslin, but her companion was dressed in the most shocking bright green creation and a headpiece bedecked with any number of feathers and ribbons. *That's* what attracted my attention, to begin with, until I saw Miss Fairchild. Our eyes met and… that was it. I knew I was in love—' He broke off and gave a loud sigh. 'Oh, Tristan, if you could only have been there.'

'I am glad I was not,' retorted his uncle, grimacing. 'I think I might have been very unwell!'

Freddie waved this aside. 'I mean I wish you could have seen her. Then you would understand. She is the most beautiful creature! Face and figure quite perfect. Dark hair, coal-black eyes, an ivory complexion— exquisite!'

'So what did you do?'

'What could I do? I touched my hat as she went past.'

'You disappoint me. I thought you would have immediately stepped up and demanded an introduction.'

'If only I could have done so! Good God, Tris, I am not so lost to all good manners, you know. As it happens, it was a good thing I didn't jump in. Mrs Conyer told me the old lady is Mrs Ancrum, one of Bath's most respected residents and a stickler for propriety. Fortunately, the Conyers are acquainted with her and they presented me when we…er…happened to meet in the Pump Room.'

Tristan felt a smile tugging at his lips. 'Goodness me. Shakespeare, the Pump Room—you grow old before your time, Nevvy.'

Freddie grinned. 'I am merely getting in practice for when I have to take you there, my aged guardian! But enough funning.' He put down his empty glass and leaned forward, fixing Tristan with his trusting blue eyes. 'Tris, I am serious about this, I want to make her an offer, but I need to make sure I have your permission, first.'

'And your mother's agreement. She is your guardian, too, remember.'

'Yes, yes, but Mama will not be a problem. She would never deny me my happiness. But that is not the only thing, I do not gain control of my inheritance until I reach five-and-twenty, so, until that time, I shall need an increase in my allowance, if I am to set up my own establishment.'

'Naturally,' murmured Tristan. 'What do we know of Miss Fairchild, save that she is the most beautiful female you have ever clapped eyes on? What relation is she to this Mrs Ancrum?'

'None. Natalya is an orphan. She lives in Sydney Place with her aunt and uncle. Mr and Mrs Pridham. They live very quietly, but they are perfectly respectable. And you are not to be thinking they have been putting Natalya in my way. Quite the opposite, in fact. She is closely chaperoned whenever she goes abroad, at balls she is permitted no more than two dances with any gentleman, and whenever I have called at the house Mrs Pridham ensures we are never alone. They never give one the least encouragement.' His cheerful, open countenance clouded slightly. 'To be frank, they are downright discouraging! That is why I want to make sure I have your blessing before I proceed.'

'And have you mentioned it to your mother?'

'Not yet. She has been in London with Grandmama, did you know?'

'Yes. She wrote to tell me she had watched the procession of King Louis from Hyde Park to Grillon's.' Tristan's mouth turned down. 'I have no doubt the crowds will be even worse when the rest of the Allied Sovereigns arrive in June.'

Freddie waved this aside as an irrelevance. 'She should be back at Frimley any day now, so I am on my way there to see her.' He gave Tristan a boyish smile. 'I thought I would stop off first and talk to you. I know that if you do not object, Mama will be happy.'

'And how long do you plan to remain at Frimley?'

'Oh, a week, perhaps two.' He added, shyly, 'I thought, when I return to Bath, I might take with me an invitation from Mama for Natalya to visit her at Frimley.'

'I see.'

Tristan sat back and sipped his wine, digesting all he had heard. He was loath to dash Freddie's hopes, but he was sure that his sister Katherine would be aghast at the idea of her only son taking a bride about whom they knew nothing.

He said, 'I think it behoves us to find out a little more about the lady before you ask my sister for her blessing.'

'Pridham is a gentleman and Lya is accepted everywhere in Bath. I cannot see that anything else is important.'

'You might not, but you may be damned sure your mother will! What do you know of Miss Fairchild's parents, or her fortune?'

Freddie jumped to his feet, a mutinous look on his face.

'Are you forbidding the banns, Tristan? Because, by heaven, if you are—'

'Oh, sit down, you young hothead, I am not forbidding anything, but your mother will need to be re-assured before she will give her permission to your forming an attachment at your age.'

'But she will come around to it, once she knows Natalya.'

'I am sure she will, but in the meantime, she could make things very uncomfortable for the lady.'

'Aye, so she could. Hell and damnation, Tristan, I have already written to Mama and told her I am com-ing to stay!'

'Well, that need not change. She will be delighted to see you, I am sure. Only do not mention Miss Fair-child. At least not until I have made a few enquiries of my own.'

'Oh?' Freddie looked suspicious. 'How are you going to do that?'

'By going to Bath, what else?' Tristan grinned. 'At my advanced age, it might benefit me to…er…take the waters.'

'Oh, oh, *devil take it*!'

The pianoforte resounded with an inharmonious dis-cord as Natalya slammed her fingers down upon the keys. It expressed her mood perfectly, but she felt guilty for her outburst and immediately glanced around to make sure she was alone.

She took a deep breath. There was no point in taking her frustration out on the poor instrument. The piece was well within her ability, but she had not touched the pianoforte all week, that was the simple truth. She was tired of spending her time at her studies when other young ladies were out riding and walking and sallying forth for picnics. True, very few of her aunt and uncle's acquaintances invited her to join such outings—with the exception of the Grishams, most families in Bath kept their distance—but even when she *was* invited, the Pridhams often refused, saying her studies were more important. Why, it was only this year that she had been allowed to attend the balls at the Assembly Rooms!

Uncle Pridham had assured her everything would change in June, when she reached one-and-twenty, but until then the strict regime of study must be maintained. She could hardly refuse to see the tutors employed by her uncle, but she could spend her time reading or sketching rather than practising at the pianoforte. It was a tiny act of rebellion and she was not particularly proud of it. She was grateful for her aunt and uncle's efforts on her behalf, but sometimes she wished they would not try quite so hard.

There was a knock at the door and the music teacher was shown in. Natalya turned to him with an apologetic smile.

'I fear you are going to be very disappointed with me this week, Mr Spark…'

Later, at the Assembly Rooms, Natalya sought out her friend Miss Grisham, a lively redhead in a gown of lemon muslin. She sat down beside her with an exaggerated sigh.

'I am late, Jane, I know it. Pray do not scold me, I have had the…the *devil* of a day. Aggie is at outs with me because I tore my new muslin gown and forgot to tell her and there is nothing more uncomfortable than a maid's sulks, you know. Then I had to endure two hours of Italian conversation and, to cap it all, Mr Spark read me a lecture because I had not perfected Mr Handel's *Sarabande*.'

'Much you care for that,' replied her friend, smiling. 'But what was it you said about Italian, Lya—has Mr Pridham managed to find you a new teacher?'

'Yes, we had our first lesson this morning. Although I wonder my uncle should put himself to the trouble. It is little more than a month now until I come of age and he knows I intend to give up my studies then.'

'And is he young and handsome, this new teacher?' Jane asked her.

'He is neither of those things.' Natalya shuddered. 'He is very short and very dark, with lascivious eyes and a wet mouth. I fear, if he had the opportunity, the *signor* would try to make love to me and I should be obliged to stab him with my hatpin. Thankfully, my aunt insists I am *never* alone with any member of the male sex.' She giggled. 'I know I have complained about that in the past, but in this instance, I am extremely grateful.'

'And so you should be, Lya,' replied her friend. 'The Pridhams take extremely good care of you, you know.'

'Yes, I do know. I am aware how fortunate I am to have such caring guardians, but it is all so, so *stifling*!' She sighed. 'I only wish I knew what they mean by it all.'

'To keep you safe, of course. To protect your reputation and wrap you in a positive *cloud* of respectability in order that you can make a most advantageous marriage!'

Natalya shook her head, all desire to laugh gone. 'I do not think that can be the case. Else why did they discourage Lord Austwick from making me an offer? He is as rich as Croesus and an earl to boot. And why am I to have all these extra lessons? Music, French and Italian. Russian history, to say nothing of the geometry and philosophy and all the other things I studied while at school! No woman is educated to this level merely to become a *wife*!'

Jane thought that a very good joke and she said nothing more, knowing her friend would be scandalised if she knew Natalya was in earnest. The disadvantage of receiving such an extensive education was that one learned a great many things that were usually kept hidden from young ladies. At school, Natalya's tutors had been happy to feed her voracious reading habits, with the result that she knew a great deal more about the ways of the world, including the fact that many otherwise respectable gentlemen had liaisons with women other than their wives.

Marriage was a commercial matter; mistresses were for enjoyment. Many men set up a mistress and kept her in luxury, merely to amuse and entertain them. At the select and very expensive educational establishment where she had spent her childhood, several girls were openly acknowledged as the children of one or more noble parents, but born out of wedlock.

Natalya suspected she was the product of such a liaison, even though no one had ever spoken of it. With the happy optimism of youth, she had not thought too deeply about it, until the past two years, when she had begun to attend balls and assemblies.

'You must learn how to go on in society,' Mr Pridham had told her. 'You need to know how to dance and converse and to be at ease in company.'

And she *had* learned. She enjoyed the company and the dancing, but it was not long before she realised she was different. She became painfully aware that, with the exception of elderly Mrs Ancrum and the Grishams, she was tolerated, rather than widely accepted by the high sticklers of Bath society. That did not discompose her, neither did the lack of friends worry her, for she was far too busy to feel lonely, but whereas most chaperons actively encouraged their charges to attract the attentions of eligible gentlemen, the Pridhams went out of their way to keep potential suitors at bay. She wondered why that should be and just what her aunt and uncle had planned for her.

Her thoughts were interrupted when Mrs Grisham came up to them in a rustle of silken skirts.

'Now, now, girls, what are you doing, sitting here with your heads together? That is no way to attract dancing partners! Jane, here is Mr Carrey come to beg the pleasure of your company for the next dance.' She gestured to the young man beside her, who flushed slightly.

'Yes, indeed, Miss Grisham, if you would do me the honour?'

'Off you go now, Jane, and I shall sit here and keep Miss Fairchild company.' With a good-natured laugh she took her daughter's place beside Natalya and patted her hand. 'Well, well, my dear, 'tis a sad crush in here tonight, and no mistake, but if you sit up straight, my dear, and smile, I am sure you will not have to wait long for a partner. I do not know what Alice Pridham is doing, letting you skulk in a corner like this.'

'My aunt is with her friends, ma'am, and I slipped away to talk to Jane.'

Mrs Grisham tutted. 'That is no way to get yourself noticed.'

'Really, ma'am, I am very happy to sit here.'

'Nonsense. A young thing like you should be on the dance floor and giving us the pleasure of seeing you tripping about!' She glanced up and ended with a note of satisfaction, 'And we shall not have to wait much longer for that pleasure, I fancy!'

Mr Pridham was approaching, accompanied by a stranger whose appearance was drawing admiring glances from the ladies as he crossed the room. If the gentleman was aware of the stir he was creating, he showed no sign of it. His style was not flamboyant, but he had an understated elegance, from his light brown hair, cut fashionably short and gleaming in the candle-light, to the toes of his dancing shoes. Natalya could find no fault with his appearance. His dark coat fitted without a crease across his broad shoulders, the white waistcoat was buttoned smoothly over his flat stomach while tight breeches and silk stockings clung to long, powerful legs.

Closer inspection showed his lean countenance was undeniably handsome but he was not smiling and his dark brows were drawn together, as if he was here for duty rather than pleasure. Natalya noticed, too, that her uncle was behaving oddly. Never a genial man, he was decidedly ill at ease as he performed the introductions.

'Natalya, my dear. Lord Dalmorren is wishful to dance with you.'

Dalmorren. She had heard the name before, but where? She looked again at his countenance. He looked familiar, but it was a fleeting impression and she dismissed it as a mere fancy.

The gentleman bowed. 'I would be honoured if you would stand up with me, Miss Fairchild.'

Natalya thought his satin waistcoat and the intricately tied cravat hinted at a man of fashion. A man of ease and pleasure. Yet his voice was as serious as his demeanour and she could read nothing from his hard, slate-grey eyes. She was even more intrigued.

With a faint smile of acceptance, she rose and placed her fingers on his proffered arm. The fine wool sleeve was soft as silk to the touch, but beneath she was aware of iron hard muscle. Perhaps he was a sportsman, more at home in the saddle than the ballroom. That might account for his rather cold manner. However, when they began to dance, his lithe grace sent a frisson of pleasure running through her and Natalya's heart gave a little skip. She spent most of her time dancing with awkward young men or elderly friends of the Pridhams. It was pleasant, for once, to have such an accomplished partner. Her curiosity in the man grew.

'Are you newly come to Bath, my lord?' she ventured.

'I arrived in Bath two days ago.'

His reply was curt, but she excused him since the movement of the dance was about to separate them. When they came back together, she tried again.

'You are perhaps an acquaintance of my uncle?'

'I never met him before in my life.' Natalya looked at him in surprise and he continued, 'The Master of Ceremonies introduced us. I wanted to dance with you, you see.'

He smiled suddenly and she almost missed a step. Quickly she dragged her gaze away from him. She felt winded by the effect that smile had upon her. It transformed his face, warming his eyes, inviting her to smile back. It was a new experience for Natalya. She was at once frightened and excited. Exhilarated. Heavens, so this was the sensation that changed females from rational beings into simpering, giggling idiots. She had always scoffed when other girls had spoken of it and now here she was, blushing and tongue-tied merely because a man had smiled at her.

'How, how flattering,' was all she could manage to utter.

Thankfully, they separated again and she assumed what she hoped was a look of polite enjoyment. It was not only to cover her confusion. Aunt and Uncle Pridham did not like her to show interest in any gentleman and they would be closely watching her progress with Lord Dalmorren.

After two dances, Tristan led his partner off the floor, wondering what Freddie saw in Miss Natalya Fairchild. True, she danced gracefully and she had a dark beauty, no doubt about it. She was a little taller than average and her figure was good. Her complexion was flawless and the hair piled upon her head shone like a raven's wing. Freddie was wrong about her eyes, though, he thought now. They were not black, but a deep, deep brown.

But for all that she lacked personality. She had made nothing but commonplace utterances during their time together. No different from the debutantes one came across in town. Tristan began to feel the familiar ennui creeping over him. In other circumstances he would bow, walk away and forget the chit, but Freddie had declared this was the woman he wanted to marry and, if he was to blurt this out to his doting mother, Katherine would immediately apply to Tristan as joint guardian for advice. Clearly, then, he must discover something he could pass on.

He glanced now at the young lady on his arm, trying to be charitable. Perhaps she was shy. When he had observed her from across the room she had looked animated enough, talking and laughing with her friend, but it was possible she was overawed by the occasion and needed to grow a little accustomed to his presence.

'Perhaps, Miss Fairchild, you would do me the honour of standing up with me again before the end of the evening.'

'Alas, my lord, that is not possible. My aunt and uncle do not allow me more than two dances with anyone.'

'I see. Very commendable. Then I shall call upon you in the morning.'

She showed no sign of being flattered by his attentions. There were no maidenly blushes, merely a slight inclination of the head and a cool response.

'Mrs Pridham will be delighted to see you, I am sure, but you will not find me at home. I shall be at my drawing lesson tomorrow morning.'

'Later in the day, then.'

'I shall be studying astronomy.'

'Wednesday?'

'I have dancing lessons in the morning and botany in the afternoon. And Thursday,' she added, after an infinitesimal pause, 'I study politics, currently Russia's part in the recent wars.'

Tristan bit back an oath, but not quite quickly enough, and she gave a choke of laughter.

'Oh, dear! Pray do not take it personally, my lord. I am telling you nothing but the truth. My days are indeed very busy.'

'If you are trying to discourage me, Miss Fairchild, you are succeeding admirably!'

'I am? Oh, dear. I am speaking no more than the truth. My aunt and uncle are eager that I should continue to improve my mind. I play chess regularly, too.' She looked up at him, dispelling any notion that she was shy. 'Does the idea of an educated female frighten you, my lord?'

Her face was alive with mischief and he felt a sudden drumbeat of alarm.

By heaven, that look is enchanting! It is no wonder Freddie is smitten.

He wanted to respond, to continue the conversation, but Mrs Pridham came bustling up.

'Ah, Natalya. There you are, my dear!'

He saw the laughter fade from those dark eyes as her aunt took her arm.

'Have you forgotten this next dance is promised to Lord Fossbridge?' Mrs Pridham turned to Tristan, bestowing on him a smile that was somewhat forced. 'I am sorry I must carry her away, my lord, but you understand how it is.'

In his mind he quickly sorted through the persons Mr King had presented to him that evening. If he remembered correctly, Fossbridge was an aged fellow, old enough to be Natalya's grandfather. Certainly not his rival. Or rather, not Freddie's rival, he corrected himself. *His* interest in Miss Fairchild was purely on behalf of his nephew.

He bowed. 'I understand perfectly, ma'am. However...' Mrs Pridham halted and gave him an enquiring look '... Miss Fairchild has been telling me of her interest in astronomy. May I be so bold as to invite you both—and Mr Pridham, naturally—to join me as my guests at Mr Walker's lecture this Friday? It is to be held at the Exhibition Rooms in Bond Street. As you know, ma'am, I am newly arrived in Bath and to attend such an event alone...'

He let the words hang, his tone of voice and expression inviting her to sympathise with him. As he had hoped, Mrs Pridham was flustered, torn between a flat refusal and wanting to oblige him.

'Why—why, that is very kind of you, my lord. We had not thought. That is—'

Tristan cut in ruthlessly. 'I am delighted that you

have accepted, ma'am, thank you. I shall call at Sydney Place in good time to convey you all to the lecture.'

With a smile and a bow, he walked away before she could say more. Now all he had to do was to recall where the devil he had seen the advertisement for the lecture and obtain tickets, which at this late stage might require him to pay out an extortionate amount to persuade someone to give up their seats. He would also need to hire a carriage grand enough and large enough to convey them all to the Exhibition Rooms. The Dalmorren travelling chaise would not do at all, since it could not accommodate more than two persons.

His eyes narrowed slightly and he muttered grimly, 'I hope you appreciate what I am doing for you, Freddie. And I hope she is worth it!'

Chapter Two

On Friday evening, Natalya dutifully made her way to her aunt's bedchamber at the front of the house for approval. She stood for a moment, regarding herself in the cheval mirror, then turned about so quickly that the skirts of her pink muslin flew out like an umbrella.

'Well, Aunt, will I do?'

She threw a slightly defiant look at Mrs Pridham, who was watching her with a critical eye.

'Very pretty, my dear,' she said at last.

Natalya put a hand to the lace shawl that covered her shoulders.

'Do I really need to wear a fichu? The neckline is very modest.'

'Your uncle and I would prefer you not to draw the attention of all and sundry tonight.'

'Really, Aunt, I am at a loss to know why you buy me fashionable gowns, if you do not wish me to attract attention.'

'You need to learn all the graces, my dear, and that includes how to dress to advantage.'

'But why, ma'am?' Natalya pressed her. 'For what role am I being prepared?'

'Why, to be a lady, my dear, what else?' Her aunt's eyes slid away from Natalya's questioning look. 'Goodness, is that the time? Lord Dalmorren will be here soon and I have not yet finished my preparations. Oh, well, Mr Pridham must entertain him, when he comes!'

'I could go down, Aunt, since I am ready.' Natalya knew her suggestion would be rejected, but she made it all the same.

'Without a chaperon? Good heavens, no.'

'But why not? He can hardly seduce me in your drawing room, with servants just outside the door.'

'This is no time for frivolity, Natalya,' was the crisp reply. 'A young lady can never be too careful about her reputation, especially one in your situation. Now, enough chattering. Off you go to your room and let me get on.'

Natalya left her, but instead of returning to her room she paused on the landing, staring out of the window, across the street towards the lush green of Sydney Gardens. It made no sense. Her education had been equal, if not better than most young men would receive, Bath's finest modistes supplied her gowns with no thought to the cost, but she could not see that the purpose of this was to find her a husband.

When she had left school and joined the Pridhams in Bath she had been seventeen years old, eager and excited about the future. She had asked them if she was to have a London Season, only to be told that it was not necessary. They had given no reason, merely told her that Bath held sufficient amusements. Amusements, yes, but to what end? She had spent the last four years in Bath and any gentleman who showed the slightest interest in her was positively discouraged.

A movement caught her attention and she looked down as a large coach and four drew up at their door and Lord Dalmorren emerged. She smiled when she recalled how his invitation to them all to go to the astronomy lecture had taken Mrs Pridham by surprise. He had given her no time to utter a refusal and Natalya appreciated his ruthless tactics, but her smile faded as she watched him disappear into the house. It was not that she did not want to attend the lecture, but she remembered how she had reacted to His Lordship's attentions on the dance floor. How his smile had caused her heart to behave most alarmingly. It would be difficult to relax and enjoy herself when she knew her aunt and uncle would be watching and listening for the slightest hint of a flirtation between herself and Lord Dalmorren.

As instructed, Natalya waited until the Pridhams had both gone down to the drawing room before she made her appearance. Her uncle was talking with Lord Dalmorren, who did no more than incline his head in greeting when Natalya came in. Almost immediately Mrs Pridham suggested they should be going, saying she would not want to keep His Lordship's horses standing any longer than necessary in such a cold wind.

Lord Dalmorren handed the ladies into the waiting

carriage with polite civility. He said nothing on the short journey to Bond Street and when they reached the Exhibition Rooms, he took a seat at the end of the row, next to Mr Pridham. Natalya should have felt relieved that he had shown no interest in her at all. Instead she felt a vague disappointment. But *why* should she be disappointed? She had done nothing to ingratiate herself with him at the Assembly Rooms. Why, he had even suggested that she was trying to discourage him! She peeped along the row. He was deep in conversation with her uncle. Perhaps he really did want company this evening, yet she found it difficult to believe that a gentleman as self-assured as His Lordship would be ill at ease in attending a lecture alone. He was an *ainigma*, as her Greek tutor used to say.

At the interval everyone moved into the next room, where refreshments were set out on a long table. There were no seats and in the crowded room the Pridhams were soon drawn into conversation with an acquaintance, leaving Natalya to drink her tea with Lord Dalmorren. Good manners dictated that they should not stand in silence.

'It is certainly very full tonight,' she remarked, looking about her. 'There is not a seat to be had. You were fortunate to obtain four tickets at such short notice, my lord. I understand they were in great demand.'

'I was, wasn't I?'

She was not fooled by his bland reply and could not resist asking him if he had been obliged to purchase them from other ticket holders.

'Now why should I want to go to so much trouble?'

'That I do not know,' she said, seriously considering the question. 'I cannot think you are trying to fix your interest with me.' She met his eyes and flushed a little. 'Pray do not think this is any false modesty on my part, I am aware I did not particularly *shine* at the Upper Rooms on Monday and I do not have the advantages of birth or a fortune to recommend me.'

'No, you do not.'

She gave an uncertain laugh. 'Goodness, that is blunt speaking indeed. You are nothing if not honest, my lord!'

'I beg your pardon, but from the little I know of you I believe you prefer honesty, so I am compelled to say that I came to Bath for the sole purpose of seeking you out, after a young relative of mine mentioned you to me. Frederick Erwin.'

'Oh, Mr Erwin!' Natalya recalled now where she had heard Lord Dalmorren's name before. It explained that feeling of recognition, too. Freddie's eyes were more blue than grey and his hair much fairer, but there was a definite similarity between the two men. She smiled. 'Ah, yes. I hope he is well?'

'Very well. He is paying a visit to his mother at present. In Surrey.'

'Oh. I thought he had gone to town.'

'No, he came to Dalmorren to see me. He is my ward, you see. His mother and I are joint guardians of his inheritance which, by the bye, will not be under his control for another four years.'

Understanding dawned and, with it, indignation. She

said, 'Are you telling me this in case I have…designs…
upon Freddie?'

She did not miss the faint look of surprise when she
said the name. Why should she not? She and Freddie
were friends, and it was His Lordship's mistake if he
thought it suggested they were anything more. How
dare he be so presumptuous!

'And do you?'

His words were a challenge and she felt a flash of
anger, but before she could respond Mrs Pridham was
at her side and she could do no more than send the odious man a glare of rebuke.

'People are beginning to return to their seats, Natalya. Shall we go in?'

There was no jockeying for position, but Natalya
could never afterwards explain how she found herself
sitting between Lord Dalmorren and the Pridhams.
A glance showed they were not pleased with the situation, but short of her aunt insisting they should exchange seats and causing the sort of disturbance they
abhorred, there was nothing to be done. Natalya put up
her chin and stared pointedly at the lectern, waiting for
the speaker to appear.

'To continue our conversation,' Lord Dalmorren
murmured, 'I was about to ask how well you know
my nephew.'

'Mr Erwin is a very charming gentleman. I would
like to think we are friends.'

She was about to add that they were nothing more

than friends, when her aunt's fan came down in a sharp tap on her arm.

'Enough talk now. Mr Walker is about to speak again.'

Natalya lapsed into silence. She fixed her attention upon the speaker, but the seats were very close and she was painfully aware of Lord Dalmorren beside her. The slightest move and her shoulder brushed his sleeve. She could not help glancing at his muscular thigh, only inches from her own. The man was like a magnet, drawing her closer, and it was an effort not to lean against him. The idea was unsettling. Disturbing. It was also very annoying, because Natalya considered herself an intelligent, sensible female. She was not given to fanciful ideas and had often mocked her schoolfriends when they sighed and pined over some man.

With great determination she dragged her attention back to Mr Walker and tried to concentrate upon his talk. The only stars that interested her were in the night sky, not in her eyes!

Despite her best efforts, during the days that followed, Natalya could not forget Lord Dalmorren. She found herself thinking about him almost constantly. When someone mentioned his name to the Pridhams as they came out from church, she strained her ears to listen. She learned the Dalmorrens were an ancient family and a rich one, so the Pridhams could not object to his lineage or his fortune. Why, then, were they so loath to pursue the acquaintance? Why were they keeping her a virtual prisoner?

Natalya had always been chaperoned, but for a whole week following Mr Walker's lecture her aunt or uncle insisted upon escorting her personally to and from her various lessons. Mr Pridham even decided they should forgo all evening engagements. It was thus over a week later that she and Lord Dalmorren met again.

It was the regular Monday ball at the Assembly Rooms and she spotted his tall figure across the room. She thought he might ignore her. After all, he had not called at the house and had made no attempt to see her since the lecture. He had thought she wanted to marry Freddie. Perhaps he had realised it was not the case and no longer had any interest in her.

Natalya's disappointment at that thought was severe. Not because she felt any particular liking for him, she told herself, but since Freddie Erwin had left Bath there were so few young gentlemen for her to dance with, certainly none as accomplished as Lord Dalmorren. That was all it was. A very natural wish to dance with someone who was neither a schoolboy nor an octogenarian.

Aunt Pridham pinched her arm. 'Lord Dalmorren is coming over,' she hissed. 'After accepting his invitation to Mr Walker's lecture, we could not refuse when he asked if he might dance with you. Goodness knows I suppose he must entertain himself somehow while he is in Bath, but *you will not encourage him*, Natalya, do you understand me?'

And there he was, standing before her, smiling and looking even more handsome than she remembered.

'This is our dance, I believe, Miss Fairchild.'

Her chin went up and the tiny spark of rebellion within flickered a little brighter. Why should she not encourage Lord Dalmorren? Why should she not enjoy a man's attentions, even a mild flirtation, if it were offered? What harm could there be in it?

Then he smiled and, when she felt the full force of his charm, all her rebellious spirit faded like mist before the sun. She was so nervous around this man she doubted if she would even be able to dance, let alone flirt with him!

Natalya took his arm and accompanied him to the dance floor, just as she had two weeks earlier. This time, however, she was aware that her pulse was beating a little faster and she was far more conscious of his presence. Just the touch of his hand made her jump. It was not merely her aunt and uncle's scrutiny that made her concentrate on her steps. She felt awkward, tongue-tied, as if she might burst into flames if she allowed herself to enjoy the dance. She kept her conversation to the mundane, giving little more than monosyllabic replies, and by the time he escorted her off the floor at the end of the dance she felt thoroughly wretched. Any liking he had for her would surely be at an end.

'And that is a good thing,' she told herself as she watched him walk away and solicit the hand of pretty, blonde-haired Verena Summerton for the next dance. 'Aunt and Uncle have told me he is only amusing himself, which I knew already. He as good as told me that he is in Bath to ascertain if I am a suitable bride for his nephew. No, my girl. You might find him charming, and amusing and fascinating, but you had much better stay away from him if you do not want to find yourself weeping into your pillow at nights!'

It was a noble resolve and Natalya found it quite easy to keep to it until the end of the evening. She had no partner for the last two dances and the Pridhams were signalling to her from across the room. She had just begun to make her way around the edge of the dance floor towards them when Lord Dalmorren stepped in front of her.

'Will you honour me, Miss Fairchild, by joining me for the next set?'

You have another chance. He wants to dance with you again!

She knew she should refuse, but the words would not come, for he was smiling down at her and all she could think of was how much she wanted to dance with him. Silently she gave him her hand and allowed him to guide her to the remaining space in one of the sets that was forming.

Natalya fixed her eyes on the top button of her partner's waistcoat, not daring to look at the Pridhams. They would be angry and she would have to endure a tremendous scold on the way home, but that was later. Now she was determined to enjoy herself. She would show him that she was no brainless ninny. She would impress him with her intelligence and wit. At least, she would if she could drag her gaze away from that waistcoat.

'I do not think I have ever known a lady so busy,' he remarked, as they waited for the music to begin. 'Your every waking hour appears to be occupied.'

'My aunt and uncle are anxious for me to improve myself by extensive study.'

'And consequently, you do not have a moment to yourself.'

'They are at pains to hire the very best tutors for me.' She added after a moment, 'Even my attendance at these assemblies is part of my education.'

'Is it, by heaven!'

'Why, yes. Every young lady needs to be able to dance.'

'Every young lady needs to be able to converse in a sensible manner,' he retorted.

That stung, all the more because she recognised the justice of it. Natalya threw him an angry look, but the dance had begun and she was obliged to hold her tongue as they stepped and turned and circled, but when the dance brought them back together, she immediately assured him that she could converse sensibly.

'Every attempt to talk to you at the Exhibition Rooms was frustrated by your aunt and uncle. How is an acquaintance to progress under such circumstances?'

Thank heavens they separated at that point, for Natalya felt her cheeks growing hot with a flush of quite irrational pleasure. Was it possible he still wanted to become better acquainted with her, despite her dismal attempts at conversation? The idea nagged at her as the dance progressed to its conclusion.

At that point she half-expected her uncle to come and drag her from the dance floor, but when that did not happen she stood, tongue-tied, waiting for the second dance to begin.

'I agree, a lecture is hardly the place for idle chatter,' Lord Dalmorren continued as if there had been no break in their conversation. 'However, discussion should follow, at some point, perhaps even debate, if the lecture was sufficiently interesting. Are you never allowed to speak to anyone?'

'Of course! I am not a prisoner.'

Even as she uttered the words, Natalya remembered how confined she had been this past week. She glanced across the room to where her aunt and uncle were standing. They were watching her with ill-concealed rage that she had disobeyed them. She knew she was kept very close, but that had never worried her before. Her friends had told her of flirtations involving stolen moments and secret assignations, away from the critical gaze of chaperons, but Natalya had never wished to slip off and meet someone.

Until now. The idea was unsettling, but it could not be ignored and she discovered that the small spark of rebellion had not quite been extinguished. When the music finally stopped and her partner reached for her hand to escort her off the floor, she drew a deep breath.

'Tomorrow is my art lesson,' she remarked. 'However, my tutor is gone to Bristol to visit his family and, if the good weather holds, I shall be walking to Beechen Cliff with Jane Grisham, to spend the day sketching vistas of the city.'

Heavens, what was she about? It was almost as if she was two people, one of them observing the other in horror. Even the sight of the Pridhams, who were watching their approach with angry impatience, could not stop her. She was shocked to hear herself continue with almost innocent nonchalance.

'Jane's maid will be with us, although the poor woman is always so tired after the steep ascent that she invariably falls asleep.'

'Is that so, Miss Fairchild?'

There was a note of teasing laughter in his voice, but Natalya dare not look up at him for fear she would flush scarlet. They were but a few steps away from the Pridhams. She released his arm and moved across to stand beside her aunt, who was tapping her foot angrily on the floor and directing a look at Lord Dalmorren that was positively glacial. Impervious to this cold reception, he exchanged a word or two with Mr Pridham, then, with a smile and a bow, he withdrew.

Natalya watched him walk away and could not decide whether she wanted to see him at Beechen Cliff in the morning and it was this conundrum, rather than the angry rebukes of her aunt and uncle, that resulted in a sleepless night.

Chapter Three

May had barely begun, but it was more like high summer, with the sun shining down from a cloudless sky when Tristan set off in the direction of Beechen Cliff. His conscience was far from easy as he ascended the steps leading up to the famous landmark. What in heaven's name was he doing, keeping an assignation with a young woman of whom he knew so little? It was not the actions of a gentleman. He argued that he owed it to Freddie to find out more about Miss Fairchild, since her guardians were playing their role with excessive zeal.

He frowned when he thought of the two weeks he had spent in Bath. Confound it, he should have asked Freddie how the devil he had managed to become sufficiently acquainted with Natalya Fairchild to fall in love. Had she made assignations with him, too?

He realised that he only had Natalya's word for it that she would be with friends. What if she was alone and this was some convoluted ploy to trap him into marriage? It would not be the first time some unscrupulous female had tried to snare him. It was one of the reasons he now spent so little time in London, where his bachelor status made him a target for every matchmaking parent. His lip curled. If that was indeed Miss Natalya Fairchild's intention then she would soon discover her mistake and it would prove conclusively that she was not a fit wife for Freddie.

When he eventually reached the top of the cliff, Tristan had to admit the climb was worth the effort. Whatever else occurred today he would remember this view of Bath. The city was spread out before him, the Abbey soaring majestically over the neighbouring buildings and the river twinkling, jewel-like, in the sun.

Soft voices and laughter caught his attention. A short distance away Natalya and her friend were sitting on the grass, sketchpads on their knees, while behind them, stretched out on the grass, was a buxom maidservant. The young ladies were wearing bonnets to protect their complexion from the sun and one of them had thoughtfully placed an open parasol to shade the maid's head as she slept.

It all looked very innocent and any casual observer would think him a gentleman out for a stroll who had come upon the group by pure chance. His mind was relieved on one point, she was accompanied, and there was a maid present, even if she was sleeping. Tristan stifled his conscience and approached.

'Good morning, Miss Grisham, Miss Fairchild.'

'Oh, Lord Dalmorren.' The note of innocent surprise in Natalya's voice did not fool him and neither, judging by the look of speculation on her face, did it deceive her companion, who looked up from her sketching to address him.

'Are you come to take in the view, my lord?'

'I am. It was recommended to me. Most strongly.' He smiled at Natalya and was rewarded by seeing her blush.

'Such a warm morning, is it not, my lord?' remarked Miss Grisham. 'Perhaps you would like to join us for a little while, I am sure you will wish to rest after your exertions.'

'Thank you, I will.' He sat down on the grass between them. 'But pray do not let me stop you working. I will just sit here and enjoy the...er...scenery.'

Miss Grisham giggled, but Natalya remained silent and became even more intent upon her drawing.

Great heaven, he thought in disgust. Did I just say that? I sound like an out-and-out scoundrel!

It was not his normal style at all. He lapsed into silence. After all, he had said he would not disturb them, had he not? For several minutes they remained with only the birdsong, the buzz of bees and the gentle snores of the maid to disturb them. Then Jane Grisham gathered up her sketchbook and pencils.

'I want to capture the view from another angle and that bush over there is blocking my view of the foreground.'

She went off to sit down at some distance away, on the far side of the sleeping maid, and Tristan berated himself for a fool. It was such an obvious ploy to leave him alone with Natalya. She must have planned this. Confound it, the little minx was a hardened flirt.

Then he caught sight of her face and changed his

mind. She was either a superb actress or she was as ill at ease as himself. His anger subsided and he gave a little inward shrug. He had wanted the opportunity to become better acquainted, so he had best get on with it.

He ventured a comment on the astronomy talk and was rewarded by an answer. He tried again and the conversation continued, a little uncertain at first, but gradually it became easier until they were chatting away with all the freedom of old friends. From astronomy they moved to history and politics, then by degrees to the recent war with Bonaparte. When she asked him if he would go to London for the forthcoming peace celebrations, Tristan grimaced.

'My mother and sister were in London recently and wrote to tell me the crowds were extraordinary. I much prefer the quiet of the country to such a spectacle.'

She chuckled. 'I believe the presence of the Allied Sovereigns in London will cause quite a stir.'

'Town will be as full as it can hold with crowds pushing and shoving and trying to catch a glimpse of the great men. Will you go?'

'No. I thought my uncle would wish to go. He has always been most interested in reports about the war, especially the Russian campaigns. He sent to London for newspapers, specifically to read about them. But he says we are to remain in Bath.'

'And are you sorry?'

She paused to consider before answering.

'I should enjoy the spectacle of the procession when they arrive from the Continent and to see these leaders that I have read so much about. It is a very special moment in history.' She was silent, her gaze wistful, then she shook her head and gave a little laugh. 'Not that I have any special reason to be there. I should only be adding to the crowds. So, no, on reflection, I shall not be sorry to remain here with my aunt and uncle.'

'Are the Pridhams the only family you have?' he asked her.

'They are my guardians,' she said carefully. 'I understand I am an orphan.'

Her choice of words intrigued him. He said, 'You do not know?'

'I do not. I know nothing of my parents.'

She was uneasy with his questioning and he said no more. Instead he let the quiet of the warm day settle around them. He watched as she plied her pencil with quick, deft strokes. When his eyes strayed to her profile, he thought that she herself made an attractive picture. That straight little nose, the dainty chin and the high cheekbones gave her face a beauty that would last well beyond her youth.

His lips quirked.

I have misjudged Freddie, he thought. The boy has shown good taste in choosing this lady as the object of his affections.

Natalya looked round. 'Something amuses you, my lord?'

He disclaimed quickly, saying, 'No, no, an old joke, merely.' He added, 'You draw very well.'

'Thank you. I am better at drawing landscapes than people, I think. My tutor despairs of my portraits.'

'My sister could never master perspective.'

'You come from a large family, my lord?'

'One sister, that is all.'

'And she is Freddie's mama?'

'You sound surprised, Miss Fairchild.'

She blushed. 'Forgive me, it is just that…she must be somewhat older than yourself.'

'Yes. Katherine is some sixteen years older than I. There were five other children between us, but they did not survive infancy.'

'Oh, how sad for your parents. And for you, too. No doubt it brought you closer to your sister.'

He shrugged. 'Not really. I was five when she married Erwin. If anything, I saw more of Freddie than his parents did. He is Katherine's only child. His father died four years ago and he was left to our joint guardianship. Did Freddie not mention it to you?'

'No.' She added a few more deft lines to the paper, then paused to study the result. 'We were not as close as you seem to think, my lord.'

'No? I had the impression the two of you were about to form an alliance.'

She laughed at that. 'Heavens, no. Whatever gave you that idea?'

'Oh, merely something Freddie said to me.'

'Then you misunderstood him, my lord. We are friends, nothing more. If your nephew thinks differently, then I am very sorry for it. I assure you I have not knowingly misled him.'

'Thank you for your clarification, Miss Fairchild.' The relief he felt at her answer rocked him and he felt the need to explain himself. He said, 'Freddie confides a great deal in me, you see. I hold him in considerable affection. Not only that, I take my responsibilities as his guardian very seriously.'

'I am glad to hear it. But, forgive me—' she shot a quick look at him '—you look very young to be *anyone's* guardian.'

The words sounded innocent enough, but he had the distinct impression she was teasing him.

He said stiffly, 'I have been head of my family for several years.'

'But you might have inherited that title as a schoolboy,' she pointed out. 'How old are you?'

Damn her impertinence!

'Not that it is any of your business,' he ground out. 'I am eight-and-twenty.'

'And Freddie is not yet one-and-twenty,' she replied cheerfully. 'The same age as me. He is far too young to be considering marriage.'

'But *you* are not.'

She stared at her sketchpad, working with fierce concentration.

'Believe me, my lord, I have no thoughts of matrimony.'

The mood had changed. She had grown serious and he was sorry for it. He tried for a lighter note.

'I was under the impression that was the *only* thought in a young lady's head.'

'Not in mine!' Her pencil slipped, putting a jagged line into her picture, and she gave a little huff of dismay. 'Oh, dear, now it is ruined!'

'Not at all. You can add a bird to your sky, Miss Fairchild.' He put out his hand. 'May I show you?'

She gave him the sketch pad and pencil and watched as he deftly turned the line into a wing, followed by a few more lines that transformed it into a bird, soaring high over the rooftops.

She laughed. 'It is perhaps more the size of an eagle than a pigeon, but you have rescued my drawing. How clever of you.'

She held her hand out for the pad, but Tristan held on to it.

'Not yet. I would like to see a little more of your work.'

He began to turn the pages and she gave a little sigh.

'You will find it very commonplace. My tutor says I should practise more…'

She trailed off as he turned over another page and came face to face with a portrait of his nephew. He looked up at her, his jaw tightening.

'So, you and my nephew are merely friends, are you, Miss Fairchild?

Natalya looked in dismay at the portrait. It was the best likeness she had ever achieved, quite recognisable as Freddie Erwin although it was far from perfect. The face was too lean, the bone structure well defined with a strong jawline and nose and the mouth sensuous but firm.

'You draw the man you want to see,' Monsieur Cordonnier, her drawing master had said, more than once, when he had studied her portraits. 'The man of your dreams, perhaps, *mademoiselle*?'

Her heart sank. She had made Freddie look far more mature and handsome than he really was. A lucky accident that had delighted Freddie, but his uncle was clearly not so pleased. She tried to explain.

'We were at the Grishams' house, it was a sketching party. Freddie asked if he could sit for me. Ask Jane, she will tell you!'

She hated to sound so defensive. So guilty. Lord Dalmorren was studying the pencil sketch and made no effort to call across for her friend to corroborate her story.

'It may be crude, madam, but it is clearly recognisable. It is very flattering, too, and much better than any of the others in here. I would say you have had plenty of practice with your subject.'

'No! It was mere chance that I managed to draw him so well!'

'You expect me to believe that? You have captured his likeness unmistakably.' He flicked quickly through the rest of the sheets. 'You have sketched half-a-dozen ladies, but not one other gentleman. That tells its own tale.'

'It tells you nothing!' she retorted, snatching the pad from his hands. 'If you look closely you will see where I have torn out several pages. Those were portraits that were too unsatisfactory to keep! You are determined to think the worst of me.'

'On the contrary, I came here today determined to think well of you.'

'I do not care a jot for your opinion!' She scrambled

to her feet and hastily gathered up her pencils and shawl. 'I shall bid you good day, Lord Dalmorren, and would be obliged if you would go away now!'

Natalya turned on her heel and hurried across to Jane, who had been resolutely concentrating on her sketchpad. However, when Natalya plumped down beside her she looked up.

'Good heavens, Lya, you look positively murderous! What has Lord Dalmorren said to you?' She leaned closer, her face alight with curiosity. 'Did he flirt with you?'

'Hush!' Natalya glanced anxiously towards the maid, as much to gain time as to make sure the servant was still slumbering peacefully.

She would dearly have liked to pour out her indignation to her friend, but that would not be wise. Jane was a year younger than Natalya and a poor confidante. She had always envied Jane her close friendship with her mother, but she knew her young friend was likely to blurt out any secrets to Mrs Grisham, and if the Pridhams should learn of her encounter with Lord Dalmorren, who knew what they might do? Instead she allowed her anger another outlet.

'He could have been forgiven for thinking that was my purpose in coming here,' she retorted. 'Really, Jane, you should not have moved away and left me alone with him!'

'But I thought that is what you wanted me to do!' replied Jane, looking mystified.

'No! I merely wanted to be able to…to converse with

him without my aunt and uncle present to scrutinise our every syllable!'

'Well, you have now had the opportunity. And by the way Lord Dalmorren stormed off I should say you have quarrelled right royally.' She sighed and put her hand on Natalya's arm. 'Oh, do tell, Lya,' she begged. 'What happened?'

Natalya bit her lip. 'He was…insulting.'

'Ooh.' Jane's wide eyes grew even rounder. 'What did he say?'

'It…it was not so much what he said.' Natalya was floundering. 'He…he did not admire my drawing.'

It was a poor excuse and she waited for her friend to question her further, but Jane accepted it without demur.

'How unchivalrous of him! And unjust, too. Why, you are the most accomplished artist of anyone I know, Lya. No doubt he thinks himself quite above his company!'

'No, no!' Natalya began to regret that she had said anything. 'I think he was merely being honest.' She tried to pass it off with a laugh. 'I am so used to people praising my work that I have grown quite conceited! Come, let us not give it another thought. We should make the most of this lovely day to finish our drawings.'

Tristan did not return to the city via the steps, but followed the longer, gentler slope that descended to the river. It was a pleasant walk with extensive views over the countryside, but it was lost on him. All he could see was the portrait of Freddie. Natalya had made him impossibly handsome. He strode on, swiping at the long grasses with his cane. Damnation, if that was how she saw Freddie, how she thought of him, then she must be very much in love. But if that was the case, why the devil could she not admit it?

He went back over his meeting with Freddie. He had almost written off the boy's protestations as youthful infatuation, but if the lady returned his regard then matters were more serious than he had first thought. His nephew might not have control of his fortune for the next four years, but he would be free to marry as he chose, once he was one-and-twenty in October. Freddie had mentioned that one of Bath's highest sticklers was friendly with Miss Fairchild—now what was her name? Ancrum, that was it. Perhaps he should make efforts to become acquainted with the lady. If Freddie was determined to marry Natalya, he needed to learn as much about her as possible. And quickly.

With that intention Tristan took himself to the Pump Room the following morning, his eyes raking the little groups of the old and infirm until he saw his quarry. With a quiet word here and there, he made his way through the crowd towards an elderly lady in a lavender silk gown trimmed with bright green ribbons and with a startling array of green ostrich feathers curling about her turban. She was leaning heavily on her stick while sipping the famous waters from a small cup. He did not approach the lady directly, but made his way first to Mr and Mrs Conyer. He engaged them in conversation and after a few moments, with the finesse worthy of a diplomat, he engineered an introduction to his quarry.

'Mrs Ancrum.' He bowed over her hand. 'You are acquainted with my mother, I believe?'

'Lady Dalmorren?' The old woman looked at him, her faded eyes surprisingly shrewd. 'Ah, yes, I knew her as Maria Aynsworth. She was several years my junior and we lost touch after I retired to Bath. How does she go on?'

'Remarkably well, ma'am, thank you.'

'Give me your arm, my—no, I shall not stand on ceremony with the son of so old a friend, I shall call you Tristan!—give me your arm, my boy, and we will take a turn about the room. I am better if I do not stand still for too long.' Tristan obliged and she continued, 'Is your mother in Bath with you?'

'No, ma'am. She has gone to stay with my sister at Frimley.'

'I had heard she still resides at Dalmorren.'

'Why, yes, ma'am. I am not married and the house requires a mistress.'

'And that is why you are in Bath, is it? To find a wife?' She noticed his slight stiffening and gave a cackle of laughter. 'Your attentions to Natalya Fairchild have been noted. You cannot get away with anything in Bath, my boy. Hotbed of gossip.'

'Obviously. Although I thought I had been most careful not to single out Miss Fairchild.'

'Anyone braving the Pridhams' displeasure enough to dance twice with that young lady would arouse comment.'

'She does appear to be uncommonly hedged about,' he replied cautiously. 'Do you know why that should be, Mrs Ancrum?' When she did not reply he added, 'My nephew, my sister Katherine's son, has shown a decided partiality for the lady.'

'And the Pridhams sent him to the rightabout, did they?' She shrugged. 'He will recover.'

'But I happen to believe Miss Fairchild is not indifferent to him. If that is the case, then his mother will want to know a little more about her. The Pridhams are most discouraging, but I was told that you are good friends with the young lady.'

'But you weren't told that I am a gossip!'

He smiled. 'No. As you so rightly pointed out, there is gossip aplenty in Bath. I am looking for truth.'

She turned her head and gave him a long, considering look, but did not speak.

He said at last, 'Mrs Ancrum, why are the Pridhams so discouraging?'

'I can tell you nothing.'

'Is that because you know nothing?'

'It is not my place to speak of such things.' She released his arm and held out her hand to him. 'I will wish you good day, Lord Dalmorren.'

Thus dismissed, Tristan could only take his leave of Mrs Ancrum, but he left the Pump Room with far more questions than he had entered it.

Chapter Four

Following the outing to Beechen Cliff, Natalya determined to put Lord Dalmorren out of her mind. Tristan Quintrell might be the Nineteenth Baron Dalmorren, as she had discovered after browsing through her uncle's copy of *Peerage & Baronetage*, but he was not worthy of her consideration, since he chose to think ill of her. How could he believe she was in love with Freddie Erwin!

She liked Freddie, who would not? After all, he had not been put off by her aunt's and uncle's attempts to discourage him. She appreciated that and with so few real friends in Bath she enjoyed his company, but although only months separated them in age, he was far too much of a boy to appeal to her. No, she preferred gentlemen of a more serious character. Ones, moreover, with whom she might discuss more than last week's ball or the latest play. Someone well read and with wide-ranging knowledge of the world.

Someone very like Tristan Quintrell, in fact.

No! She must not think of him.

* * *

Natalya was obliged to tell herself the same thing several times over the next few days, for he remained stubbornly in her head and no amount of study could dislodge him. When she picked up her book on astronomy, she recalled sitting beside him at the lecture and their all-too-brief discussions on the subject. When she had her dancing lesson, she remembered his lithe grace at the Assembly Rooms, and when she joined the Grishams for a nature ramble with their old governess she found her thoughts wandering off. She wondered if His Lordship was still in Bath. If he would look for her in vain at that evening's Dress Ball, which the Pridhams had decided it was not necessary to attend.

Waking to an overcast sky and steady rain did nothing to lift Natalya's spirits the next morning. The day stretched before her. Friday was designated a study day, when she would read various informative works, usually of history or philosophy, and discuss them with Mr Pridham. They had read Voltaire and Rousseau together in French. More recently she had finished Mrs Wollstonecraft's *A Vindication of the Rights of Woman*, which had not been one of Mr Pridham's recommendations, and she was now making her way through all six volumes of *The History of the Decline and Fall of the Roman Empire*, but even the thought of Mr Gibbon's very readable work could not make her look forward to the day with any great enthusiasm and it was with relief that she received an invitation to go out.

Aggie brought the note to Natalya while she was

breaking her fast in her room and she lost no time in seeking out her aunt and uncle. She found them in the drawing room, engaged in their usual morning pursuits; Mr Pridham reading the newspaper aloud to his wife while she worked at her embroidery.

'Good morning, Aunt, Uncle.'

Mr Pridham put down his newspaper and nodded towards the sheet of paper in her hand.

'Ah. Mrs Ancrum's invitation to you to take tea with her.'

'Yes.' Natalya was aware that all correspondence was taken first to her uncle and she pushed aside the familiar spurt of irritation. 'As you are aware, sir, she asks if I might be permitted to remain for dinner, too, if I am not engaged.' She looked to her aunt. 'May I accept, ma'am? If we have no other engagements this evening, then there is no need for me to hurry back.'

She waited hopefully. Mrs Ancrum was one of the few people in Bath of whom Mr and Mrs Pridham approved and she was relieved but not surprised when, after a glance at her husband, Mrs Pridham agreed she might go.

'Thank you!' Natalya beamed at her. 'If the rain has stopped, then Aggie can walk there with me, but she need not remain. Mrs Ancrum says she will send me home in her own carriage after dinner.'

'I hope you will manage an hour at the pianoforte before you go out,' put in Mr Pridham, glancing at the clock. 'Mrs Ancrum's patronage is important for you, my dear, and you must not neglect her, but you must work on your accomplishments, too. Especially now.'

Natalya looked up and was about to enquire what he meant by the last remark when her aunt came forward and touched her arm.

'Well, well, that is a treat for you, Natalya. When you go, you must be sure to give Mrs Ancrum our regards. Now, what do you say to practising your music this morning, my dear? I have an hour free to sit with you while you play and you know how much I enjoy listening to you. Shall we go to the drawing room now?'

It was less than a mile from Sydney Place to the Paragon, where Mrs Ancrum lived in some style. Natalya's maid waited only until her mistress had been admitted to the house before walking on to Milsom Street to carry out an errand for Mrs Pridham. Natalya breathed a sigh of relief. Whenever she left the house her aunt insisted she should be escorted by her maid or a footman and if she joined her friends it was on the understanding that they were similarly accompanied. Her visits to the Paragon were the only ones where she felt she was not under constant surveillance.

She was shown into the drawing room where she found Mrs Ancrum alone and sitting in her favourite wing chair beside the fire.

'No, no, pray do not get up on my account, ma'am,' she said, crossing the room and planting a kiss upon her hostess's faded cheek.

The old lady's hand came up briefly to touch her shoulder. 'Bless you, child, you are like a ray of sunshine!'

Natalya blushed and turned away the compliment with a laugh.

'That is because, despite the rain earlier this morning, it is such a warm day and my face is glowing from the exertion of walking here! But how are you, ma'am? In prime twig, I see. Pomona-green suits you, it matches your eyes.'

'Flatterer. Now, ring the bell, my love. We shall have tea and catch up on all the gossip. Why, it must be a full week since I have seen you.'

The afternoon passed pleasantly with no lull in the conversation. Mrs Ancrum gave her young friend a spirited account of all she had done and seen since they had last met and, as she did not believe in holding back her opinions, Natalya was vastly entertained by her comic descriptions of the people she had seen at the Pump Room.

'Overdressed frights, for the most part,' declared Mrs Ancrum, with a blatant disregard for the garishly coloured flounces and ribbons of red and purple that adorned her own gown. 'And the Conyers were there, Mrs Conyer wearing another of her eye-catching gowns. Bright yellow silk with so many frills and flounces I swear she looked just like a dandelion! And it is not at all helped by the fact that she is as broad as she is tall!'

'No, no, you are too cruel, ma'am,' Natalya protested, laughing. 'She is a most agreeable lady. Always cheerful, which, considering her health, is a virtue, I think. Such a generous nature, too. I can overlook her bright colours because she is always so kind when we meet.'

'And why should she not be kind to you?' exclaimed Mrs Ancrum, bridling.

'Not everyone thinks as highly of me as you, ma'am,' said Natalya, blushing a little.

'Well, they should!' came the gruff retort. 'And their son was here in the spring, was he not? I remember he came with them, once, to the Pump Room.'

'Yes, Mr Gore Conyer. A very pleasant gentleman.'

Mrs Ancrum helped herself to another small cake and said casually, 'He had a friend with him, I believe. A Mr Erwin. Handsome young buck, if I recall. I believe you danced with him, Natalya.'

'I danced with both gentlemen, ma'am.' Natalya eyed her hostess warily, wondering where this was leading.

'But I hear you found Mr Erwin the more agreeable?' Mrs Ancrum laughed. 'Oh, do not poker up, Natalya, you know I am one for plain speaking.'

'So, too, am I and I should like to know what has brought on this sudden interest in Freddie Erwin!'

'I met his uncle earlier this week. Lord Dalmorren. He was asking about you.'

'He had no right to do so!'

'He appears to think you and his nephew are in love.'

Natalya blushed furiously, which only added to her indignation. 'Ooh, how dare he, when I expressly told him it is nothing of the sort!'

'If you showed such vehemence in your response then he may well have thought the lady doth protest too much,' murmured the old woman, her shrewd eyes fixed on her young guest. She laughed suddenly. 'Now drink your tea, my love, and calm yourself. Then you can tell me everything.'

'There is nothing to tell,' replied Natalya. 'Freddie Erwin is a pleasant young man and we danced together several times. He and Mr Conyer joined one or two of the outings got up by the Grishams, but there were plenty of other young ladies present besides Jane Grisham and myself. Verena Summerton and Laura Spinhurst, to name but two of them.'

'Then why should Lord Dalmorren be asking about you?'

Natalya put down her cup. The old lady was too shrewd to believe any prevarication.

She said, 'He saw a drawing I had done of Mr Erwin. Not a good one, but…flattering. He thinks it shows I have formed a…a *tendre* for his nephew but it is nothing of the kind. I merely kept it because it was better than most of the portraits I have attempted.' She gave a tiny shrug. 'It is true that Freddie and I became friends, but you will not be surprised to know that my aunt and uncle did everything they could to discourage him from calling.'

'In my opinion, there is nothing more likely to aid a love affair than opposition.'

The old lady was watching her closely, but Natalya merely smiled and said with perfect sincerity, 'Not in this case, ma'am. When Mr Erwin left Bath, we parted with nary a pang. At least,' she added, her brow furrowed, 'not on my side.'

'And if the young man *has* formed an attachment, do you think you could return his regard?'

Natalya hesitated.

'Marriage to an agreeable man would be a way of escaping the stifling care of the Pridhams,' she said slowly. 'But it is not to be considered. They will never agree to it.'

'In a few weeks you will be one-and-twenty, Natalya. You will not need their consent.'

'True.' Natalya stared at her hands for a long moment. 'I wish I knew why my aunt and uncle are so protective. Why they discourage every gentleman who even looks at me! They insist I am a lady, there is no curb on the amount they spend on my clothes and my education, and yet…' She fixed her eyes on Mrs Ancrum. 'We have never spoken of it, but I think, I *believe*, you know something of my parents, ma'am. I pray you will tell me!'

The old lady threw up her hands. 'Do not ask me, my love, I do not *know* anything. The Pridhams are good, respectable people, if a little Puritan in their outlook. Have they not promised they will explain everything to you on your birthday?'

'Well, yes.'

'There you are then! In the meantime, if young Mr Erwin is indeed serious in his intentions, if he loves you, then your lineage will not matter in the least.'

Natalya shook her head. 'I wish I could believe you, ma'am, but I know it is not the case. Every book, every guide on genteel living I have ever read says differently. If I should turn out to be, to be a—'

'Do not even think of it!' Mrs Ancrum interrupted quickly. 'I cannot believe the Pridhams would have in-

troduced you into Bath society if there was anything
amiss with your birth. They are merely being over-
diligent in their protection of you. No, this Mr Erwin
would be a good match for any young lady and you
would be wise not to discourage him. And to that end,
you should not antagonise his uncle!'

At the mention of Lord Dalmorren, Natalya gave a
long sigh.

'I am afraid it is too late for that, ma'am. Our last
encounter ended very badly. He can have no wish to
continue the acquaintance now.'

Mrs Ancrum chuckled. 'Then you have an opportunity to make it up with him, for he is coming here for
dinner tonight!'

Mrs Ancrum's maid showed Natalya up to the guest
room, where she washed her face and hands and sat
down at the mirror to tidy her hair before dinner.

'I should have gone home,' she told her reflection.
'When she told me she had invited Lord Dalmorren to
dinner, I should have left the house immediately.'

Instead she had allowed herself to be persuaded to
remain. Mrs Ancrum had told her the Grishams were
coming, too, together with their son and daughter.

'You know I enjoy the company of young people,'
she had said. 'It is just a little party, with my old friend
Colonel Yatton invited to make us an even number at
dinner, but nothing to displease your aunt and uncle. No
dancing, of course, although I hope I might persuade
you and Jane to play for us. You are such a clever puss,

your accomplishments alone should convince Lord Dalmorren that you are an eligible match for his nevvy!'

Natalya put down her hairbrush and stared into the mirror—she did not want to be an eligible match for Freddie Erwin. She knew Freddie was not the reason she had decided to stay. It was Tristan. She berated herself for using his name, even in her thoughts, but she could not stop the dizzying swoop of her insides at the prospect of seeing him again.

'It is merely because our last meeting ended so unsatisfactorily,' she told herself as she pinched her cheeks to provide a little more colour. 'One should never part on a quarrel.'

She sat back, turning her head this way and that to study her reflection. If she had known there were to be guests, she would have worn something a little more dashing than her periwinkle-blue sprigged muslin.

'But if Mrs Ancrum's note had mentioned that there would be guests,' she told her reflection, 'Aunt Pridham would have refused to let me come!'

There was a knock on the door and Mrs Ancrum's maid peeped in.

'The mistress says to tell you she has gone down to the drawing room, miss.'

'Thank you.'

Natalya rose and shook out her skirts, then, with a final glance at her reflection, she straightened her shoulders and hurried down the stairs.

Mrs Ancrum's oldest friend, Colonel Yatton, arrived first, followed by the Grishams, who bustled in with all the energy and goodwill of a happy family. Mr and Mrs Grisham greeted Natalya in their usual friendly fashion, their son Henry bowed over her hand while Jane squealed with delight and hugged her.

'What a wonderful surprise, Natalya, I did not know you were to be here tonight.'

'That is because I was not sure she would be,' Mrs Ancrum replied for her.

'Well, we are very pleased Mr and Mrs Pridham could spare you,' put in Mrs Grisham, smiling at Natalya.

Lord Dalmorren entered and was greeted cheerfully by his hostess, who advised him not to stand upon ceremony, but to come in and join them all.

'Just an impromptu little dinner, my lord,' she said, giving him her hand. 'You know everyone, I believe.'

'I do, ma'am, thank you.'

He glanced around, nodding to everyone and finally turning to Natalya.

'Miss Fairchild.'

She made her curtsy, determined not to blush under the scrutiny of those hard grey eyes, trying not to think how well he looked, immaculate in black tailcoat and light-coloured breeches, a diamond winking from the folds of his snowy cravat. She knew a moment's panic when she thought he might approach, but his attention was claimed by the Colonel and the gentlemen were all soon engrossed in a conversation which lasted until it was time to go in to dinner.

Mrs Ancrum was an excellent hostess and conversation flowed between her guests as readily as the wine that accompanied the meal. Natalya was relieved to be seated at a distance from Lord Dalmorren, but she was contrary enough to wish he might occasionally look her way. A foolish idea and impolite, too. How odd it would look if he ignored his immediate neighbours to stare at her! She dragged her attention back to her end of the table and threw herself into an animated discussion on the merits of Lord Byron's poems.

At the end of the meal, Mrs Ancrum rose and invited the ladies to accompany her to the drawing room, where Jane carried Natalya off to the sofa, leaving her mother and their hostess to occupy the chairs flanking the fire.

'Have you made up your differences with Lord Dalmorren?' Jane whispered. 'He seems very agreeable this evening.'

'I am sure he has forgotten that silly incident.' Natalya tried to pass it off with a laugh. 'He did not like my drawing of his nephew, that is all.'

'The sketch you made of Mr Erwin, when he came to Bath in February?'

'Yes, that's the one. We were all agreed at the time that it was not very good.'

'I remember it now; you were very cross with yourself for not being able to capture his true likeness.' Jane's brow cleared. 'That explains everything. From His Lordship's conversation with Mama at dinner, one can tell he is extremely attached to his family. Although, it was very wrong of him to disparage your drawing,' she added quickly. 'And he should not have been angry if you took offence at his criticism. It was very rude to storm off without a word of farewell.'

'He did not *storm off*,' Natalya protested. 'I...um...
I think perhaps he was late for an engagement.'

Natalya was uncomfortable that her friend should
think ill of Lord Dalmorren. He had misconstrued the
situation between herself and his nephew, but that was
not entirely his fault. However, it was impossible to explain it all to Jane and Natalya did not try. Instead she
turned the subject and chattered on about fashions and
the weather until the gentlemen came in.

Mrs Ancrum called to them from her place by the
fire.

'I am glad you did not linger over your brandy. I
have promised to return Miss Fairchild to her home
by midnight.'

'Indeed?' cried Mr Grisham, glancing towards the
clock. 'Then we should waste no time in asking the
young ladies to entertain us with music!'

A short discussion ensued as to who should play first
and at last Natalya was persuaded.

When she walked over to the pianoforte, Lord Dalmorren followed, saying he would move the candles
for her.

'Home by midnight?' he murmured as she took her
seat at the pianoforte. 'Just like Cinderella.'

She ignored that, but she could not resist muttering,
'I hope you will find my playing more acceptable than
my painting.'

'That rankled, did it?' She saw a smile tugging at
the corners of his mouth. 'I beg your pardon. To own
the truth, I thought your drawing was very good. It was
the subject matter that concerned me.'

'My lord, I assure you there is no reason why it should,' she told him earnestly. 'I have no designs upon your nephew.'

'Perhaps it is more that Freddie has designs upon *you*.'

She could read nothing from his tone or his grey eyes but mild amusement. Her heart lifted as she ran her fingers over the keys and began to play. They were no longer at odds and she was surprised how much that pleased her.

Natalya returned to Sydney Place just before midnight in Mrs Ancrum's ancient but serviceable barouche and entered the house to be informed that the master and mistress were waiting for her in the drawing room. They greeted her kindly, brushed aside her apologies for keeping them up so late and enquired if she had enjoyed herself.

'Very much,' she replied truthfully. 'Mrs Ancrum had invited a few friends to join us for dinner. Her whist partner, Colonel Yatton, of course, and the Grishams were there, too, with Jane and Henry. Oh, and Lord Dalmorren,' she added casually. 'I understand his mama was a good friend of Mrs Ancrum, in her youth.' She salved her conscience with the thought that it was not exactly a lie, although 'an acquaintance' were the words Mrs Ancrum had actually used.

'Lord Dalmorren?' Mr Pridham sat up in his chair. 'I hope he did not make you the object of his attention this evening.'

'Not at all. I barely spoke to him all night.'

She need not tell them that they had sung a duet together, or that she had played for him while he entertained the company with an Italian love song. Or that he had looked into her eyes several times during his performance, as if he had been singing just for her, a thought that had caused her to miss more than a few notes of her accompaniment.

'In fact,' she added, trying to send their thoughts in another direction, 'I spent more time talking to Henry Grisham.'

Her uncle waved a dismissive hand. 'We all know young Grisham is dangling after Miss Spinhurst. He is no threat.'

'Threat?' Natalya jumped on the word. 'I am surprised you do not keep me locked in my room, if you consider any gentleman's attention to be a threat.'

'If I had my way, my girl, I would do just that!'

'Your uncle is funning!' put in Aunt Pridham hastily. 'It was very kind of Mrs Ancrum to invite you. I shall write her a note in the morning, thanking her.'

'Better than that, Aunt, you may thank her in person,' replied Natalya sweetly. 'Mrs Ancrum will be calling here tomorrow morning. She has invited me to join her on a drive to Lansdown Hill, if you do not object? We were talking about the Battle of Lansdown tonight and she expressed a desire to see the monument.' She looked from her aunt to her uncle. 'You do not mind if I accompany her, do you? She had asked Colonel Yatton to escort her, but he embarks upon a course of treatment at the hot baths tomorrow and cannot go.' She clasped her hands together. 'After all Mrs Ancrum's kindness to me I should very much like to keep her company on this outing. I do not like the idea of her going to Lansdown without a companion. However, if you wish me to refuse I shall do so, when she calls.'

She held her breath while her aunt and uncle looked at one another.

'No, no, we have no objection,' replied Mrs Pridham at last. 'I am sure Mrs Ancrum will look after you and one must undertake these outings when the weather permits, I understand that.'

'Thank you.' If the Grishams had been having this conversation, Jane would have flown across the room to kiss her mother's cheek, but Aunt Pridham did not encourage such shows of affection, so Natalya merely smiled and dropped a slight curtsy. 'If you will excuse me, I am excessively tired and will go to bed now. It is very late.'

Bidding her aunt and uncle goodnight, she made her way up the stairs, not to think about the pleasures of the forthcoming outing, but to recall the delights of the evening and Lord Dalmorren serenading her. Just the thought of his voice, a rich, powerful tenor, sent a shiver down her spine. All the way to her toes.

Chapter Five

The monument on Lansdown had been erected in the last century, to commemorate the heroism of Sir Bevil Grenville and his Cornish pikemen at the Battle of Lansdown during the Civil War. Natalya had seen it before, but she was very ready to enjoy another outing to Lansdown Hill, where on a clear day one could enjoy views over the rolling countryside.

When Mrs Ancrum's barouche pulled up in Sydney Place, the hood was down and Mrs Ancrum was making use of her parasol. Natalya climbed in beside the old lady and allowed the footman to drape a rug across her knees, but it was hardly necessary, for the day was warm as well as sunny. She made herself comfortable while Mrs Pridham exchanged a few words with Mrs Ancrum.

'It is very kind of you to take such an interest in Natalya, ma'am,' her aunt concluded.

The old lady waved away her thanks.

'Nonsense, I enjoy her company.' She added, in her

blunt way, 'I thought last night she was looking a little peaky. She spends far too long cooped up at her studies and not enough time in company.'

Mrs Pridham's smile became a little rigid.

'We are eager for her to have every accomplishment, ma'am.'

'Then you will not object to today's little jaunt,' replied Mrs Ancrum, casting a triumphant glance towards Natalya. 'Purely educational!'

She ordered the coachman to drive on, waved one regal hand to Mrs Pridham and settled back in her seat with a sigh.

'Lord, how the Pridhams do object to any trip of pleasure. I am even more sure they must be Puritans.'

Natalya giggled as she put up her own parasol. 'Pray do not be ridiculous, ma'am.'

'Hmmph. I am sometimes surprised that they allow you to come out with me.'

'They allow it because you are highly respected and your friendship counters any rumours concerning my birth. I am excessively grateful to you, ma'am. I am well aware that without your patronage I would not be so readily accepted in Bath.'

Mrs Ancrum shushed her and reached out to take her hand.

'Anyone who knows you must admire and respect you, Natalya. I wish I might do more to refute the rumours.'

'Can you not, ma'am?' Natalya turned to look at her.

'Not as much as I would like.' The old lady squeezed her hand. 'Your birthday is only a few weeks away now,

my dear. I am sure the Pridhams will explain everything then.'

'But what if—what if my worst fears are confirmed?'

'Pish! If there was anything disreputable about you it
would have come out by now,' she said cheerfully. 'The
Pridhams are far too circumspect about you, that is all.
It is their reticence that causes people to speculate.'

Natalya could not deny it had added to her doubts
about her parents. Her aunt and uncle were kind enough,
but they kept her at a distance. She could not recall ever
receiving a warm kiss on the cheek from her uncle,
or being hugged by her aunt. She could not deny they
treated her well, spared no expense in looking after her,
but they did it out of duty. Not affection.

'No,' continued Mrs Ancrum. 'A respectable marriage would do a great deal to help, if only the Pridhams could see it.'

Natalya kept silent about her own thoughts on this.

'That is the reason I invited Dalmorren to join us
last night,' continued Mrs Ancrum. 'I want him to see
what a good wife you would make for his nephew. I
know he would get little encouragement from your aunt
and uncle.'

Natalya bit her lip. 'Perhaps they have other plans
for me.'

'What plans should they have, other than to see you
comfortably established? No, when you reach one-and-
twenty I am sure you will discover that your birth is perfectly respectable.' She stopped and seemed to struggle
with herself, then she said with unwonted force, 'But

even if that should not be the case, your true friends will stand by you, never fear.'

Natalya wondered sadly how many true friends she had, but as Mrs Ancrum abruptly changed the subject at that point she followed her lead, pushing doubts about her future to the back of her mind. It was futile to speculate. Uncle Pridham had promised to tell her about her family when she came of age and after that she would be able to make her own choices for the future.

Lansdown Hill was every bit as delightful as Natalya remembered. When they alighted from the barouche, she gave Mrs Ancrum her arm and they strolled to the monument, where, at her elderly friend's behest, she related the story of the battle and they took a moment to remember the lives lost and the suffering of those caught up in the more recent battles in France and the Peninsula.

They were making a final perambulation of the monument when a rider appeared and stopped some distance away. As they watched, he dismounted, secured his horse to a tree branch and came striding towards them.

Mrs Ancrum stopped. 'Bless me, it is Lord Dalmorren!'

Natalya had already recognised him and she felt the blush rising through her body. She kept her eyes lowered as Mrs Ancrum called to him.

'Good day to you, Tristan. This is a surprise.'

'Really, ma'am?' There was the merest hint of a drawl in his voice. 'Have you forgotten that I told you I would be riding up here today?'

Natalya looked up, startled, but Mrs Ancrum's countenance was all innocence.

'It quite slipped my mind,' she said. 'But now you are here you can give me your arm, if you please, while we continue our walk. Poor Natalya must find me a burden.'

'Not at all, madam. And, if you recall, we were about to return to the barouche.'

'That was to spare you the exertion of supporting me longer that was necessary. Now that Tristan is here he may take your place. In fact, he can give you his other arm and we can take a closer look at Sir Bevil's statue.'

Natalya bit her lip, torn between amusement, embarrassment and indignation. His Lordship, on the other hand, appeared to be completely at his ease. He laughed.

'Mrs Ancrum, you are the most outrageously designing creature. You deserve that I should whisk Miss Fairchild away and leave you to your own devices, but *that*, I suspect, might suit your purposes even better!'

The old lady chuckled. 'Stop it, Tristan, you are putting my young friend to the blush!'

'*You* have already done that,' Natalya told her, cheeks flaming. She said crossly, 'I am minded to leave you both and walk back to the carriage alone!'

'Pray do not do that, Miss Fairchild.' He put up one hand. 'Mrs Ancrum merely wishes to help. Let us be frank about the matter, your aunt and uncle put every obstacle in our way, but I should like to know you a little better.'

Recalling her own disastrous attempt to arrange such

a meeting, Natalya knew not what to say. Tristan smiled down at her.

'If you return to the carriage now, Mrs Ancrum will feel obliged to accompany you. Surely you do not wish to curtail her pleasure?'

'Of course she does not,' said that lady. 'Come, my lord, you may give me your arm and Natalya may walk along beside us with perfect propriety. No one can complain about that!'

The matter was settled. They turned back to the monument and Natalya was persuaded to repeat her account of the battle. Lord Dalmorren appeared genuinely interested and gradually, under his gentle questioning, she relaxed and began to enjoy herself, although she could not be persuaded to take his arm.

'How pleasant this has been,' declared Mrs Ancrum, when at last they strolled back towards the barouche. 'I am so glad we met you here, Tristan. Perhaps you would like to join us for refreshments at the hostelry just down the hill?'

Tristan demurred and glanced towards Natalya, who gave in to the promptings of her rebel self to say, 'You would be very welcome, my lord. Mrs Ancrum would appreciate your escort back to the Paragon, too, I am sure.'

'Very well, then, if you do not object, I should like to join you.'

He smiled, transforming his rather stern features into something much softer and Natalya felt again the sudden tug of attraction. Heavens! Perhaps the Pridhams were right to keep her so confined, if she could be affected by a gentleman on such a short acquaintance. It occurred to her that there were other gentlemen, including Freddie Erwin, whom she had known for longer than Tristan and yet she felt not the slightest spark of attraction.

She stole another glance at him as he escorted Mrs Ancrum towards the waiting carriage. He was every inch a fashionable gentleman with his tall hat and boots polished to a mirror-like gloss. In fact, she thought he looked even better in riding jacket and buckskins than in his black evening coat. The frightening thing was that she had had several gentlemen pointed out to her as handsome, but not one of them made the breath hitch in her throat, or made her stomach swoop when they looked her way.

They reached the carriage and she waited for Lord Dalmorren to hand her in, steeling herself for his touch. Yet despite thinking herself prepared, she could not prevent her fingers trembling in his grasp or the sudden giddiness that attacked her.

'Steady now.'

He helped her up the steps and she managed to sit down, but even then, when she was settled beside Mrs Ancrum, her spine burned where he had supported her. She could still feel his hand on her back, strong and secure.

'Well, how fortunate that we should meet with His Lordship,' remarked Mrs Ancrum as the carriage began to move.

Natalya dragged her eyes away from the sight of

Lord Dalmorren, riding beside the barouche on a glossy black hunter.

'You planned this.' She glared at Mrs Ancrum. 'Just as you planned last night's little party. You are trying to, to throw us together.'

'I only want to give Lord Dalmorren the opportunity to know the real you, Natalya. The clever, lively, accomplished young lady that *I* know, not the insipid obedient little doll that the Pridhams would like you to be. If he takes a shine to you, he will support young Mr Erwin when he makes his offer. And heaven knows you will need some support, for I fear you will get very little from your own family.'

'Freddie Erwin is not going to propose to me. And I would refuse him if he did,' Natalya told her. 'I do not love him, ma'am.'

Mrs Ancrum looked as if she was about to say one thing, then she changed her mind. She smiled. 'I am sorry for it, if that is the case, my love, but I understand. You must think me a foolishly interfering old woman.'

'Oh, no, ma'am, no! I know you have my interests at heart, truly I do, but believe me when I say that I would not be happy marrying Mr Erwin.'

'Then I have quite mistook the matter.'

'You and Lord Dalmorren both,' muttered Natalya, bitterly.

'But I hold by my belief that it is better for you to be given a little more freedom than you are granted by your aunt and uncle. How can you learn to be easy in a gentleman's company if you only see him when you are hedged about by chaperons?'

She gave in. 'You are perfectly correct, ma'am. Sometimes I feel quite…quite *shackled* by my life. My every word, every look is scrutinised.'

'Oh, my poor dear,' exclaimed Mrs Ancrum with ready sympathy. She patted her hands. 'You must enjoy yourself when you are with me, then. I shall keep you safe and I will not let you stray beyond the bounds of propriety, but I should like you to know more freedom than you are generally given.' A roguish twinkle appeared in her eyes. 'Try a little flirtation with Lord Dalmorren, if you wish. Since you tell me you are not intending to marry his nephew, it cannot hurt!'

Natalya forced a laugh and shook her head. She said nothing but she thought, with some alarm, that such an idea must not be given room to grow. A flirtation with His Lordship could do her a great deal of damage!

The hostelry where Mrs Ancrum had bespoke refreshments was situated almost halfway down Lansdown Hill. When they arrived Lord Dalmorren quickly dismounted to help the ladies step down from the carriage. They were clearly expected, for Natalya had barely alighted when the landlord and his wife both ran out to welcome the visitors. They were shown into the private parlour, where a cold collation had been set out and wines, lemonade and ale were arranged on a sideboard.

Natalya found she was very hungry. She sat down at the table with her companions to enjoy her meal and afterwards Mrs Ancrum declared she needed a rest before resuming her journey. Natalya made her comfortable in the only armchair and placed a glass of wine on a little table at her elbow.

Tristan was pouring himself a tankard of ale, but she knew he was watching her. She glanced around. The only other seating in the room apart from the chairs round the table was a large wooden settle. If she went to sit there, would Tristan join her? Natalya wondered. Would he sit close, their shoulders, possibly their thighs, separated by only a few thin layers of cloth? Her cheeks grew hot and she was alarmed to discover how much she liked the idea.

'Will you take a glass of wine, Miss Fairchild?'

Tristan was standing at the sideboard, waiting for an answer. She dare not look at him for fear he might read her lustful thoughts.

'A little lemonade would be very welcome, thank you.'

She returned to the table and sat down. At least its thick wooden top would provide some sort of barrier between them. She felt a little hysterical. She was being nonsensical. There could be no danger sitting here in this room with Mrs Ancrum present. But her hand still shook as she accepted the glass of lemonade from Tristan.

He could not but notice and she tried to laugh it off.

'I think I must be a little tired. The fresh air...' She tailed off lamely.

'And being out so late last night.' His eyes glinted. 'Cinderella.'

The memory of their enjoyable evening flooded

back. How he had stood beside her while she played, turning the pages. Singing with her.

Singing *to* her, gazing at her while he sang *cara mia. Stop it, Natalya!*

She sat up a little straighter. 'What nonsense. Midnight is not late at all. It was merely that Mrs Ancrum had promised her maid would escort me home and my aunt had no wish for me to inconvenience anyone.'

'I see,' he replied gravely. 'The Pridhams take great care of you. Which of them is your blood relation?'

She stared into her lemonade, turning the glass slowly between her hands.

'I do not know,' she said, her voice low. 'My uncle has promised to explain everything on my birthday. The fourth of June. I will be one-and-twenty.'

'Ah. Then you will be free to marry whomsoever you wish.' He leaned forward. 'But why must Pridham wait until then to tell you about your parents? Why can he not tell you now?'

'I think that might have something to do with trustees.' She saw his brows rise and spread her hands. 'I must have some, I think. There has been no lack of funds for my upbringing, but I do not think it is entirely within the Pridhams' control. Occasionally, when Mr Pridham is angry he says, *If I had my way,* which makes me wonder if perhaps he receives instructions from elsewhere.'

'That would suggest that you are not a pauper, then.'

'No.'

Neither did it prove she was an eligible match. She glanced towards the armchair, where Mrs Ancrum was dozing. The old lady's reticence to tell her what she knew only added to Natalya's suspicions that she was baseborn. If that were so, there was nothing she could do about it. No respectable man would marry her.

Tristan shifted on his chair. 'After the fourth of June your uncle will not be able to forbid the banns. If Freddie returns and proposes, will you accept him?'

She was about to repeat once again that she had no interest in his nephew when she recalled Mrs Ancrum's words, that if a man loved her, he would not care about her birth. If Freddie did care for her, and if he was intending to make her an offer—and Tristan's presence in Bath suggested that was the case—then perhaps she should accept him. After all, marriage to a good, kind man must be preferable to the fate she feared awaited her, if she was illegitimate.

'Well, is it so difficult a question?'

His voice sounded harsh and unfriendly to her overstretched nerves.

'Not at all,' she snapped. 'However, Freddie has not yet asked me to marry him. And in any case,' she added, goaded by his scowl. 'I shall wait until I attain my majority before making any decisions about my future!' She pushed back her chair. 'Mrs Ancrum is stirring. It is time we were going. Perhaps, my lord, you will summon the carriage.'

When Tristan reached George Street he dismounted and handed the reins to the waiting servant. He did not enter his hired house, but stood on the flagway, pulling off his gloves and frowning as he watched his man lead the horse away.

The more he saw of Natalya Fairchild the more he liked her, but that did not make her any more eligible a match for his nephew. Katherine would want to know something of her future daughter-in-law's pedigree and every avenue he had tried so far had come to a dead end. He could not even discover anything about the Pridhams, although they appeared to have a considerable income.

No one knew or was willing to divulge anything about Miss Fairchild's natural parents and even Natalya had not been told. His doubts and fears might yet be allayed and she might turn out to be perfectly respectable, even an heiress, but the more Tristan saw of Natalya the more he was convinced she was not the bride for Freddie. They might be the same age in years, but she was far more mature.

Her interests, too, differed wildly from those of his nephew. Freddie was still finding his way in the world, whereas Natalya read widely and she had definite opinions. Marriage between them could only end in disaster. He was too much the boy and she needed a man.

Such as yourself, I suppose?

The thought brought him up with a jolt. He wanted to laugh it off, brush it aside, but there was more than a grain of truth in it. She attracted him—not just her beauty, but her lively wit, the humour that made her eyes sparkle with mischief, her readiness to argue her case, yet she was still willing to consider opposing points of view. Whatever else she might be, she was no milk-

and-water maid, to knuckle down meekly beneath her husband's thumb and he was convinced that husband should not be Freddie. In fact, Tristan realised, he disliked the idea of anyone marrying Natalya.

With something like a growl, he shook off the disturbing thoughts and made his way into the house. The footman who opened the door was startled into silence by having his master's hat, riding crop and gloves thrust at him and commanded in terse accents to have a decanter and glasses fetched up immediately.

Tristan strode on, not waiting for the man to reply, and went in to the drawing room almost without check, only to come to a halt just inside the door.

'Ah, there you are, Tris.' Freddie jumped from his chair, grinning. 'I have been waiting for you!'

Chapter Six

'Freddie.' Tristan pushed his wayward thoughts to one side and nodded at his nephew. 'When did you get back to Bath?'

'This morning. Your letter to Mama, telling her you had taken a house in Bath for the summer, could not have been better timed. I had been there for nearly a fortnight and was desperate to get back here, so I told her I was coming to join you. I have seen Hurley and he has arranged everything, prepared rooms for me and my man and had the bags taken up. I asked for wine to be brought in, too. I hope you do not mind, Tris, but you must be rattling around here all alone and cannot object to putting me up.' He noticed his uncle's hesitation and flushed slightly. 'I can always find a room at the White Hart, or the Star, if it is inconvenient.'

'It is not inconvenient at all,' replied Tristan. 'I would have preferred you to give me a little notice, that is all.'

'Excellent! I did not like to presume and told Platt not to unpack my bags until I had spoken to you,' came the sunny reply. 'But I will do so, as soon as we have drunk a glass together. What will it be, Tris, Madeira? Or the claret is very good, I tried a glass while I was waiting for you.'

'Claret, then. And it should be good. It is from my cellar at Dalmorren Manor.' He waited until Freddie had supplied him with a glass of wine before speaking again. 'How is your mother?'

'In fine spirits. I took your advice and did not mention Miss Fairchild to her, although I did prepare the ground, telling her I thought it was time to settle down.'

'Oh? And how did she take that?'

'Not well. She started planning parties for me at Frimley, to introduce me to the families there, but I told her I was not in that much of a hurry. I said it can wait until my birthday in October.'

'Did you, by heaven! And what excuse did you give her for coming back to Bath? Oh, of course,' drawled Tristan, his voice heavy with sarcasm. 'You were coming to visit me.'

Freddie beamed at him. 'Yes. Has it not worked out well? But tell me, Tris, have you met Miss Fairchild? What do you think of her?'

Tristan took another sip of his wine and pretended to savour it. He had been expecting the question, but still felt unprepared to answer.

'She is very pretty,' he said at last.

'Pretty! Tris, she is the most beautiful woman I have ever seen!'

'Ah, but then, you have not seen very many yet, have you? Now don't fly up into the rafters, my boy, I am only stating the case. Very well, let us agree that Miss Fairchild is beautiful.'

'And is she not accomplished?'

'Extremely.'

Freddie's brows snapped together. 'You are going to add a rider,' he accused his uncle.

'Merely that we know nothing about her birth.'

'What does that have to say to anything? I love her!'

'As you have told me, on numerous occasions,' retorted Tristan. 'However, as your guardian, it behoves me to know something more about the lady.'

'Then approach the Pridhams and ask them. Tell them Lya and I want to be married.'

'They do not encourage young gentlemen to dangle after their ward.'

'As I am very much aware! However, once they hear from you that I am serious and that I have the means to support a wife, they will come around, I am sure. And besides, Lya will be of age soon, then we will not need their consent.'

Tristan said cautiously, 'Have you spoken to Miss Fairchild of your feelings?'

'Well, not in so many words. She is always so hedged about by chaperons that we have not been able to speak plainly, but she must know of it.'

'She has never slipped away to meet you in secret?'

Freddie looked shocked. 'Good Lord, Tris, Lya would never do anything so…so improper. How could you even think it?'

'No, forgive me. But she has given you reason to hope your suit would be successful?'

For the first time in the interview, Freddie looked unsure.

'Not as such. I did come close to declaring myself on several occasions, but for some reason or another the moment was never propitious. And her aunt and uncle are always so vigilant, we had no opportunity to converse alone for more than a few minutes at a time. However, now that you are here to support me, I will get to it as soon as maybe.' He grinned at Tristan. 'And I have another ally! I told Grandmama about meeting Mrs Ancrum in Bath and she has written a letter that I am to deliver to her. That will put me in credit with the old lady, I am sure!'

'But not necessarily with the Pridhams,' murmured Tristan. 'Or my sister, when she learns of the reason for your return to Bath.'

Freddie dismissed this with a wave of his hand.

'You mean my marriage to Lya? Mama will come around, when she sees how much in love we are. What objection can there be?' Freddie finished his wine and pushed himself out of his chair. 'Now, I'd best go and tell Platt to look out my evening coat and we can sit down for a snug little dinner together.'

Freddie hurried away, leaving Tristan to pour himself another glass of wine. Natalya had assured him she was not thinking of marriage. Until today. When he had asked her directly if she would accept an offer from Freddie, she had prevaricated. Was she waiting to know what her own fortune might be?

He shifted uncomfortably. He had not thought her mercenary, but if she was penniless then any marriage would be preferable to destitution. And then there was that portrait she had drawn of Freddie. It was too intimate and far too handsome, portraying Freddie as the man he might become, rather than the boy he still was. Surely she could not have drawn that if she did not feel something for the boy.

Tristan decided he must observe them together. If they were truly in love, then he would have to reconsider, but his instinct was to dissuade Freddie from proposing marriage to Natalya, to do everything in his power to prevent the match. The problem was, he suspected his judgement was flawed, because he himself felt a strong attraction to the lady.

Not that anything could come of that. He would not, could not become his own nephew's rival for Natalya's affections.

'Well, well, my lord, do they not make a handsome couple?' Mrs Ancrum nodded towards Freddie and Natalya, who were making their way on to the dance floor.

Tristan did not answer immediately and the old woman chuckled. 'If one believed in Fortune, one might think it was more than mere chance that has laid Mrs Pridham low with a sore throat. When Mr Pridham told me that was the reason she was not at the morning service yesterday I was very sorry, of course, but then I saw your nevvy and Miss Fairchild stealing a few words together and saw how I might do the young lovers a good turn, so I sent a note to Sydney Place, saying I had a notion to look in at the ball tonight and offering to bring Natalya.'

'Allowing him to stand up with her for a second time might not be the wisest thing, ma'am.'

'Oh, tosh, there can be no harm in it. Why, you did the self-same thing yourself.'

'Aye, and I am aware of the gossip that created!'

Another fat chuckle. 'I told you, my lord, a man cannot sneeze in Bath without it raising comment, not but what everyone believes you came to approve your ward's choice of a bride!'

'The devil they do!'

'And why not? Young Erwin never made any secret of his preference for Natalya. Speculation is rife. If you listen to gossip, which I never do.'

He grinned at that. 'But you are not averse to fuelling the gossip by allowing Miss Fairchild to dance all night with my nephew, is that it?'

'It is my belief that the more they know of one another the better. That way the affair will either fizzle out when they discover they are not suited, or they will make a match of it.'

An elderly couple was bearing down upon them and, with a nod and a smile, Tristan excused himself and moved away, leaving Mrs Ancrum to talk to her friends uninterrupted. She was right, confound it, they did make a very striking couple and danced well together. Freddie was tall, although still showing some of the lankiness of youth, and his partner, with her deep brown eyes and her raven-black hair, lustrous in the candlelight, was the perfect foil for his classically fair good looks.

The Pridhams were sure to hear that Freddie had

been showing their ward an undue amount of attention. Tristan gave an inward shrug. He was not the boy's
keeper and Mrs Ancrum was right to let them have more
time together. They needed to discover their true feelings and better they should do it here, in public, than
stealing time alone together. He turned away. Good
luck to them.

For Natalya, standing up again with Freddie was a
mixed blessing. She knew her aunt would want her to
refuse, but Freddie danced well and he begged her so
charmingly that she succumbed to the temptation, especially since she could see Lord Fossbridge bearing
down upon her and the thought of spending two country dances with him, listening to his ponderous compli-
ments and enduring his even more ponderous dancing,
was not to be borne.

If it had been Lord Dalmorren coming to solicit her
hand, she would have refused Freddie, but Tristan had
not approached her all evening, save to greet her when
she arrived with Mrs Ancrum. Not that it mattered,
she told herself as she skipped along beside her partner. She did not care in the least whether he danced
with her or not.

'By Jove, that was lively,' declared Freddie, as the
last bars of music died away. He held on to her hand.
'Shall we sit out the next? I want to talk to you.' He
squeezed her fingers. 'Please say you will, Lya. I do
not know when we may get another chance like this.'

Natalya felt a momentary panic. He was going to propose to her and she would much rather he did not. When

Tristan had asked her bluntly if she would marry Freddie, she had felt so uncertain about her future that she had seriously thought she might do so, even though she did not love him and doubted if he was truly in love with her. But when the two men had entered the ballroom together this evening, all her doubts had disappeared. She had known then that she could never marry Freddie.

Now he was smiling down at her, his face alight with hope, and her heart sank. However, there was no avoiding it now, so they had best get it over. She allowed him to lead the way to two chairs set a little apart from their neighbours. Natalya fanned herself nervously while Freddie, looking equally ill at ease, fidgeted beside her.

He laughed suddenly. 'This is not how I envisaged this moment, Lya, but if I do not speak now heaven knows when we may have another opportunity.'

'Oh, please, Freddie, please say no more.' He looked at her in alarm and she went on, with some difficulty. 'Am I—would I be correct in thinking you mean to offer for me?'

'Well, yes, but I am making such a mull of it, aren't I?'

She reached out and touched his hand. 'Dear Freddie, that is not why I stopped you. You see, I do not want—that is, I do not think you should propose to me.'

'Are you afraid your aunt and uncle would object, or that my own family would refuse to allow it?'

'I am sure of it, but I would not let that stand between us, if…if I loved you.'

'And you don't?' His blue eyes were fixed on her. 'Are you sure you could not learn to love me, in time?'

She shook her head. 'I like you very much, as a friend, Freddie, but I do not love you. And I do not think you really love me. Not the deep, lasting love that is required for a happy marriage. No, let me finish,' she said quickly, when he opened his mouth to protest. 'I fear we should not suit, my dear friend. Our interests are so different. You do not share my love of art, for instance, or astronomy. And you only enjoy music if you can dance to it. You fell asleep during the last concert you attended in Bath, did you not?'

'Confound it, Lya, what is that to say to anything? True, I do not like reading, as you do. And I cannot understand your interest in old stones or...or *history*, but I would be happy to go with you to visit the Royal Academy or the museum in London, or even if you wished to travel around England looking at ancient monuments and the like.'

This was said with such an air of dogged determination that she laughed. 'I can see by your expression that the very idea of it fills you with horror.'

'No, no, you mistake me,' he said hastily. 'I could learn to love these things, as you do.'

'Perhaps you could, but why should you do so? I am sure you would be happier with someone else.' She flicked a little glance at him. 'Jane Grisham, perhaps. You have been friends for so long I think you would suit very well.'

'No, how could you say that?' he protested. 'Lya, I knew from the first moment I saw you that I wanted you for my wife! I know what it is, you have seen how easy Jane and I are together and you are jealous. That shows you care for me!'

Smiling, she shook her head and reached up to put a warning finger against his mouth.

'Hush now, Freddie. The fact that I am not at all jealous tells me quite the opposite. I am very flattered by your offer, but believe me, I cannot love you.' He looked downcast and she reached out to take his hand. 'I hope we can remain friends.'

'I hope so, too.' He sighed. 'Ah, well. I suppose there would be a deal of opposition to our marrying now. However, in a few months we will both be of age. Who knows but I might persuade you to change your mind by then? And such a show of constancy must weigh with my mother, as well as with the Pridhams. No, you will not make me give up hope just yet.'

'Very well.' Natalya knew she was being cowardly in not making her rejection absolute, but Freddie was looking so much more cheerful she could not bear to dash his hopes. Also, she was very sure his infatuation would soon fade. 'Let us agree to remain friends, then. In truth, I should not like to fall out with you, Freddie, I have so few real friends in Bath and I count you as one of them.'

'I am honoured you should think so.'

He was still holding her hand, but when he would have lifted it to his lips, she gently pulled away, saying with another smile,

'We have been sitting together for a full quarter of an hour and I think you should escort me back to Mrs Ancrum, before she grows anxious.'

* * *

Tristan was determined not to stand and watch Freddie and Natalya going down the country dance, but he could not prevent his eyes from straying back to the dance floor. He had just decided to take a look in the card room when a jovial voice at his shoulder made him turn quickly.

'If it isn't Tristan Quintrell. Never expected to see you in this place!'

'James!' Tristan put out his hand, genuinely delighted to see his old friend. 'Last time I heard, you were in the Peninsula. You had just made major.' He looked around. 'Is your wife with you?'

James Moffatt pulled a face. 'You don't think I'd come to a ball of my own volition, do you? Dolly is here somewhere, chattering with her friends.'

Tristan laughed. They had been at school together, but had lost touch in recent years and he was content to spend several minutes catching up on the past.

'So, you have sold out,' he said at last. 'What brings you to Bath?'

'Old wounds. Took a bullet in the leg, old boy, and one in the chest that just missed the lung. It has left me devilish weak, I can tell you. In fact, this is one of my first outings. Dolly decided retiring to Bath would be just the thing for us, so she packed up everything and moved us here. Had to sell my hunters. I don't ride much now, y'see.'

He placed one hand on his chest, looking glum.

'I did not bring any of my riding horses to Bath,' Tristan replied. 'I did not think I'd need 'em.'

In truth, he had not expected to be in Bath so long. He had anticipated being here a week or so, to make Miss Fairchild's acquaintance and pursue his enquiries about her family. The only reason he had taken the house in George Street was in order to bring his mother and Katherine here, should an alliance between Freddie and Natalya prove inevitable.

'I should like to explore the countryside around Bath,' said the Major, interrupting his thoughts. 'but Dolly won't countenance any exertion until the sawbones says I am well enough and he's not keen on my doing anything more than taking a gentle airing around the city at present. Dolly won't even let me drive up to Lansdown, where I believe the view is well worth the effort.'

Tristan decided not to mention his recent ride there, fearing it might upset his friend. Instead he tried to give James's thoughts a more cheerful turn.

'That will wait until you are stronger. In the meantime, there are numerous entertainments to be had in Bath itself. The theatre, lectures, even balls such as this!'

The Major grimaced. 'We have been here a few months now and I'm afraid it's not the place for me. Too full of gossip and invalids! When the lease runs out at the end of the summer, I think we'll be off back to Berkshire. Why are you here?'

'Family matters.' Tristan did not want to elaborate.

'Ah, yes. That's your nephew over there, ain't it, Tris? Dancing with Miss Fairchild.'

'Are you acquainted with the lady?'

'I know *of* her: Local beauty.'

'I can see that. Tell me something I do *not* know.'

'Not much to tell. The Pridhams keep her closely guarded.'

'What of her parents?'

'I know nothing about 'em, old friend. Ah, here is Dolly now. She can tell you more.'

James smiled as his wife came up and took his arm. After pleasantries had been exchanged, he told her of Tristan's interest in Miss Fairchild.

Mrs Moffatt regarded him with her bird-bright eyes.

'Why, she is quite a mystery, my lord! No one knows anything about her father, but I heard tell that her mother's family has quite cast her off. Some say she was born the wrong side of the blanket, but the fact that Mrs Ancrum has taken the chit under her wing suggests otherwise. She is a pretty-behaved gel and whatever the truth may be, the Pridhams look after her pretty well.' Her gaze flickered over the dance floor. 'I'm surprised she is standing up with your nephew again. That will give the Bath tabbies something to gossip over in the Pump Room tomorrow!'

Major Moffatt laughed. 'As if they needed something! But tell me, Tris, do you ever see anything of young Framlington? And what of Naismith…?'

Tristan smiled, but was relieved at the change of subject, and by the time they parted the next country dance was well underway. He turned his attention back to the dance floor, but there was no sign of his nephew, or Miss Fairchild. His eyes raked the benches at the side of the room and he finally spotted them sitting together in one corner of the room. He could only see Freddie's profile, but Natalya's lovely face was smiling, and as he watched she put her finger to Freddie's lips, then reached for his hand.

Tristan swung away. He felt winded, as if he had taken a blow to the gut. Could anything be clearer? For all her protestations to the contrary, Natalya obviously cared a great deal for Freddie. Jaw clenched, he moved blindly towards the door, but his pace slowed before he reached it. He could not leave. Freddie might very well partner Natalya for another two dances before the night was out, if he was not checked. He remembered Dolly Moffatt's words. People were already watching, speculating about the young couple. For them to stand up together for a third time would send the gossipmongers into a frenzy.

The music had stopped and he turned in time to see Freddie escorting Natalya back to Mrs Ancrum. Tristan made his way through the milling crowd until he was close enough to catch Freddie's eye. He watched as his nephew excused himself and came across.

'Well, Tris, did you want me?' He was grinning, clearly pleased at the way his evening was progressing. 'I was about to ask Miss Spinhurst to stand up.'

'Henry Grisham is there before you,' Tristan replied, glancing across the room. 'I thought we might play a hand of cards.'

'At a ball?' Freddie laughed. 'Come now, Tris, is there no one you wish to dance with?'

Tristan took his arm. 'Humour me.'

'Very well.'

With a shrug, Freddie followed him into the card room. They found an empty table in one corner and commenced a game of piquet.

'Tell me,' said Tristan, studying his cards, 'how many other ladies have you danced with this evening, besides Miss Fairchild?'

'Why, none, as yet.' Freddie quickly selected a discard and threw it down. 'You cannot blame me for taking this opportunity to dance with Natalya. When her aunt is present, she is allowed only two dances with any man. Natalya is kept far too confined.'

'Perhaps with good reason.'

A frown crossed Freddie's cheerful countenance. 'Natalya is the woman I intend to marry, Tris. I'll not hear a word against her.'

'Neither do you want to incur censure.'

'There is no one here who would do so. Devil take it, Tris, Mrs Ancrum sees no harm in our dancing together.'

'She may not do so, but you may be sure the Pridhams will, when they hear of it.'

Freddie looked mutinous. 'Natalya deserves to enjoy herself and, if she wishes to dance with me again this evening, I will not deny her!'

Tristan frowned at him. 'You young fool, do you not realise that your attentions will reflect badly on the lady?' He saw the boy's face darken and said more gently, 'You would not wish Miss Fairchild to become the object of gossip and speculation, would you?'

He saw that his words had hit home. Freddie's boyish face grew serious.

'No, of course not, but…' He stopped, then said in a furious under-voice, 'We are merely dancing, Tris. Surely no one can think anything wrong with that!'

'This is Bath, Freddie. Most of the people here love nothing more than to see the most innocent events in a scandalous light.'

'You are right, damn you.' Freddie sighed. 'Oh, well, when we have finished our game, I will engage both Miss Grisham and Miss Spinhurst to stand up with me this evening. That will throw the tabbies off the scent.'

'It will help, certainly,' said Tristan. He put down his cards. 'My trick, I think.'

The play continued and after an hour Freddie threw down his cards in disgust.

'You win again,' he said, giving Tristan a rueful look. 'That's three games in a row. I beg your pardon, I have not really been attending to the cards.'

'It does not matter. At least you are not making a cake of yourself in the ballroom.'

'True.' Freddie cocked his head, listening to the music. 'If I am going to solicit Miss Grisham's hand, I should go and do so for the next country dance.'

'Very well. But you will oblige me by not standing up with Miss Fairchild again.'

'But she has already promised to dance The Maid of Seville with me.'

Tristan shrugged. 'Then another beau will have an opportunity to stand up with her.'

'You do not understand.' Freddie leaned across the table, saying earnestly, 'Have you not noticed? The gentlemen do not dance with her, some discouraged by the Pridhams, others because they are afraid of associating with a lady whose birth is shrouded in mystery.' He added bitterly, 'If I do not stand up with her again, she will be obliged to sit out, or to suffer dancing with the likes of Lord Fossbridge!'

'Very well, I will take your place.'

'You!'

'Yes. I was not going to dance tonight, but if it is the only way to salve your conscience, then I will do so.'

For a moment he thought Freddie would object, but then the boy grinned.

'I have to say I'd as soon you danced with Lya than anyone else, Tris. And it will give you a chance to get to know her better.'

As they strolled back to the ballroom, Tristan had to admit the idea of standing up with Natalya appealed to him. Freddie went off to find himself a partner and Tristan moved to the side to watch the set that was currently forming. He saw Colonel Yatton leading Natalya out on to the dance floor. The boy was right, Tristan admitted to himself. Most of Natalya's partners were elderly friends of the Pridhams or Mrs Ancrum.

Freddie had secured Jane Grisham's hand and as they joined the set, Tristan saw the smile that Natalya gave them. He forced himself not to scowl. She looked serene, not at all jealous to see her beau standing up with another lady. He turned away and went to sit beside James Moffatt on the benches at the side of the room. By heaven, she must be confident of her power over Freddie!

* * *

It was time. Tristan crossed the room towards Mrs Ancrum. Natalya was one of the little group surrounding the old lady, but she had her back to the room and did not see his approach. Mrs Ancrum beamed at him.

'Ah, here is your next partner, my dear, come to carry you off!'

Natalya turned, the laughter dying from her face.

'Oh. I thought Freddie…'

He bowed. 'Plans have changed. I hope you will do me the honour, Miss Fairchild?'

He offered his arm to Natalya and as they walked away, he heard Mrs Ancrum chuckle. 'Lord, how I enjoy watching the young people enjoying themselves!'

Neither of them spoke as they took their place in the set that was forming. Tristan noted the becoming flush to Natalya's cheeks. Brought on, he thought bitterly, by flirting with Freddie, even while he was dancing with another lady! He recalled the way she and Freddie had sat out earlier, deep in discussion. How she had taken his hand. The memory sliced into him like a knife.

Natalya cast a doubtful glance up at him. 'Have I done something to offend you, my lord?'

'Apart from making up to my nephew?'

She flushed, but her chin lifted a fraction. 'Freddie and I are friends.'

'That is very plain to see!'

If he had thought the music would drown out his words, he was mistaken. She glared at him.

'What do you mean by that, what are you implying?'

'That your sitting with your heads together for half an hour will set tongues wagging.'

The movement of the dance prevented them saying more and Tristan was thankful. A ballroom was no place for an argument. When they came back together, he forced himself to apologise.

'I beg your pardon, Miss Fairchild. It is not my place to reprimand you.'

The smile on her lips did not match the wrathful sparkle in her eyes.

'You are quite correct, my lord, it is *not* your place.' That determined little chin lifted even higher and she said icily, 'Not that I admit to any action that warrants a reprimand! Talking to your nephew, in full view of everyone, cannot be considered *fast*.'

She danced away from him, her black curls bouncing. She was right about that. Talking with Freddie was in no way improper, but that intimate gesture, when she had reached out and touched Freddie's mouth… The thought of it sent a bolt of pain crashing through him and he almost missed his step. Confound it, he was jealous of his own nephew!

He thrust the thought aside, horrified, and tried to concentrate on the complicated movement of the dance. By the time he and Natalya were together again he had regained his composure. She responded to his attempts at conversation warily, but when he led her back to Mrs Ancrum they were able to part with perfect civility, if not in any friendly fashion. Her response to his nod was a frosty curtsy before she turned away to smile at Colonel Yatton, who had come up to claim her hand for the next dance. Jaw clenched, Tristan strode off to the card room with never a backward glance.

Tristan glanced at his watch. It was so late he might as well remain until the end of the ball. He waited while Freddie escorted Natalya and Mrs Ancrum to their carriage, then they walked back to George Street together. Freddie, naturally enough, was ecstatic.

'What an evening! To dance the first dances with Natalya, then to be allowed to stand up with her again! I was sorry not to stand up a further time, but I see now that your dancing with her has answered very well.'

'Oh?' Tristan glanced at him warily. 'What did Miss Fairchild tell you of our dance together?'

'Why, nothing, only that you understand one another better now.'

What the devil did that mean? Tristan wondered why she had not told Freddie of his disapproval. The boy was sufficiently infatuated to take her side in any argument. But she would know that Freddie did not like to be at odds with anyone. Perhaps she was so sure of him she could afford to keep silent.

'But you were not dancing the whole time you were with Miss Fairchild,' remarked Tristan, trying to sound casual. 'What did you discuss, when you were sitting out together?'

Freddie waved a hand. 'Oh, this and that. There is so little chance to talk, you see, when she is chaperoned by Mrs Pridham.' He gave an ecstatic sigh. 'Is she not an angel, Tris?'

'I do not feel qualified to judge.'

'No? But you have danced with her. She has grace, beauty and intelligence. She is more accomplished than any other woman of my acquaintance!'

'A veritable paragon, then.'

Freddie stopped. 'Yes. She is, Tris!'

Tristan took his arm and gently moved him on. 'And has she agreed to marry you?'

'Oh, well, you know, not yet, but she will. I am confident she will. Only she thought it best to wait a few weeks. Until she is of age, you know.'

'The devil she did!' Tristan bit back any further comment. He did not know what to think. Was she a cunning little vixen, who had Freddie wrapped around her finger and meant to wed him, or was she waiting to see how much she was worth and if she could aim higher? If she discovered she was a considerable heiress, would she drop him flat?

There was also the possibility that she was the love-child of some unknown gentleman. It had crossed his mind more than once that the Pridhams might be playing some deep game, intent on catching a rich husband for their niece.

'Perhaps you should invite Mama to come to Bath,' Freddie mused. 'I am sure she will love Natalya, do you not think so?'

Tristan thought Katherine would be horrified at the thought of her only son marrying a girl whose respectable birth was not assured.

'I think we should wait a little for that,' he replied cautiously. 'The house in George Street is hired for the season, so there is no rush.' He knew his nephew was going to argue and said quickly, 'I will sound out the Pridhams. If you are serious about offering for Miss Fairchild.'

'More serious than I have ever been about anything in my life before. Dash it, Tris, have you not been listening to me?'

'I beg your pardon, Freddie, but it is very sudden. You have known the lady for such a short time.'

'I have known her since January, and it is now May!'

'Yes, yes, but you were only in Bath for a small part of the year.'

'What has that to say to anything? I fell in love at first sight!'

'Your mother is hardly likely to think that is a recommendation. What can you tell her about Natalya? What do you know of her birth, her family?'

With an oath Freddie clutched at Tristan's arm.

'Tris, pray do not refuse to support me in this! You must talk to the Pridhams as soon as maybe. When they realise I am serious in wanting to marry Natalya they cannot fail to give you some information about her.'

The flaring streetlamp made Freddie's youthful features looking even younger, but there was no doubting the earnest entreaty in his voice. Tristan sighed.

'Very well. Tomorrow I will call at Sydney Place and speak to Pridham about the matter.'

'Excellent. I knew I might rely upon you!' Freddie slipped his arm through Tristan's as they set off again. 'Now, when we get back to your house, we should open a bottle of your best claret, to celebrate!'

* * *

It was a full week before Tristan could see Mr Pridham, who had succumbed to the sore throat that had laid low his good lady. Natalya had escaped the infection, but she could not be persuaded to go out or to receive visitors, apart from the doctor and the various tutors employed to instruct her. Tristan learned all this from Freddie, who appeared to accept the situation with equanimity. His friend, Gore Conyer had arrived in Bath and the two young men joined the Grishams for various outdoor parties and picnics, as the weather continued fair.

It was thus on the Monday morning that a note was delivered for Lord Dalmorren, informing His Lordship that Mr Pridham would see him at two o'clock, if it suited. Tristan duly presented himself and was shown into the drawing room, where his host greeted him with rather forced bonhomie and offered him a glass of port wine.

'I wish I could offer you sherry, my lord, but as you know, the recent war in the Peninsula has wreaked havoc with the supplies coming in from Spain.'

Conversation continued thus, and it was not until the two men were seated, each with a glass in hand, that Tristan had the opportunity to explain the reason for his visit. Mention of Freddie brought a frown to Mr Pridham's already sombre countenance.

'That young gentleman has become a little too particular in his attentions to my niece.'

'I believe there is an attraction between them,' replied Tristan. 'It is hardly surprising. My nephew tells me they have been acquainted now since the beginning of the year. I believe there may be some understanding between them, sir, and it behoves me, as Mr Erwin's guardian, to discuss the matter with you.'

'There is no need for discussion. There can be no possibility of an alliance between Erwin and my niece.'

Tristan's brows rose. 'That is very blunt, sir.'

'I think it is best to speak frankly. This affair must be nipped in the bud before it goes too far.'

Tristan put down his half-empty glass. He had the impression that if he had finished his wine Mr Pridham would have suggested he should leave. He tried a more persuasive note.

'Surely, if the young people are truly fond of one another, we should at least consider the matter.'

'There is nothing to consider. I should be obliged to you, my lord, if you would inform Mr Erwin that his suit will not succeed.'

'He will be disappointed to hear that.' He forced himself to add, 'As, I believe, will Miss Fairchild. I had not thought my nephew such an ineligible partner. The lady certainly does not appear to think so.'

'My ward will do as she is bid,' retorted Mr Pridham. 'I have already told her she should forget Mr Erwin. There will be no repeat of last week's disgraceful behaviour in the Assembly Rooms, where they spent far too much time together and attracted no little attention.' His mouth turned down in distaste. 'You were present, I believe, my lord. I would have thought, as Erwin's guardian, you might have done more to prevent it. They have laid themselves open to gossip. I have informed Natalya that she will attend no more balls for the time being and her outings will be severely curtailed while your nephew is in Bath.'

'You are not afraid that she will rebel?' Tristan smiled. 'Young love can be very overwhelming, you know.'

'My lord, if you think your nephew might try to persuade Natalya to elope then I suggest most strongly that you advise him against it.'

Tristan's hold on his temper began to slip.

'Freddie might be in love, but he is a gentleman,' he retorted. 'He would never contemplate taking such an outrageous step.'

'I am glad to hear it.'

Tristan regarded his host steadily. 'Have you considered, sir, that your niece will be of age in a few weeks' time? She will then be able to wed anyone she chooses.'

'Rest assured it will not be your nephew!'

'Really? From what I have observed, I believe your niece is very fond of him. Surely you would not like to see her hurt.'

'That need not concern you, my lord.' Pridham rose. 'Now, if that is all, I am extremely busy.'

Tristan pushed himself to his feet. Time for a little plain speaking.

'You have made it quite clear that you will not countenance an offer from my nephew. Perhaps we should discuss *my* concerns about Miss Fairchild. You cannot be unaware that there is some talk about her parentage.'

'Idle gossip that is unworthy of attention.'

'Unworthy, perhaps, but the speculation cannot be other than damaging to the young lady.'

Mr Pridham drew himself to his full height and glared up at Tristan.

'My lord I am not at liberty to tell you anything of Miss Fairchild's history, or her parents. Nor can I give your nephew any reason to hope. I am sure he is an excellent young man but he should not, must not, offer for her.' He stalked to the door and held it open. 'I bid you good day, my lord.'

Tristan made his way back to George Street, turning over in his mind his conversation with Pridham. He had expected the man to show a little more compassion towards the young couple. Instead, the fellow had exhibited a despotic attitude that would not have looked out of place in a Gothic novel. No wonder Natalya might be tempted to marry, just to escape his petty tyranny.

Freddie had been in good spirits all week and Tristan hoped he would not be unduly disappointed by the setback. He would have to warn the boy against any hasty action, but if the pair were intent upon a union, then they should wait until they were both of age. Natalya would be one-and-twenty in a few weeks' time, Freddie's birthday was in October. Heaven knew he did not want them to marry, but if they were determined, he would not stand in their way. And, he thought grimly, he would have to coax his sister into accepting to the match.

Arriving at his house, Tristan was informed that his nephew was in the drawing room. He left his hat and gloves with the footman and went in. Freddie was standing beside the fireplace, staring down into the empty hearth, and Tristan decided to get the bad news over with as quickly as possible.

He said, without preamble, 'I will tell you now, Pridham is determined to forbid the banns.'

Freddie turned towards him, his boyish countenance pale and unusually grim.

'Is he, by Gad? Well, it seems he is not the only one who objects to my courting Miss Fairchild. I have been warned off, Tris.'

Chapter Seven

Tristan fetched two glasses of brandy and put one into Freddie's hand. The boy was still looking very white so he put one hand on his shoulder and gently pushed him down into a chair.

'Tell me,' he ordered. 'Everything, and from the beginning.'

'You know I went out riding with Gore Conyer and Henry Grisham this morning. When we got back, I took my hack to the stables behind the White Hart and was on my way here when two fellows approached me. They seemed respectable enough and they invited me into the Cock Tavern to discuss a matter of business.' He gave a slight shrug. 'They addressed me by name and I thought perhaps Conyer or Middleston had put them my way, but no—' He broke off, his brow darkening. 'Damned impertinence! They told me they had been commissioned to talk to me, to warn me that my... my *association* with a certain lady who lives in Sydney Place must cease, or it would be the worse for me!'

Tristan muttered a curse. 'You did not recognise these men?'

Freddie shook his head. 'They were not part of the Pridhams' household. At least, not that I had ever seen.'

'How did they speak—were they local, educated?'

'They were dressed respectably. Clerks, or servants, perhaps. Only one of them talked and he spoke very well.' Freddie hesitated, frowning. 'Too well, now I come to think of it. No trace of an accent. It crossed my mind at the time that perhaps he was not an Englishman. Deuced odd.'

'As you say, Freddie, damned odd. What are you going to do?'

'Do? Why, nothing. Even if I had changed my mind about marrying Natalya I should not withdraw now!' He saw Tristan's brows go up and added quickly, 'Not that I *have* changed my mind. Not at all! Damn their impudence, I am not to be intimidated by such a thing!'

'Nevertheless, I think we must take this seriously, at least until we learn more. Pridham told me he was *not at liberty* to tell me anything about his ward. A strange choice of phrase, don't you think? Perhaps there is someone else behind all this. You will oblige me by taking your groom or a footman with you when you go abroad, unless you are in the carriage.'

'Take a servant with me, everywhere? I cannot do that!'

'You can and you will. By heaven, Freddie, there is some mystery here and I am damned if I will let it go. I am determined to get to the bottom of this matter. I shall write to Charles Denham tonight. He can make discreet enquiries about the Pridhams. And about Miss Natalya Fairchild.'

'Dash it all, Tris, you don't want to involve your secretary.'

'On the contrary, Charles is the very best person to involve. He is discretion itself and he is currently in London on estate business, so he is well placed to look into this matter.' He glanced at the clock. 'I will write to him tonight. Now I must go and change for dinner.'

Freddie had finished his brandy and was looking much more like his normal self. He replied cheerfully, 'Oh, that is what I meant to tell you, Tris. I am off to dine with the Grishams and then we are all going to the Assembly Rooms.'

'Pridham has told me that Miss Fairchild will not be attending this evening.'

'That doesn't surprise me,' said Freddie easily. 'Jane Grisham called on Lya earlier this week and heard that Mr Pridham had kicked up a dust about our sitting together for so long at last Monday's ball. He is keeping her very close for a while, but Jane has promised to carry any messages we may have for one another.'

'You might wish to change your mind, then. About attending tonight's assembly.'

'No, I thought I might as well look in. Gore Conyer and Henry will be there, so we will have a merry time of it.'

'While Natalya sits at home alone.'

A faint flush coloured Freddie's cheeks. 'Oh, well, it is not as if *my* sitting at home, too, will do her any good. Better that I am seen out and about in Bath, then the Pridhams might think there was nothing so very serious in our meetings after all and relax their guard.'

'I believe they are taking the matter far more seriously than that, Freddie. Have you not considered that it might well have been Pridham who set those fellows on to you?'

'That would be a hare-brained thing to do. He must know that no true gentleman would allow himself to be frightened off by a few threats. However, I will take the carriage tonight, just for your peace of mind, dear Uncle!'

With that he hurried away, seemingly far less concerned with the events of the day than Tristan.

After a week's confinement in Sydney Place, Natalya was allowed to go abroad again with her friends, on the understanding that she was always accompanied by one of the Pridhams' trusted servants, who was given strict instructions never to allow their young mistress out of their sight.

Mr Pridham had informed Natalya of his interview with Lord Dalmorren and stressed to her that he would in no wise countenance an offer from Mr Erwin. Natalya listened to him in silence, eyes downcast, but was so incensed by his manner that she made no effort to convince him that she was not in love with Freddie.

When she had asked him what he had told Lord Dalmorren about her parentage, his angry response that there was nothing to tell was so full of bluster she was more convinced than ever that there was something shameful in her past. Something so bad that no man would ever want her, if he knew of it. The thought was so lowering that when she next met Freddie, at the Grishams' picnic party, his protestations were like balm to her wounded spirits.

The picnic was an annual event, traditionally held on the first fine Monday in June, but this year a spell of early warm and settled weather had encouraged them to bring it forward to the end of May. The Grishams invited all their friends and acquaintances to join them and on the appointed day, old and young alike gathered outside their house in Royal Crescent. From there they would make their way together to Lansdown Hill by carriage or on horseback. By the way Mr Pridham had frowned up at the clear blue sky when they left Sydney Place, Natalya guessed her uncle and aunt would have preferred to stay away, but they had accepted the invitation some weeks ago and it would have been difficult to withdraw without offending the Grishams. Thus it was that Natalya was allowed to ride out on her beautiful grey mare while the Pridhams were accommodated in one of the open carriages.

Natalya noticed Freddie riding into the Crescent on a rangy bay hack. He was accompanied by Lord Dalmorren on the black mare that she thought more suited to the hunting field than on the cobbled streets of Bath. When their eyes met, Tristan touched his hat to her, but did not approach, and she saw him frown as his nephew trotted up and greeted her with unfeigned delight.

In the happy confusion of arrivals, it was a simple matter for Freddie to draw Natalya a little away from the others for a private word. He was outraged by her

uncle's refusal to agree to an engagement and fumed
for some moments over her incarceration.

'What with your uncle's attitude, and the threats,
I am tempted to elope with you this minute, if you'd
agree!'

'Threats?' She looked at him closely. 'Is there something I do not know?'

He hesitated. 'I had not meant to tell you, Lya, but
I was warned off!'

She listened in growing horror as he related the incident and, when he had finished, she reached out and
touched his arm.

'Oh, Freddie, then you might be in danger if you are
seen too long in my company!'

'Dash it all, Lya, I am not going to be bullied into
staying away from you.' He saw her anxious frown and
said quickly, 'Forgive me, I should not have said anything. I do not set any store by it, I assure you. In fact,
it is very likely that I misunderstood the fellows and I
have it all wrong. A couple of ruffians, making empty
threats. And quite unnecessary, too, since Tristan had
already called upon your uncle and he refused even to
consider an offer from me.' He grinned. 'Is it any wonder, when Tristan told me of it, that I was too angry to
think of anything other than running off with you?'

'No, indeed! I was angry, too, at first, when Uncle
Pridham told me he had rejected your suit. Indeed, I
felt so rebellious that I could not bring myself to tell
him I had no intention of marrying you! Nevertheless,
I am appalled that someone should threaten you.' She
shivered and cast an anxious glance over her shoulder.

'Perhaps it would be best if we do not talk together for too long at any one time. Come along, let us get back to the others.'

He nodded. 'Very well, although I am… I am *dashed* if I want anyone to think I am no longer your suitor! That would make me appear quite lily-livered.'

She smiled, but said nothing. As they turned to rejoin the main group Natalya noticed that Lord Dalmorren was watching them. The brim of his hat shadowed his face, but she was sure he was frowning.

'Freddie, could it have been *your* uncle who set those men on you?'

'Tristan?' He burst out laughing at that. 'By heaven, Lya, what an idea! No, if Tris wanted to prevent the banns he would tell me to my face. He would not resort to such underhand tactics. But do let us forget all about that now. The sun is shining and I want us to enjoy ourselves. And if you do not object, I should like to go on very much as we did before. I still hope you will change your mind about me, you know.'

'I am convinced we should not suit, Freddie, but I confess I would not wish you to avoid me altogether.' She flushed. 'I am aware there are rumours about my birth. It would be such a blow to one's pride, you know, not to have *any* suitors.' She tried to make light of it, but could not help adding anxiously, 'Only I do not wish to put you in any danger.'

'Dash it, you have no need to worry about me, my dear. I shall be on my guard in future, trust me. But remember I am your friend, Lya. You can call upon me if ever you need help.'

Natalya was touched by this, but they were too close to the others for her to reply and they trotted up to join the riders following the carriages as they began to move out of Royal Crescent.

Freddie went off to ride alongside Jane Grisham and almost immediately they were engrossed in conversation. Natalya thought how comfortable they looked together. Perhaps they might even make a match of it one day. Jane's family were wealthy and well respected in Bath. There were no questions over her parentage, no objection to her as a bride for any gentleman.

'Suffering pangs of jealousy, Miss Fairchild?'

Natalya looked around to find Lord Dalmorren beside her and was mortified to feel a blush heating her cheeks.

'Not at all, my lord. Freddie is free to talk with whomsoever he chooses.'

'And you are not?'

'You know I am not!'

'Why should that be, Miss Fairchild?'

'You have spoken to my uncle,' she countered. 'What did he tell you about me?'

'Nothing. He saw no reason to say anything about you, since he would not even consider Freddie's suit.'

'Then you know as much as I.' Suddenly she was tired of the pretence. 'I have no idea who my mother was, or my father. I am accepted in Bath because the Pridhams are rich and claim me as their kin and also because of Mrs Ancrum's patronage, but although the local families allow me to associate with their daughters, I am not considered a suitable match for their sons.

Or for anyone.' She thought of the threats Freddie had received and shivered. 'You would be advised to stay away from me.'

'No, why? I am responsible to no one for my actions. If I ride beside you, it is because I want to do so. I enjoy the company and conversation of an intelligent woman. Many men do, you know, Miss Fairchild.'

She stared straight ahead, blinking away a sudden rush of tears.

'Now what have I said to make you cry?'

'Why, nothing, I am merely being foolish.'

She forced a smile. His words confirmed her fears. She had read of girls being educated to a high standard and given all the accomplishments to amuse a rich and powerful man. Not with the aim of becoming his wife, but his courtesan.

Tristan watched the play of emotion in Natalya's face and could not understand it.

'Have I upset you?' he asked abruptly. 'Perhaps you think I am trying to flirt. I assure you that is not the case.'

'No.' An unsteady laugh accompanied the words. 'I acquit you of that, my lord. I believe you were being kind and I am very grateful.'

The humble note in her voice irked him. He said roughly, 'I do not want your gratitude.'

'Then what do you want of me?'

Her eyes were gleaming with angry defiance, but there was something more in their depths. Fear. She was wary as a wild creature.

'Why, nothing,' he replied. 'Merely to talk with you. And to see how well you ride. Perhaps you have not noticed, but we have reached a stretch of flat ground and some of the others are preparing to gallop. Shall we join them?'

The anxious look fled.

'I should like nothing better!'

They turned their mounts and trotted up beside the rest of the riders. There were calls from parents and those in the carriages for the riders to be careful, but they went unheeded. Soon they were all spread out and speeding over the turf. For the first part of the gallop Tristan kept his horse in check, following Natalya as she galloped towards the front of the pack. Not for her a gentle canter while she remained upright in the saddle, looking calm and elegant. Natalya was bent low over the grey's neck, urging her on while the skirts of her riding habit billowed out in an azure cloud behind her. His hired mare covered the ground at an easy pace while he watched in admiration the way Natalya controlled her spirited mount. They had drawn level with the leaders when he gave the mare her head, surging forward to overtake everyone and thundering onwards to the end of the gallop, a hedge that enclosed a field of sheep.

He pulled up and swung the mare around to discover he was well ahead of the others and he had time to watch Natalya galloping the final few yards towards the hedge, where she brought her horse to a stand with the ease of an accomplished rider. She was transformed, her cheeks and eyes glowing from the exertion and a smile of unalloyed pleasure lighting her face. He glanced about to see if Freddie would take the opportunity to approach her, but his nephew had pulled up beside Miss Grisham and they were already turning to walk their horses back towards the road.

Tristan trotted over to Natalya and she greeted him with no sign of their earlier restraint.

'That hunter of yours goes like the wind,' she told him, sending an appreciative glance towards his mare.

'Yes, I was fortunate to find such a fine animal at the stables.'

'That is a hired mount?' Natalya's brows went up. 'She is much better than the usual run of job horses.'

'She is indeed. Possibly a recent addition, from the stable of some gentleman who has been obliged to sell up. I have reserved exclusive use of her until further notice.' He added, 'If I had known I should be riding out so much, I would have brought my own horses.'

His quizzing glance reminded Natalya of their meeting on Lansdown Hill and she felt a flush stealing into her cheeks. She leaned forward to run a hand along her own mare's glossy neck.

'After you passed us, Bianca was desperate to catch up, but it was a forlorn hope.'

'Do not despise her efforts, she is a game little mare. Fleet, too. You ride well, Miss Fairchild.'

'Thank you. It is something I enjoy, very much.'

'Who taught you, your uncle?'

'No. I learned at school.'

'Indeed? I know little of these matters, but I think that is unusual.'

'Is it? We were encouraged to do so, but then the

school was situated in a very remote area of Yorkshire and there were few carriage roads.'

'And what was the name of this school, Miss Fairchild?'

'Miss Norwood's Academy. A very select establishment for…'

He waited for her to finish. She looked very solemn for a moment until she noticed he was watching her. She gave a little smile.

'I have always enjoyed riding, especially over the wild moorland. Unfortunately, my uncle allows me no more than an occasional outing from Bath, and even then, except for Lansdown, there are so many farms and small fields, there is little opportunity for hard riding.'

'True, unlike Devon, where I have a hunting lodge.'

Tristan stopped, aware that he had been about to say how much he would like to take her there and to ride out together, over the hills and moors. She was watching him, waiting for him to finish the thought and he cleared his throat.

'The country is very different from this,' he ended awkwardly.

'I suppose it must be.' She looked back the way they had come. 'The carriages are making heavy work of the hill. I expect my uncle would like me to wait for them to catch up.'

'Or we could ride on to the picnic site with the others.'

She looked at him, her eyes twinkling with shy but unmistakable mischief. 'Yes, we could.'

They turned their horses and followed the other riders the few hundred yards to where the picnic had been set out for them. Natalya chattered away quite freely and Tristan found himself wishing that the picnic was another mile away. All too soon they reached the servants' carriage, where grooms were waiting to take care of the horses while the guests made their way to the picnic rugs and baskets of food laid out a short distance away.

Tristan jumped down and went across to help Natalya dismount. The Pridhams' groom came running up to overtake him.

'No need to fret, my lord, I'll help Miss Fairchild.'

'Nonsense, I'll do it. Stand back.' His tone brooked no argument and the servant reluctantly stepped aside.

As Tristan lifted her down, Natalya gave him another of her mischievous glances.

'Poor Forbes, he has orders to look after me, you see.'

'And what harm do the Pridhams think will come to you here, in company?'

His hands were still on her waist and as he looked down into her smiling face, he knew the answer to that question, for he had a sudden desire to pull her close and capture that inviting mouth with his own. As if aware of his thoughts, she blushed and looked away from him. With an effort Tristan released her, but could not resist taking her hand and pulling it on to his arm. It was the courteous thing to do, he told himself, but as they walked on the silence between them was charged with an awareness that neither of them would risk naming.

Although chairs were available, most of the riders preferred to make themselves comfortable on the rugs and Natalya accepted an invitation to sit down with

Laura Spinhurst and Jane Grisham. Freddie was close by, but she felt safer there than with Tristan. She had thought she might faint when he lifted her down from the saddle. That moment of helplessness when he held her in his arms had set her heart fluttering, but she had managed to maintain her composure until he had set her on her feet. If that was not bad enough, he had then looked down at her and the glow in his eyes had made her stomach swoop in the most frighteningly delightful way. Even now, thinking about it set her heart thudding and her skin still tingled where his hands had rested around her waist.

She tried to listen to the conversation going on between Jane, Laura and Freddie, but her eyes kept wandering to Tristan. He did not sit down, but strolled around, exchanging a word with various acquaintances, and when the carriages arrived he walked over to help the ladies to alight. She wondered if they, too, would feel the same electric tingle of excitement at his touch.

'Heavens, Lya, was that a sigh?' Jane Grisham demanded in playful tones. 'Are you tired of our company already?'

'I know the cause,' declared Laura. 'It is because Mr Erwin has left us.'

Natalya had not even noticed that Freddie had gone. She hastened to assure her friends that was not the case, but they did not wish to believe her.

'What a wasted opportunity, Lya,' Jane commiserated with her. 'If you had planned it better, you might have had a good twenty minutes alone with him! It is too late now, Mr and Mrs Pridham are already making their way over and they will make sure you have no occasion to speak to him privately.'

'You appear to be on very good terms with Lord Dalmorren,' Laura observed.

'She needs to be, if she is to marry his nephew,' opined Jane. 'After all, we know the Pridhams will do all they can to oppose the match. Not that *that* will matter after Saturday, will it, Lya? Because that is your birthday and you will be one-and-twenty. Then you will not need their permission!'

'Well, I do not know how you can bear it,' declared Laura. 'To be constantly escorted wherever you go and not to be allowed to stand up for more than two dances with a gentleman.'

'She did manage to dance several times with Freddie when Mrs Ancrum escorted her to the Assembly Rooms,' Jane pointed out.

'Yes, but then poor Lya was locked in her room for a whole week,' exclaimed Laura. 'You were probably fed on bread and water!'

Natalya laughed. 'No, no, it was nothing like that, I assure you!'

Jane touched her arm, saying eagerly, 'But we have hit upon a plan to rid you of your chaperons, Lya, at least for an afternoon. We are holding another sketching party at Royal Crescent on Thursday next. Mama will speak to Mrs Pridham and tell her you will be collected and returned in our own carriage, so there will be no need for you to be accompanied by your dragon of a maid.'

'Aggie is not a dragon, Jane!'

'But you will not deny the Pridhams have instructed her to keep a close watch on you,' said Laura. She leaned closer, her eyes shining. 'What will you do, when you attain your majority—will you run off and marry Freddie?'

'No, of course not!'

'Well, that is what everyone is saying will happen,' retorted Miss Grisham, pouting.

'Oh, Jane, surely you do not expect Natalya to tell us her plans!' exclaimed Laura, laughing. 'Or Freddie, either.'

'We have no plans,' Natalya insisted, flustered. 'Now can we please talk of something else?'

Tristan gave Mrs Ancrum his arm to walk the short distance from the carriage to the chairs set out for the comfort of the more elderly members of the party.

'I am glad to see young Erwin doesn't sit in Natalya's pocket,' she remarked, nodding to the three young ladies sitting together. 'I hear Pridham refused to allow the boy to make an offer.'

'Really, ma'am? *How* did you come to hear that?'

'Now don't you fly up into the boughs, my lord! You know how word spreads in Bath, there's no stopping it. Everyone knows your nephew is dangling after Natalya.'

Tristan said cautiously, 'Perhaps Miss Fairchild does not wish to marry him.'

'If that was the case, then I think she would have given him an indication of it! Natalya is not one to give a young man false hope.'

He did not reply. Having observed Freddie and Natalya all day, he was not at all convinced there was a strong attachment between them, but he knew he could no longer trust his own judgement. He did not *want* Freddie and Natalya to be in love and for the most selfish of reasons.

'Ah, do sit down and join us, Mrs Ancrum,' Mr Grisham waved and called out as Tristan approached with his companion. 'We are talking of the imminent arrival of the Allied Sovereigns. It is little more than a week away now.' He turned to his neighbour. 'No doubt you will be going, Mr Pridham?'

'No, sir. We remain in Bath. I have no interest in these visiting foreign dignitaries.'

'Have you not?' Mrs Grisham fluttered her fan. 'Oh, that surprises me, sir, because I recall Mrs Pridham telling me she has a relative working at one of the embassies. What a spectacle it will be, I am sure. I vow I am so excited that we are able to go and to have obtained rooms overlooking the procession route, too!'

'Aye, we was quite fortunate there.' Her husband chuckled. 'It was not cheap, but Jane and my dear lady were adamant that we should go!'

'I was,' affirmed Mrs Grisham, 'but I was also determined that we should not miss dear Natalya's birthday party. We intend to set off the following morning.'

'Oh, never say you will travel on a Sunday,' exclaimed Mrs Pridham, looking shocked.

'I am afraid it cannot be helped,' Mr Grisham told her. 'It is nigh on a hundred miles and cannot be done comfortably in a day. We need to be in town by Monday evening to see the procession on Tuesday.' He laughed. 'I only hope the royal party is not delayed in France.'

'Well, I confess I shall be very happy to remain in Bath,' declared Mrs Pridham. 'The crowds in London will be quite unbearable, everyone bustling for a view of the Allied Sovereigns. I believe there are any number of entertainments arranged for them.'

'To say nothing of various visits out of London, including Oxford, I believe,' added Mr Grisham.

'Good heavens,' declared Mrs Ancrum, laughing. 'I hope they all have strong constitutions so they are not laid up from the crossing!'

Having escorted Mrs Ancrum to her chair and brought her a glass of wine, Tristan moved away to sit down beside Natalya.

He said, 'With the Grishams going to London, perhaps you regret now that you do not go.'

'Not at all. Jane has promised to write to me and I shall enjoy hearing all about it.'

'And there will be reports in the newspapers.'

She laughed. 'I do not think we shall lack descriptions of all the celebrations! But I dislike crowds and pomp and London is sure to be very hot and very busy. No, I shall prefer to be here.' She looked at him, saying shyly, 'Shall you go, my lord?'

He shook his head. 'Thankfully, my presence will not be required in town. And like you, I would rather avoid the crush.'

'Then, perhaps you will come to my birthday party on the Saturday.' She flushed a little. 'Mrs Pridham said I might invite whomsoever I chose and Freddie is coming, so perhaps you would like to come and keep an eye on him.'

The last words were uttered with a hint of defiance and he laughed. 'My nephew is at liberty to go wherever he chooses, Miss Fairchild. I am not his keeper. But for all that, I should be delighted to come along, if I may.'

A day in the fresh air was the perfect excuse for Natalya to retire early, but she lay in bed for a long time with her hands behind her head, gazing out of the window at the moon. Everyone had declared the picnic a great success and Natalya had enjoyed it, especially riding with Lord Dalmorren. She blushed as she remembered how he had helped her to dismount. The feel of his hands on her waist, the sudden suspicion that he was going to kiss her and her shocking realisation that she would very much like him to do so.

The idea of Tristan wanting her made Natalya shift restlessly in the bed. There was no doubt that she found the man dangerously attractive. She liked him, but not in the safe, friendly way she liked Freddie. She blushed again when she recalled how she had invited him to her party. She had told herself it was in order that he might see that she and Freddie were no more than friends, despite the rumours, but in her heart she knew it was because she wanted to see him, to talk to him. Her heart gave a little skip. Perhaps she might even flirt with him.

The pleasurable anticipation that accompanied the idea was soon pushed aside by other, more worrying thoughts that had nagged her all day. The threats Freddie had received. He had dismissed the idea that his uncle was behind them, but it *was* possible, if Tristan considered him a rival. If Tristan was base enough to threaten his own nephew, then she wanted nothing to do with him. And if he was innocent, as Freddie believed, then he might be threatened, too. But who would do such a thing?

She had spent much of the ride back from the picnic pondering that question. As soon as she arrived back at Sydney Place, she requested a private word with her uncle and told him about the threats made to Freddie. He had looked genuinely shocked by the news and his subsequent denial that he knew anything about them rang true. He was pompous enough to believe that, having rejected Freddie's suit, no one would gainsay it and he would think no more of the matter.

She pulled the covers a little higher around her. Freddie was anxious no one should think he had given in to intimidation and withdrawn his suit and she had been happy to go along with it, but now she wished they had made it plain to everyone that he was no longer a suitor. She should have told Jane and Laura as much today.

And Tristan. More than anyone she wanted Tristan to know she had no interest in his nephew!

'Well, he will know soon enough,' she announced to the darkness. 'On Saturday I shall be one-and-twenty. I shall be able to decide my own future.'

But would she? That very much depended upon what she learned of her parentage. Also, although there appeared to be no shortage of funds for her upbringing, she was not aware of any fortune that she could call her own and, without money, how would she live? Despite her education, it would be very difficult to earn a living as a teacher or governess without references and she doubted very much if the Pridhams would help her to go her own way.

The thoughts went round and round in her brain until at last she turned over and snuggled down beneath the covers.

'It is no good speculating,' she muttered into her pillow. 'Hopefully the Pridhams will have some good news for you on your birthday. Then you can decide upon your future.'

Chapter Eight

The invitation to the Grishams' sketching party arrived the following morning, but despite Mrs Grisham's assurances that Natalya would be escorted to and from Royal Crescent by her own very superior maid, Mr Pridham insisted that Aggie should go with her. Natalya tried to argue.

'Surely it is not necessary for such a short journey,' she reasoned. 'It is not as if I am fresh from the school-room. And besides, what possible harm can come to me in Bath?'

'Once you attain your majority you will be free to act as you wish,' he returned heavily. 'Although I hope you will allow yourself to be guided by older and, I hope you will agree, wiser heads.'

'And will you tell me then who I am?' she asked, momentarily diverted. 'I should like to know something of my history. Indeed, I think I am entitled to know.'

She did not miss the nervous look that her aunt threw at Mr Pridham, but he remained resolute.

'Trust me, Natalya, all will be revealed in the fullness of time. You must have a little patience, if you please.'

'I believe I have been very patient, Uncle! Ever since I left school and came to live with you, I have asked you to tell me who I am, but you have fobbed me off.'

She saw the muscle twitch in her uncle's cheek, a sure sign that he was growing angry.

'No expense has been spared in your education or your upbringing,' he retorted. 'You should be grateful that so much care has been lavished upon you.'

'And I am grateful, sir. Indeed, I appreciate everything you and Mrs Pridham have done for me, but I should like to know *why* you have done it and where the money has come from!'

'And you shall know, but not yet.'

'To return to the Grishams' invitation,' Mrs Pridham broke in, before Natalya could press her husband further. 'Your lessons will be completed by noon so there is no reason you should not go. However, it must be in our carriage and with your maid in attendance. Come, Natalya, we are not being unreasonable.'

Natalya observed how her aunt's mouth stretched to a smile, but it never reached her eyes. She had learned that the expression meant there would be no more discussion and she gave in.

Two days later, she set off in the carriage with her maid for Royal Crescent.

As she expected, the Grishams' drawing room was crowded with familiar faces, mainly young ladies, although a smattering of gentlemen were in attendance, including Freddie. Those who did not wish to draw were expected to pose for the others, but recalling the confrontation with Tristan when he had seen her portrait of his nephew, Natalya chose this time to make a likeness of Mrs Grisham, who was good-natured enough to sit in the corner for the whole of the afternoon, demanding only that she should be supplied with tea, cake and conversation.

Freddie did not appear overly put out by Natalya's choice and he happily agreed to sit for Jane Grisham to take his likeness. It seemed to Natalya that they were getting on very well and doing far more talking and laughing than sketching. However, when the groups re-formed after stopping to partake of refreshments in the form of tea or lemonade and cakes, Natalya's friends conspired to prevent her drawing anyone except Freddie. He cast her a laughing, rueful glance and suggested they should take the vacant seats by the window.

'Your friends are determined to throw us together,' he murmured as they sat down.

'Yes, and I am very sorry for it. I beg your pardon, Freddie, I would not wish to make you uncomfortable.'

'I am not, I assure you.' He was silent for a while, then said, 'I am quite reconciled now, you know. To not marrying you.'

'I am glad of it, but pray, hush now. After my last, deplorable effort to capture your likeness, I am determined to do much better this time!'

Her pencil was flying over the paper as she concentrated, taking frequent glances at his profile as the drawing progressed.

'I am resigned to the fact that you cannot love me,' he told her, his eyes fixed on a spot across the room. When Natalya followed his glance she realised he was looking at Jane Grisham and a smile tugged at her lips.

She said, 'Admit it, Freddie, I have not broken your heart.'

He looked for a moment as if he would argue, then he gave a long sigh. 'You must think me very fickle.'

'No, merely a trifle impetuous. You offered for me far too quickly, you know.' She sketched a few more lines before sitting back and looking at him. 'Next time you should wait a little longer. Make sure of your feelings before you speak.' She stopped, her pencil poised in mid-air and gave a little crow of laughter. 'Good heavens, I sound very much like a maiden aunt!'

He grinned at her. 'But the advice is sound, Lya!'

She sobered. 'Then let us make it clear to everyone that we are not going to be married and as soon as possible. I have not forgotten those threats against you, Freddie.'

'That is one very good reason to carry on with the pretence,' he retorted, frowning. 'I'm dashed if I will let anyone think I have given in!'

'No one will think that at all, but the Pridhams might be more comfortable about your attending my party!'

He smiled at that, but it was a little forced.

'Actually, I am not sure I should attend,' he told her. 'I received a letter from my mother today. She has heard from an old friend of hers who lives in Bath that we are to be married.'

'Oh, no!'

'Alas, yes. Mama is distraught. She is very angry with Tristan, too, for she knows he is in Bath and thinks he has been keeping this from her. Which is true, but only because he was convinced the whole thing would fizzle out.' He added without rancour, 'And he was right, too, damn him.'

'Oh, dear, we should not have kept up the pretence.'

'No, that's not it, Lya. The lady in question saw us at the Assembly Rooms, the night Mrs Ancrum escorted you.'

'When we danced together several times.'

'Yes.' He nodded. 'She put two and two together and, well, that was it. She dashed off a letter to Frimley immediately, assuming that Tristan's presence at the ball meant the match had the family's blessing.'

Natalya put a hand to her cheek. 'Oh, Freddie!'

He sighed. 'Mama is a widow, you see, and not in the best of health. She depends upon Tristan to look out for me and this letter has put her in quite a pelter.'

'Oh, your poor mama. You must go and reassure her that there is no cause for concern.' She hesitated. 'And you should tell Lord Dalmorren so, too. Before you leave Bath.'

'Thank you, yes, I think it would be best. After all, he will know soon enough.'

'I really think you should go to Frimley as soon as maybe,' she urged him. 'If you wait for my party, it will be another full week before you reach your mother. Just think how anxious she will be by then.'

'Do you really think I should do that? You would not mind?'

Recalling the threats made against him, Natalya was relieved that he was leaving Bath, but she thought it best not to say so.

'I do not mind in the least,' she told him. 'I shall miss you, but I truly believe you should make all haste to speak to your mama in person.'

'You are right, by Jove. I shall set to work on it immediately.' He jumped up. 'I can make all the arrangements today and be off at dawn.' He crossed the room to say a few words to his hostess but before leaving he returned to Natalya and took her hand. 'Adieu, Lya, and thank you!'

He pressed a kiss upon her fingers and turned away, but at that moment Lord Dalmorren entered and Freddie was obliged to stop before he reached the door.

'Why, Tristan, I did not know you were coming!'

His cheerful greeting carried across the room to Natalya, but the shock of seeing Tristan set her heart thudding in her chest and Freddie's parting words were lost to her. She pretended to concentrate upon her drawing, but from the corner of her eye she saw him clap his uncle on the shoulder and hurry off.

She felt breathless and giddy, half-hoping, half-dreading Lord Dalmorren's approach, but her next surreptitious glance showed her that he had been intercepted by Mrs Grisham.

Natalya breathed deeply, trying to compose herself,

dismayed at Tristan's power to disconcert her. There was no reason for her to feel uncomfortable, she was doing nothing improper. Then she looked down at the sketchpad. This latest drawing of Freddie was no better than her first attempt. If anything, it was worse. She had not been able to capture his boyish looks and once again she had made his face too lean, too serious.

Tristan was making his way across the room towards her. Natalya looked up and the breath caught in her throat. She gave a second, horrified glance at her sketch pad. There was no doubt. The flat planes of the face, the straight nose and strong chin, even the hard, penetrating eyes. The face she had drawn belonged to Tristan, not his nephew.

Oh, good gracious, what was wrong with her! Natalya quickly shut up the pad and put it behind her as Tristan sat down on the chair so recently vacated by Freddie. She would die rather than have him see that drawing!

'Good afternoon Miss Fairchild.' His voice was perfectly pleasant, but she was painfully aware of the shadow of suspicion in his eyes. 'What did you say to my nephew that sent him flying from the room?'

'He is making arrangements to visit his mother,' she told him. 'She has heard rumours that we are to be married and he wishes to reassure her it is not true.'

'Or is he merely putting her off the scent?'

'No! There is no possibility of our marrying.' She threw him a glance of pure exasperation. 'I wish you would believe that I do not *want* to marry Freddie!'

'But does he want to marry *you*?'

She bridled. If he thought her so unsuitable a bride, let him stew in anxiety over his nephew a little longer.

'That is for Freddie to tell you, not I.'

She picked up her sketchbook and rose from the chair, but as she went to walk away Tristan reached out and caught her wrist.

'I hope you are not playing fast and loose with Freddie's affections, madam!'

Her lip curled. 'I would never do such a thing!' Slowly she shifted her glance to his fingers. 'Now you will unhand me, if you please.'

Tristan watched Natalya walk away, head high, back ramrod straight. He cursed himself for handling the situation so badly. He had come to the Grishams expressly for the pleasure of seeing her, talking to her, but the first thing to catch his eye as he entered the room was the sight of Freddie pressing a kiss on her dainty hand. He had seen the way she smiled at Freddie, how her eyes followed him as he left her side, and he was conscious of a burning desire to have her look at him in that way.

The wave of jealousy that crashed over him shook him to the core. He wanted to believe her when she said she would not marry Freddie, but the boy's demeanour as he was leaving the room, his barely suppressed elation, was not that of a man recently rejected by his lover.

Rational thought was subsumed by anger and suspicion. Tristan saw his hostess bearing down upon him again and dragged together his scattered wits. He apologised for calling, explained he had been looking for his nephew and now had only to follow him back to

George Street. With that he left, knowing he looked and sounded quite distracted.

'Lord Dalmorren did not stay long,' remarked Jane, packing away her pencils. Natalya, who was sitting beside her, said nothing. She was still shaken from their encounter, unhappy that they should be at odds.

Jane continued, 'Apart from a word with Freddie as they passed and to take his leave of Mama, he spoke only to you, Lya. What did he say?' She leaned closer. 'Did he come expressly to forbid the banns?'

'No!' How Natalya wished she and Freddie had made it clear that he was no longer courting her. Well, that must be mended and she would begin immediately. She said, 'There is no question of my marrying Mr Erwin. We have decided we should not suit.'

To her chagrin, Jane gave a little crow of laughter.

'Oh, Lya, what a fib! When he has been sitting in your pocket ever since he first came to Bath!'

Natalya gave up and moved away. It did not matter. Tomorrow Freddie would be on his way to Surrey and everyone would realise very soon that it had been nothing more than a harmless flirtation that had run its course.

Tristan was up early the following morning to see Freddie off. Over dinner last night, the boy had told him of the letter from his mother and explained he was going to tell her there were no truth in the rumours of his forthcoming marriage to Natalya, but still Tristan could not be easy. He had not pressed him but now, as they walked out to the post chaise, he knew he could not put it off any longer. Damnation, he was the boy's guardian as well as his uncle.

The house servants were all indoors so he stopped Freddie on the doorstep, out of earshot of the postilions and Freddie's valet, who was holding open the carriage door for him.

'Freddie, forgive me, but have your feelings for Miss Fairchild truly changed, or have you withdrawn your suit because of what happened at the Cock Tavern?'

'Damnation, Tris, I am not one to run shy because of a few threats!'

'No, I know that, but,' Tristan forced himself to ask, 'are you still in love with her?'

'If I was, do you think I would be leaving Bath and missing her birthday?' When he had jumped into the carriage, the valet closed the door and scrambled up on to the box beside the driver. Freddie let down the window and put out his head.

'If you are anxious about what Mama will say about this business with Natalya, pray do not be, Tris. I am off to put her mind at rest.'

With that he gave a cheery wave and put up the window as the carriage pulled away. Tristan made his way back into the house, realising that the boy had not quite answered his question.

The Pump Room was crowded when Natalya entered with her aunt and it was some moments before she saw Mrs Ancrum. Excusing herself, she made her way across the room.

'I thought I should not see you here,' declared Mrs Ancrum as Natalya came up to her. 'Why, it must be past noon by now!'

'It is, but Mr Pridham insisted we finish our studies.' She rolled her eyes. 'Russia's role in the recent war! I suppose he thought it would be of interest, since the newspapers are full of the Tsar's visit to England next week. But it is the last morning I need spend on such matters,' she said, eyes twinkling. 'I have decided to give up all my lessons. There shall be no more Italian, or drawing, history or anything else, as from today!'

'Oh, is today of special significance?' asked the old lady, feigning innocence. 'Ah, yes, it is Friday. The third of June, I think.'

'You are quite right ma'am, and tomorrow is the fourth. You are a wicked tease!'

Mrs Ancrum was delighted with this reply and she laughed. 'Did you think I would forget your birthday, my dear? You know I rarely go out of an evening, but I shall be at your party tomorrow night, you may be sure.'

'I depend upon it,' Natalya replied. 'You shall be my guest of honour.'

'What? I thought that would be young Mr Erwin.'

'No, indeed, even if he was coming.'

'Is he not?'

Natalya shook her head. 'He is gone into Surrey for a while.'

'To apprise his mother of his forthcoming nuptials, no doubt. Oh, do not colour up so, my love, everyone in Bath has heard the rumours.'

'But there is no truth in them, ma'am. I am *not* going to marry Freddie Erwin.'

Mrs Ancrum frowned at her. 'And why not? Have you allowed yourself to be browbeaten by your Uncle Pridham? Or has Lord Dalmorren said something to you?'

'Oh, His Lordship disapproves of me,' she said bitterly, remembering their last meeting. 'He thinks me a most unsuitable bride for his nephew!'

'Well, he has no reason to do so!'

'Does he not, ma'am? Can you be sure of that?'

For once Mrs Ancrum looked less than certain, but she rallied quickly and told Natalya not to be so anxious.

'I am sure Pridham will make everything clear to you in the morning. And if it is not quite what we would wish for you—' the old lady patted her cheek '—well, we shall see!'

Natalia awoke to a sunny morning that augured well for the day. Her birthday. Aggie bustled in with her hot chocolate and she sat up in bed, a little thrill of excitement shimmering through her. She had given up asking her aunt and uncle about her parents. 'When you are older' was the constant response. Well, today she *was* older. She was one-and-twenty. Today she would at last learn the truth.

As soon as she had dressed and broken her fast, Natalya made her way to the drawing room where she found her aunt and uncle waiting for her. Mrs Pridham came forward to greet her and acknowledged the occasion by awkwardly kissing her cheek. Her husband fetched a leather box from the mantelshelf and held it out to Natalya.

'Your mother's pearls,' he explained. 'I thought you might like to wear them for our little party this evening.'

She opened the box and gazed at the contents. On a bed of blue velvet nestled a single string of pearls and matching drops for her ears.

'They are beautiful, sir, thank you.' She looked up. 'These belonged to my mother, you said. Will you tell me something about her?'

Natalya waited expectantly. Her uncle shifted from one foot to the other and would not meet her eyes. She noticed that her aunt had returned to her seat and was nervously pleating the skirts of her morning gown and then smoothing them out again. All the old dread resurfaced. The fear that she was an unwanted lovechild, an abandoned foundling. She felt quite sick.

'Please, please tell me,' she whispered, hot tears burning her eyes. 'However unwelcome, however unpleasant the truth may be, it cannot be worse than my imaginings.'

Her uncle shook his head. He said solemnly, 'It was my intention to explain everything today, but unfortunately circumstances have changed. You must be patient a little longer.'

'Patient! I have been patient all my life, sir.'

'I know, but we cannot tell you yet, Natalya.'

'You mean you will not!' She dashed a hand across her eyes. 'I am forced to conclude that my…my history is too shameful to bear.'

Her aunt uttered a protest, but Mr Pridham silenced her with a look.

He said sharply, 'Pray control yourself, Natalya, you are becoming hysterical. Your story is not as hopeless as you think.'

'Is it not?' She glared at him.

He put up one hand. 'Come, my dear, there is no need to distress yourself. All I ask is that you bear with us a little longer.'

'How *much* longer, sir?'

'You will know all before the week is out.'

'Can you at least tell me if my birth is…respectable?'

Mr Pridham walked over to the fireplace. He appeared to be wrestling with his conscience and Natalya waited in silence. At last he spoke.

'A vast amount of money has been spent upon your education and your upbringing, Natalya. You may be assured that would not have been the case if it was not expected to yield a significant return.'

Her brows drew together. 'You make me sound like an investment.'

He did not smile, nor did he deny it. He said in his usual, measured tones, 'Mrs Pridham and I value you greatly, my dear. You know we were unable to have children of our own and we have tried to give you every advantage under our care. I hope you appreciate that, Natalya.'

'Yes, sir, and it is not that I am ungrateful, but—'

'Good, good.' He cut her short. 'Now, I promised you should decide if you wished to continue with your education, so tell me—am I to send a note to your dancing master, asking him not to call this morning?'

The interview was over. Natalya knew she would learn nothing more from her aunt or uncle now. Tantrums and hysterics would avail her nothing, so she gathered up her pride and made herself respond calmly to his question.

'Yes, if you please. I have already informed Monsieur Cordonnier that I will not require more drawing lessons from him. Nor do I wish for further instruction in Italian from Signor Merino. As to my music lessons, perhaps they should continue, for a while at least.'

'An excellent idea.' Uncle Pridham was clearly relieved that she had not made a scene and he continued with ponderous humour, 'We would not wish you to grow bored in Bath, would we? Very well, very well. Off you go, my dear. If you have nothing else to do, then I am sure Mrs Pridham would appreciate your help in preparing the house for your party this evening.'

'I would indeed,' said her aunt. 'There is a great deal to be done, but you will need to put an apron over your gown, Natalya.'

'I will go and fetch one, ma'am.'

Natalya left the room, disappointment weighing heavily upon her spirits. It was useless to protest further; her aunt and uncle would only remind her again that they had looked after her very well for the past four years and that she owed them a very great deal. They had given her everything.

'Except love,' she muttered as she made her way to her room. 'Except love.'

Chapter Nine

Natalya spent the rest of the morning helping her aunt with the arrangements for the party, but when Mrs Pridham suggested she should spend the afternoon resting she begged to be allowed to go out.

'I am far too excited to sleep,' she explained. 'It is such a lovely day that I am sure a walk in Sydney Gardens would do me no harm. I shall take Aggie with me, for propriety.'

It took her a little while to persuade her aunt to agree, but finally she was allowed to fetch her wrap and her parasol and to sally forth with her maid in attendance. However, after strolling under the trees for a few minutes, Natalya left the gardens and set off at a brisk pace along Great Pulteney Street, much to the consternation of her maid.

'Miss, miss wherever are you going?' cried Aggie, hurrying along beside Natalya. 'The mistress won't like it.'

'My aunt will never know,' declared Natalya, 'unless you tell her.' She heard the maid's frightened gasp and added reassuringly, 'We are going to call upon Mrs Ancrum. There can be no objections to such a visit.'

Her maid continued to lament all the way to Pulteney Bridge, where Natalya stopped and turned on her.

'If you are so set against it, you may go back if you wish, Aggie, but I am going on to see Mrs Ancrum.'

'But what if the mistress asks me where you've been?'

'There is no reason why she should do so,' replied Natalya. 'And if she does, you may tell her you could not prevent me.'

'Which is true enough,' muttered her maid. She looked at Natalya's determined face and heaved a loud sigh. 'The mistress has told me often and often that I am not to let you go out alone.'

'There you are then.' Natalya set off again. 'Come along!'

She arrived at the Paragon just as Mrs Ancrum was returning from the Pump Room in a chair. When she saw Natalya hovering on the pavement, she called out to her.

'Miss Fairchild, what a pleasant surprise! Go on into the house, my dear and these capital fellows will follow.'

Natalya went indoors and watched as the carriers brought the chair up the steps and into the hall. One of them carefully helped their passenger to alight and she rewarded them generously for their efforts.

After the ladies had divested themselves of their coats, Natalya followed her hostess to the drawing room while Aggie was despatched to the nether regions of the house, where she could while away the time drinking tea and gossiping with Mrs Ancrum's servants.

When they were both settled comfortably in the drawing room with the tea tray and a plate of small fancy cakes before them, Mrs Ancrum gave her young friend a wide smile.

'Well, this is a pleasure I did not expect today! How are you enjoying your day, my dear?'

'It has been sadly disappointing,' Natalya told her bluntly. 'I had hoped that I would learn something of my family, but my uncle says I must wait even longer. Mrs Ancrum, from remarks you have made I believe you know something of my history. Dear ma'am, I should be very much obliged if you would tell me.' She read a refusal in the old lady's countenance and went on quickly. 'Forgive me if I appear very forward, but for the past four years the Pridhams have refused to tell me who I am. *What* I am. They promised I should learn the truth once I attained my majority, but now they tell me that is not possible and I am... I am *desperate* to know.'

'Oh, my dear, how uncomfortable for you! But I might be doing more harm than good in speaking out. It is only conjecture. I have no proof, you see.'

'Then I pray you will tell me what you *believe* is the truth.' Natalya clasped her hands tightly together. 'You have always been such a kind friend to me, ma'am. Anything you can tell me would help.'

After an inward struggle Mrs Ancrum nodded. 'Very well. I think your mother was a young lady called Elizabeth Faringdon. She was the only child of an old school-friend of mine. Eliza was a sweet gel and I was very fond of her. Her mother died when she was very young and Eliza used to spend a great deal of time with us at Ancrum Hall. We were never blessed with children, you see, and it was such a pleasure to have her in the house. Then her father married again and the new Mrs Faringdon naturally wanted her stepdaughter at home with her.

'I saw little of her after that, until her come-out. I was in London for her first Season but, bless the child, she was so giddy with excitement she had little time for an old lady like myself and the Faringdons did not encourage her to visit. You see, they had great hopes of her marrying well. I believe there was an earl and a marquess showing an interest, but, as I understand it, Elizabeth only had eyes for one man.'

Natalya caught her breath. 'My father?'

'Yes. I believe so. He was a diplomat from one of the embassies.'

'You know his name?'

'Unfortunately not. I saw him only once, when he was walking in Hyde Park with Elizabeth, but we were never introduced. He was a good-looking young man, but her parents were against her marrying a foreigner.' The old lady shook her head, her mouth turned down. 'It was very badly handled. They tried to force a match with the Marquess, but Elizabeth ran off with her diplomat.'

'Is that all you know, ma'am?' asked Natalya, when the silence had stretched on for an agonisingly long time.

'All I know for certain,' she replied cautiously. 'She

never contacted me, you see. I heard the diplomat fled the country and Elizabeth was cast off without a penny.'

Mrs Ancrum stopped, her face working as old and painful memories intruded.

'I wish with all my heart that I had made more effort to tell Eliza that I was her friend, that she might confide in me during that short London Season. But there, I thought it best not to interfere. The Faringdons would tell me nothing, save that they had disowned her, irrevocably. I tried to find Elizabeth, but without success, and later I heard that she had died giving birth to a daughter.'

'To me.' Natalya put her hand to her cheek. 'The only thing I have ever known is that my mother died when I was born.'

'Sadly, that is not an uncommon occurrence, my dear.' The old woman sighed. 'When the Pridhams brought you to Bath four years ago I was struck by the resemblance between you and Elizabeth. Not in colouring—you have that from your father, I think—but occasionally you have the look of her, the way she had of tilting her head to one side if something intrigued her. And you have her laugh, I think.'

'But you cannot be sure.'

'No. Alas, my dear, I cannot prove anything. Oh, I asked questions, but the Pridhams denied any link. However, I was made aware in no uncertain terms that if rumours about this ever got out, if you ever learned of it, you would be removed from Bath. Their reaction convinced me you were Elizabeth's child, but I could not bring myself to tell you, if it meant I should never see you again.'

Natalya bit her lip. 'And my parents did not marry?'

'I do not know. Perhaps I should have tried harder at the time to discover what had become of you, but Ancrum's health was deteriorating and we were obliged to move here in order that he might take the waters. Then, when you came to Bath, all those years later, I was afraid to look too hard, lest I should find irrefutable proof that you had been born on the wrong side of the blanket, as they say. I decided the best thing I could do was to be on hand to give you my support.'

'Your friendship has done much to silence the gossip,' said Natalya. 'For that I am very grateful.'

'At my age one does not worry about the niceties of a wedding ceremony. And besides that...' Her fingers tightened on the arms of her chair and she added fiercely, 'You have more breeding in your little finger than most of the so-called ladies of my acquaintance!'

Natalya sighed. 'Society would not agree with you, ma'am. I cannot expect to make a respectable marriage if my birth is in question.'

'Nonsense. That will not matter to a man who truly loves you!'

'Perhaps not, but it *will* matter to his friends and his family.'

Natalya saw from the look on her elderly friend's face that she acknowledged the truth of that. Any man who married her, if she proved to be illegitimate, would be shunned, pilloried by society. How could any couple expect to be happy under such circumstances, no matter how much in love they were?

Mrs Ancrum gave a loud sigh. 'I am so sorry, Natalya. I should not have told you.'

'Yes, you *should* and I am very glad you did, ma'am. Now I know the truth, I can plan for my future.'

'Natalya, we do not know if it *is* the truth!'

'I cannot believe my aunt and uncle would be quite so reticent if they were not ashamed of my origins.'

Mrs Ancrum had no answer to that and for a while silence reigned, broken only by the ticking of the clock.

At last, Natalya sighed. 'It grows late. I should get back.'

'What will you do?'

'I need to talk to the Pridhams. Until today they were my legal guardians and they have looked after me for four years. I owe them something for that, I think.' She rose and went over to kiss the old lady's cheek. 'Thank you for being honest with me, ma'am.'

Mrs Ancrum gripped her arm. 'I shall always be your friend, my love. Come to me, if you are in need.'

In need! Destitute, perhaps, if she quit the Pridhams' house. She pushed aside the thought and summoned up a smile.

'Thank you, I will remember that. And you *will* come to my party this evening?'

Mrs Ancrum patted her cheek. 'Nothing would prevent me, my dear!'

Natalya walked slowly back to Sydney Place, trying to decide what she should do. If Mrs Ancrum was correct, she was the natural daughter of a gentlewoman, but as such, why spend so much upon her education and on teaching her the accomplishments society required of a lady? It would have cost less to provide her with a dowry sufficient to tempt an impoverished gentleman.

Or they might have placed her with some acquaintance who required a governess. Why were the Pridhams so anxious to keep her single? Was she destined to become the plaything of some rich man? Her extensive reading had taught her such things happened. Perhaps she was intended for some fate so dark, so unthinkable she dare not imagine it?

Oh, fiddlesticks, be sensible, Natalya! You are not the heroine of some Gothic novel! This is Bath, for heaven's sake. You would do well to stop allowing your imagination to run riot and demand your uncle tell you the truth!

Fortified by this self-administered homily, Natalya quickened her step and she entered the house, determined to seek answers immediately. However, she was thwarted when she learned that Mrs Pridham was lying down in her room and Mr Pridham had gone out and would not be returning until dinnertime. Natalya could do nothing but curb her impatience and wait.

Aggie nestled the final white rosebud into her mistress's black curls.

'There, miss. As pretty as a picture!' She met Natalya's eyes in the mirror and beamed in delight.

Natalya wished she could share the maid's unalloyed pleasure. No fault could be found with her hair, swept up to accentuate the graceful line of her neck and arranged in artfully loose curls about her head. The white roses looked like stars against her raven locks and had been chosen to complement her white-satin gown with its overdress of white muslin, embroidered with silver.

Natalya sat very still while Aggie clasped the single string of pearls around her bare neck, then she slipped the matching ear-drops into place. The faint iridescence from the pearls provided the only hint of colour and Natalya thought she looked like a statue, pale and bloodless. She had had no opportunity to speak privately with her aunt or her uncle and the speculation still whirled about in her head, despite her attempts to convince herself there was a reasonable explanation for everything.

Behind her, she heard Aggie give a loud, ecstatic sigh. 'You look like a princess!'

The idea made Natalya laugh. That was one solution that had not occurred to her, although it was probably no more unlikely than her lurid imaginings. Heartened, she bit her lips and pinched her cheeks to put some colour in them before she made her way downstairs.

A few guests had been invited to join them for dinner. Mrs Ancrum and the Grishams were there, as well as Lord Fossbridge and Colonel Yatton, and Mrs Pridham had made a point of inviting Laura Spinhurst and Verena Summerton, along with their parents, to ensure Natalya had young friends of her own at the table.

My aunt and uncle have gone to a great deal of trouble for my birthday, thought Natalya, as she walked into the crowded drawing room. *Your suspicions are not only nonsensical, they are ungrateful, too.*

Smiling, she took a glass of wine. It was her birthday. Tomorrow she would ask her aunt to tell her about her parents, but this evening she would try to forget all about that and enjoy herself.

Candles were already burning in the windows of the Pridhams' house when Tristan arrived. He supposed he was what would be called fashionably late, but he had debated whether to come at all. Finally he had decided he should attend, if only to take his leave of Natalya. After all, with Freddie no longer in Bath there was little reason for him to stay. Nor was there any reason to come to the party, for that matter. In truth, he had been surprised to receive the formal note from Mrs Pridham, following Natalya's invitation for him to attend, but when he walked into the crowded drawing room he realised that everyone of standing in Bath had been invited to celebrate Miss Fairchild's coming of age.

He soon noticed, however, that apart from young Grisham he was the only bachelor present under sixty. A wry smile twisted inside him. The Pridhams saw him only as Freddie's uncle, not a suitor for their niece's hand. What the devil did they mean by keeping her so hedged and protected? Was there some secret about her birth that they dare not tell a prospective husband? Perhaps they were merely eccentric. Well, if that was the case, Natalya was one-and-twenty now and she could choose to do whatever she wished.

The double doors between the two reception rooms on the first floor had been thrown open, but even so the room was crowded and, since everyone was trying to make themselves heard against the chatter, it was noisy, too. He saw Natalya standing beside Mrs Ancrum's chair and crossed the room towards her. She was bending a little to catch something the old lady was saying and he was afforded the delightful view of her creamy breasts rising from the low-cut corsage.

Sudden and unexpected desire slammed through him and he fought hard to conceal it. He dragged his eyes to her face, but even that was not without its dangers. By heaven, but she was beautiful. Hauntingly so with her white gown almost glowing in the candlelight. The arrangement of her black hair, piled high on her head, accentuated the long, slender neck with its single strand of pearls. The fine bones of her face were as cleanly defined as sculpted marble. An ice maiden, he thought. Then she looked up and he saw there was fire in her eyes, which were huge and luminous beneath the gently arching brows. She held out her hand to him.

'Lord Dalmorren. I am so pleased you could come.'

He bowed over her fingers. The smile trembling on her lips lifted his spirits. Tristan glanced towards Mrs Ancrum, but she was already deep in conversation with Colonel Yatton, sitting beside her. He turned back to Natalya.

'You are looking very well this evening, Miss Fairchild.'

She looked down at herself and grimaced. 'I feel like a sacrificial virgin.'

'Oh, why should that be?'

He was still holding her fingers and he wondered now if their slight tremble had not been a pleasurable reaction to his touch, but fear. His heart swelled with the urge to protect her.

'You may confide in me,' he murmured. 'You have my word I shall respect anything you tell me.'

Emotion flashed across her face. Surprise, perhaps, and relief, although for what, he had no idea.

'That is very good of you.' Her voice was low, serious, but she shook her head. 'It is nothing. A mere irritation of the nerves.'

Not good enough, Natalya, you are unhappy and I want to know why.

'It is very hot in here. Let us walk across to the open window.' He lifted her fingers on to his sleeve and for a moment he rested his hand over hers. 'Why should you be nervous? It is your birthday. A day for rejoicing, surely.' He paused for a heartbeat. 'Are you missing my nephew?'

'Freddie? No, not in the way you mean. Naturally I would have liked him to be here. As a friend.'

The look she gave him was reassuring, but he had to be certain. Suddenly it was vitally important that he did not misunderstand her.

'And you really have no plans to marry him?'

They had reached the window, where the barest breeze wafted in, bringing with it the faint rustling of the trees in the park. He scooped two glasses of wine from a passing waiter and gave one to Natalya. She took a sip, staring down into the street below. He waited in silence, enjoying the view of her profile, with its straight little nose. There was the slightest droop to her mouth and he wished he might take that determined little chin between finger and thumb and tilt her face up to him. He wanted to kiss away the unhappiness that hung about her like a cloak.

At last she turned to him. 'I will not marry Freddie and I have told him so. I confess it would be tempting to know my future was secure, but he is too young.'

'He is but a few months younger than yourself.'

'In *age* we are almost equal, yes, but...' She gave a wry smile. 'I like him too much to tie him down. In another few years he will meet the love of his life, a young lady who will suit him far better than I.'

'I think so, too.' She flinched and he added quickly, 'I am saying I believe you are not suited, not that you are in any way an unsuitable bride.'

'You do not know that.'

The words were so low he almost missed them.

'And you do?'

She hesitated and he waited again, hoping she would confide in him. After a long, long moment she laughed, not very convincingly, and took another sip of wine.

'Of course not. But as for marriage, how can any of us predict the future, my lord? I believe many happy unions are born from the most unpromising beginnings.' She turned her back on the window and smiled, 'But this is all too serious for today. Freddie told me that you are a member of the Royal Society—do tell me what that is like! Do you attend many lectures, do you know many of the fellows?'

He followed her lead, describing some of the lectures he had attended. Natalya showed a gratifying interest in all he said, especially when he told her of the talks about ancient Egypt. Her questions were pertinent and he was persuaded to describe for her his visits to the British Museum.

'I should like to see the Egyptian antiquities,' she told him. 'I believe the collection is now quite extensive, following our success there against Bonaparte.'

'The artefacts are quite fascinating, but as I understand it, they are nothing compared to the ruined temples and the pyramids in Egypt itself. I should like to go there and see them for myself, now the war is over.'

'So, too, should I. Very much.' Her eyes were shining at the thought of it and she flushed slightly, as if embarrassed at her enthusiasm. A little laugh escaped her. 'I have travelled so little that even London would be a novelty for me! How I envy those who made the Grand Tour, before the war with France put an end to such things. Just imagine how exciting it must be, to visit the capitals of Europe, to put to use all those languages I have learned. Ah well, it is not impossible that I shall visit Egypt one day, if...'

He smiled. 'If what, Natalya?'

She shook her head and he had the impression she stifled a sigh.

'Nothing. I am being nonsensical.' She looked up, saying brightly, 'Have you been to Stonehenge? We went there last year to explore the great stones and I was most intrigued. I should so like to know who built them and for what purpose.'

'You enjoy speculating about the past, then?'

Her eyes dimmed a little.

'More so than the future.'

She had withdrawn from him. He wanted to ask her what she meant, but she was looking past him, her face once more a polite mask. He heard the rustle of silks as Mrs Pridham came up and took her niece's arm.

'Natalya, my dear, Lord Fossbridge has been waiting this past half-hour to speak to you.' She turned to Tristan, all smiles and condescension. 'Pridham and I are quite delighted you could come this evening, my lord, but I hope you will excuse me if I carry Natalya away, there are so many of her friends who wish to speak to her.'

Tristan bowed and stood aside. He had not missed the wistful, almost anxious note in Natalya's voice as she mentioned the future. What was she afraid of? Confound it, his secretary should have found out something about the girl's background by this time! He would write Charles another note. Or better still, he would go to London himself.

But why bother with all that? What is Natalya Fairchild to you?

The thought brought his head up quickly. He was not sure he was quite ready to admit that, even to himself.

Natalya felt Tristan's eyes on her as she went about the room. Not that he was standing apart, staring at her, as Freddie had been wont to do when he first came to Bath. Lord Dalmorren was too much of a gentleman for that. However, she could not shake off the feeling that he was observing her and she could not deny she would have liked to watch him, too.

She thought the evening would be an intolerable bore

if he was not present. He was not the only well-travelled, educated man here this evening, but he was certainly the most attractive. He had a way of looking at her as they conversed as if she was the only other person in the room. As if every word she uttered was of importance to him. Earlier she had found herself studying his handsome face, wondering how it would feel if he kissed her. She thought he wanted to do so, if she had read correctly the warm glow in his eyes as he carried her off to the window to talk.

Stuff and nonsense, Natalya! The man was merely being polite.

Her eyes kept straying back to him throughout the evening. True, he looked to be happy enough conversing with the Grishams, then with Major Moffatt and even old Colonel Fossbridge, but she thought he might find occasion to speak to her again before the party ended.

At least, she hoped he would do so.

Eleven o'clock and still the reception rooms were full. Natalya might not be considered quite the thing by most of the high sticklers in Bath, but she noted that none of them had refused an invitation to celebrate her coming of age. They might regard her doubtfully, even ignore her in the street, but they were determined to remain and enjoy the lavish supper provided by the Pridhams. Her only regret was that Jane Grisham and her family had been obliged to leave because they were travelling to London early the following morning. Apart from Mrs Ancrum, they were her closest friends and she would miss their company in Bath.

Lord Dalmorren had made no attempt to speak to her again. Perhaps he had come tonight only to assure himself that she no longer had designs upon his nephew. The thought both angered and disappointed her, although she did her best to shrug it off. If that was the case, then he was quite odious and she did not care a jot what he thought of her!

In anticipation of the crowd, Mrs Pridham had brought in extra staff to wait upon her guests and, as everyone was preparing to go in to supper, one of these newly hired footmen slipped a note into Natalya's hand. She was so surprised that for a moment she merely stared at the folded paper, then she hung back from the crowd and surreptitiously read the message.

It was a plea, couched in the most urgent terms, for her to meet the writer in the garden. She frowned at the signature, but it was too much of a scrawl. She did not recognise the writing and although she thought the signature began with an F, she could not be sure. She read the final line again.

Tell no one. Do not fail me!

Natalya caught her bottom lip between her teeth. She could think of no one but Freddie who would ask her to engage in a clandestine meeting. She frowned. Had he not yet left Bath? Perhaps he had had a run of bad luck at the gaming tables and needed funds to travel to Surrey.

Instinctively she looked around for Tristan, thinking she should take the note to him, then she changed her mind. Surely Freddie would have sent the note to his uncle if he had wanted to involve him. From all Freddie had told her she knew he thought a great deal of Lord Dalmorren. It was most likely that the poor boy was embarrassed to approach him. Dear Freddie, doubtless he was making a crisis out of something that would most likely prove to be no more than a silly, in-significant little matter.

Everyone else had left the room. Natalya crossed to the windows at the rear of the house. They overlooked the small garden, but from the lighted room she could see nothing. It was enveloped in darkness. She knew there was no way into the garden except over the neigh-bouring walls on either side, or through the coach house that opened on to the mews. If Freddie was there, then he must have bribed a servant to let him in through the house. My, how she would tease him about this!

She hurried downstairs, slipped past the kitchens and out into the garden. It was quite dark now, but still warm. A sliver of moon hung in the sky and, once her eyes had grown accustomed to the gloom, she could see the outline of the trees that lined the narrow path, although everything beneath them was in deep shadow. She felt very conspicuous in her white gown, which glimmered in the darkness.

'Freddie?' she called his name softly.

There was a movement in the shadows beside her and she turned.

'Freddie, what on earth—?'

The words were cut off as a large hand clamped a wad of cloth over her nose and mouth. She was caught in an iron grip, a strong arm around her waist almost lifting her off her feet. She struggled, trying to breathe through the material over her face. Then everything went black.

Chapter Ten

The evening passed slowly for Tristan. There was no shortage of conversation, but he acknowledged to himself that the only reason he stayed was the chance of another word with Natalya. The Pridhams seemed intent on keeping him away from her, but he was determined to talk to her again before the end of the evening.

He escorted Mrs Ancrum to supper and they were soon joined by Tristan's old friend, Major Moffatt, and his wife. No one could fault his attention to his companions, but although he listened with half an ear as Mrs Ancrum and the Moffatts discussed the imminent arrival of the Allied Sovereigns and the celebrations for the Peace arranged in London, he was all too aware that Natalya was nowhere to be seen. On the main table, Mrs Pridham was speaking earnestly to her husband and a few moments later she slipped out of the room.

'You're very distracted, Tris. Something wrong, my friend?'

Major Moffatt, sitting beside him, had leaned closer

to refill his glass. Tristan met his eyes and decided against prevaricating.

'I was looking for Miss Fairchild. Seems damned odd that she should disappear from her own party.'

The Major pushed the decanter away.

'Not sure if it is of any relevance,' he said slowly, 'but I was one of the last to come in to supper. My dashed leg, you know. I like to wait, rather than hold up everyone else. I noticed Miss Fairchild reading a note.' He continued in the same carefully indifferent voice, 'Could have been a billet-doux.'

Tristan considered. It was most likely from Freddie, apologising for his absence on her special day. Why would he do that, though, when he had taken his leave of her in person? He frowned. Besides, it was not like Freddie, who found putting pen to paper a laborious chore. After a moment he excused himself from his companions and left the supper room.

In the hall, Mrs Pridham was talking to a maid-servant. When the girl had hurried away, he approached his hostess.

'Is anything amiss, ma'am? Can I be of assistance?'

She jumped. 'What? Oh, no, no, my lord. I was… er…merely having a word with the staff. We have hired extra servants, you see. One needs constantly to keep an eye upon them.'

'Forgive me, but surely that was Miss Fairchild's maid I saw in the hall just now,' he persisted. 'I trust your niece is not ill?'

'Natalya?' Mrs Pridham gave a little trill of laughter. 'No, she is not ill, my lord. Nothing of the sort. Natalya is never ill. Only…only it has been a long day and she is a trifle fatigued by all the excitement. She has gone to her room. That is all.'

She had retired from her own party! But perhaps it was not quite so strange. There was a notable absence of young people and no dancing. Tristan felt a stab of disappointment that she did not think his company worth staying for, but he shrugged it off. Most likely she was missing Freddie a great deal more than she would admit.

Mrs Pridham touched his arm. 'Do, pray, go back to your supper, Lord Dalmorren. My niece would not wish to have any attention drawn to her absence.'

If Natalya was not coming back, then there really was no point in his staying any longer. Tristan gave his hostess a tight smile.

'As a matter of fact, I had not intended to remain so long, ma'am. I shall take my leave of you now.' She looked surprised, but he gave her no time to speak or persuade him to stay. 'There is no need to send out for my carriage,' he told her as he bowed over her hand. 'I shall walk around to the mews and find it myself. Good night to you, Mrs Pridham.'

Outside the night was balmy. Tristan regretted now that he had brought his carriage. After all, it was not far to George Street, he might easily walk. Confound it, he would much prefer to walk. Beyond the flickering street lamps, a crescent moon was sailing in a cloudless sky. He recalled what James Moffatt had told him about Natalya receiving a note and he glanced up at the moon again. It was a perfect night for a midnight assignation.

Hell and damnation! Could it be that Freddie had

duped him, that he had not yet left Bath? Perhaps Natalya had not retired. Perhaps they were even now in the garden together. Jamming his hat on his head, Tristan strode quickly to the far end of Sydney Place and made his way around the corner. As he had thought, the rear of the terrace was completely enclosed by a high wall. There would be neighbouring gardens on either side of the Pridhams' residence and the mews buildings along the back. No easy way in or out, save through the house or the coach house.

'Bah! You have let the woman get under your skin,' Tristan muttered. 'Get yourself home to bed, man.'

He found his carriage without difficulty. It was pulled up at the entrance to the mews, the driver and footman sitting together on the box. They were both slumped, the coachman's hat pulled low as if he was asleep, but he heard Tristan's approach and he straightened, elbowing his companion in the ribs to rouse him. As the sleepy footman scrambled down, Tristan exchanged a word with the coachman.

'All quiet here, John?'

'As the grave now, my lord,' replied the old retainer cheerfully.

'Now?'

The coachman grunted. 'About a half hour ago a carriage comes hurtling out o' the mews.' He jerked a thumb towards the footman, standing now beside the open carriage door. 'Poor Simon there was walking around and had to jump out o' the way.'

'You sustained no hurt, I hope, Simon?'

'No, my lord, although the driver was whipping up

his horses like the devil was on his heels!' the footman chuckled. 'John says to me that like as not they are on their way to Gretna!'

A chill ran through Tristan as a scenario took shape in his mind. Natalya slipping away from her own party. A speeding coach. It all made sense. She was one-and-twenty now, she could marry whomsoever she wished, but Freddie was not yet of age, so they would have to fly to the border. So, Freddie's leaving Bath early had been nothing more than a ruse. The chill was ousted by a white-hot rage.

'Devil take 'em both,' Tristan muttered as he jumped into his own coach, 'Drive me home, John!'

They lurched away, pulling into Sydney Place and rattling through Great Pulteney Street with Tristan scowling into the darkness, but it did not take long for his initial anger and suspicion to subside. He knew Freddie. The boy could not have deceived him so cheerfully if he had been planning an elopement. And Natalya. He recalled how anxious she had been.

'I feel like a sacrificial virgin.'

Suddenly he knew something was wrong. Very wrong.

Natalya felt sick. She was lying on a hard leather bench that lurched and swayed. A moving coach. Cautiously she opened her eyes. She could not see anything inside the carriage, but the squares of dark blue-grey sky showed her that the blinds had not been pulled down. Against the window in the opposite corner was a black outline. A woman in a poke bonnet and with narrow shoulders. The fog was clearing from Natalya's mind and cautiously she pushed herself up on the seat.

The woman put out her hand. 'Drink.'

Moonlight glinted on a metal flask. Natalya took it and removed the stopper. She sniffed cautiously, then took a sip. Water. Some of Natalya's terror eased. She took another sip, then addressed her companion with all the authority she could muster.

'You must turn back immediately.' There was no response. 'Where are you taking me?'

'No talk.'

Natalya could not recognise the accent from just two words, but it was very thick.

'This is an abduction,' she said imperiously. 'I demand you let me go.'

The woman did not move and her silence was more unnerving than anything else. Natalya felt the coach slowing and as they clattered over a bridge she fell on the door, hands scrabbling for the handle. She would jump out and risk broken bones if only she could escape! To her frustration she found the handle had been removed, as had the strap to let down the window. The woman opposite reached over and caught her shoulders, pushing her back into her seat with surprising strength.

'You stay.'

Shocked, Natalya huddled back in her corner. She was very frightened, but she was determined she would not cry. Biting her lip, she gazed out of the window. She had no idea where they were, for she rarely went out of Bath and never at night. The landscape looked strange, unfamiliar in the darkness. She shivered and rubbed her bare arms.

The shadowy figure opposite shifted, her bulky figure blocking out even more of the light as she removed her cloak and handed it to Natalya.

'Oh, so you do not want me to die of cold.' The remark was met with only silence.

Natalya threw the cloak about her shoulders. It was too dark to see, but she could feel the quality of the wool. It was heavy and expensive. Her companion was no slattern from the gutter. Natalya guessed she was some sort of servant, but whether she was maid to a countess or a courtesan she had no idea.

The carriage rattled on through the night. The faint moonlight occasionally showed the black outlines of woods or buildings, but there was no sign of life and Natalya guessed it must be very late. She had no idea how long she had been unconscious, but it had been gone eleven o'clock when she had slipped down to the garden.

They drove past a posting inn, where lights shone from some of the windows and torches flared in the yard. The sober pace of the vehicle suggested to Natalya that the driver had no desire to stop and change horses. She would be missed, at some point, but would anyone guess what had happened? Would anyone know where to begin searching for her?

How foolish she had been to slip away without telling anyone. She had thought she was safe enough in the walled garden. She frowned. Had her abductors bribed the Pridhams' servants, or had they overpowered them and left them unconscious, or bound?

The idea that someone had gone to such lengths to carry her off was frightening, but she forced herself to stay calm. She had a female for company, she must hope that was a sign they meant her no harm. Not yet, at least. While they were travelling she was safe, but she would need all her wits about her once they reached their destination, wherever that might be.

Natalya knew she should rest, but her overwrought nerves refused to give in. Sleep was impossible. She found her eyes continually opening to stare out of the window. In the far corner, her travelling companion had no such trouble. She was snoring loudly.

Quietly Natalya drew off her gloves and tried the doors and windows again, running her fingers around the frames. There was no way out, short of breaking the glass. She considered it, but not only would the broken shards be deadly, the noise would alert her captors before she could even begin to climb out.

Sighing, she sank back into her corner and stared out at the night. The sliver of moon had slipped to the horizon and in the near-complete darkness the horses had slowed to a walk. Natalya wondered what time it was. One o'clock, two? Three? Had she been missed yet, or were the guests still filling the Pridhams' reception rooms, disguising the fact that she was not present?

Natalya would have preferred a small party with only true friends such as the Grishams and Mrs Ancrum. And perhaps Freddie. She counted him among her friends now, although her aunt had been most reluctant to send him an invitation. However, Natalya had insisted, more out of stubbornness and a desire to have her way in at least one small thing. That little victory had resulted in Natalya issuing an invitation to Freddie's uncle, too, and she had discovered that her aunt was not at all averse to adding such a fashionable person as Tristan to her lists.

Tristan. Leaning her head against the squabs, Natalya stared out of the window, allowing her thoughts to move away from her predicament for a while. When had she begun to think of him by that name? It was as if she had known him for ever. She wanted so much to call him a friend, to trust him, but the feelings he aroused in her were confusing and frightening.

But not as frightening as her current situation. The woman snoring in the opposite corner was strong. From the rumble of voices overhead there were at least two men on the box. She was a prisoner and being carried far away from anyone she might consider a friend. She had never felt so alone before.

Something went past, momentarily blotting out the dim light. A horseman. Natalya banged on the window and screamed. The rider had pulled ahead of the carriage. She heard shouts, raised voices from the box, then the coach came to a stand.

In the opposite corner the woman had stirred and, although she could see nothing but shadows, Natalya guessed she, too, was alert and listening. The carriage rocked as one of the men climbed down. He opened the door and Natalya almost burst into tears when she heard a familiar voice ordering the man to climb back on to the box.

The woman in the corner muttered angrily. She rose

from her seat, but Natalya was quicker. She jumped up, pulling off the cloak as she did so. She threw it over the woman and pushed her back with all her might. Then she jumped out of the carriage and slammed the door shut behind her.

'Well done, Miss Fairchild.'

Tristan's tone was calm, reassuring. She could only see his black outline at the side of the road, the moonlight glinting off the glossy flanks of his horse. It also gleamed on the barrel of the deadly pistol he was aiming towards the driver and the guard.

'Now, ma'am, perhaps you could pick up that shotgun and throw it into the ditch. Thank you.' He stretched out his free hand. 'Time to leave, I think.'

Natalya did not hesitate. She gripped his fingers and put her foot on the toe of his boot. As she pushed off from the ground, he hauled her up and across the saddle in front of him. He muttered a terse, 'Hold on', and then they were moving past the carriage.

She heard the coachman angrily cursing his companion and ordering him to get down and find the shotgun, but Tristan had kicked his mount on and the voices were lost in the darkness. Natalya clung on as they cantered along the road until they came to a break in the hedge. Tristan slowed the horse and pushed through into an open field.

'Are you hurt?' he asked tersely, keeping the horse moving.

Natalya had been clinging tightly to him, but now she sat up a little.

'No.' She could not stop her voice shaking. 'Frightened.'

'You were very brave. Nimble, too,' he added, the harsh note in his voice replaced by a tremor of laughter.

She glanced down and saw that her white skirts were still hitched up above her knees.

'Oh, heavens!'

Somehow she managed to pull the flimsy muslin into a more decorous covering, although she guessed she was still showing an inordinate amount of ankle.

'I am afraid we cannot stop to make you more presentable,' he told her. 'We need to get away from here, out of sight of the road. They might yet come after us on foot.'

'Very true.' Natalya glanced nervously towards the road. 'Let us get on, then.'

'Very well.' He settled her more firmly across the saddle. 'Hold on tight!

Tristan pushed the hunter into a canter across the open field towards the trees on the far side. The green, unripe heads of corn brushed against his stirrups in a protesting hiss and, as a landowner himself, he winced at the thought of the damage he was doing to the crop, but it could not be helped. He had to move quickly and put as much distance as he could between Natalya and her abductors. She clung to him, arms around his waist and her head resting against his chest. He very much wanted to hold her close, but he needed to concentrate, to keep a steadying hand on the reins lest the horse should stumble. He kept up the pace and it was not until they were sheltered within the trees, out of sight of the field and the road, that he allowed the horse to slow again to a walk.

Immediately Natalya loosened her hold and sat up.

'Are you all right?' he asked her. 'Do you need to stop?'

'No, please, go on,' she urged him. 'It is not the most comfortable journey I have ever undertaken, but I shall do very well.'

His heart went out to her for her brave attempt to make light of the situation.

'I wish I could have brought a carriage for you, but there was no time.'

'Why did you come after me?' she asked him. 'How did you know?'

'You had disappeared and your aunt was looking worried, but when I asked after you, she told me you had retired. I did not quite believe you would leave your own party, but I did not question it until my coachman told me he had seen a coach driving swiftly away from the mews.' He decided only the truth would do. 'I thought you had eloped with Freddie.'

'But I had told you there was nothing between us!' She gave a tiny gasp of indignation. 'You did not believe me.'

'I *did* believe you, once I had thought about it, only by that time I was back at George Street. I sent my servants to seek news of a carriage leaving Bath at speed while I went off to the livery stables. I apologise for not bringing another mount for you, but I knew I had to act quickly if I was to catch you and even the best of the other nags at the stable would have slowed me down.'

'But why did you come alone?' she asked him. 'You might have been killed.'

His heart swelled a little at the thought that she might care what happened to him.

He said, 'I did not want to risk a scandal by involving anyone I could not trust. I did not bring my groom with me to Bath and my valet cannot ride.'

She gave a little choke of laughter.

'What an oversight, my lord. You should be more particular in your choice of servant.'

'Yes, I should.' He grinned into the darkness, relieved that she could still joke with him.

She shivered and looked nervously over his shoulder.

'Are you cold?'

'A little. I wish I had brought a cloak with me, or at least that I had not left my gloves in the carriage. My hands are chilled.'

Tristan unbuttoned his coat. 'Put your arms around me, inside my jacket.'

After a slight hesitation she did just that and his skin tingled at her touch, despite the layers of silk and linen between them. She raised her head suddenly.

'Oh, dear, how long can the poor mare carry us both?' she asked him doubtfully. 'I am no lightweight.'

Tristan laughed at that. He wanted to tell her that she weighed no more than feathers. That he would carry her himself, if necessary.

'I am sure she is up to it, if we do not press her too

hard. We will have to walk her until we can find a carriage. Or fresh horses.'

Satisfied, she leaned against him again, her arms hugging him. Her dusky curls were tickling his chin and he was tempted to rest his cheek against them, even to drop a kiss on her head, but he resisted. The situation was already delicate, he must not make it worse.

Natalya held on, settling herself into the rhythm of the mare's gait as Tristan guided the creature through the dark woods. She felt no fear, riding through the night with her cheek pressed against his chest. It was strangely comforting as if they were enclosed in a bubble where nothing could harm them. She was safe, for now, but the fear for the future still lurked and must be faced. The abduction, her uncle's refusal to tell her anything of her history or what was in store. She could not help thinking she was a pawn in some game she did not understand.

The horse stumbled and Tristan's arm tightened around her.

'I beg your pardon.' His voice rumbled in his chest and against her cheek. 'Were you sleeping?'

'No.'

She was tired now, but she did not want to sleep. She wanted to savour this moment for ever, not worried about the past, or the future, just breathing in his scent, a heady mixture of soap, wool and leather, plus something unmistakably male.

They came eventually to a lane bordered by a straggly hedge dotted with trees. Tristan brought the hunter to a stop in the shadows. Natalya straightened, reluctantly ending the pleasant reverie and forcing herself to think of what was really happening. The cool night air cleared her brain and for the first time she was aware of how oddly Tristan was dressed. He had changed his silk knee breeches for buckskins and top boots, but beneath his riding jacket he still wore the white silk waistcoat and the intricately tied neckcloth with its diamond pin, which winked when he raised his head to study the sky, trying to work out their direction. Something twisted inside; he really had made haste to follow her.

'Do you know where we are?' she asked him.

'No, but your abductors were carrying you towards the London road. I think we should head in the other direction.' He pointed. 'South.'

'Very well. After all, this lane must lead somewhere.'

She tried to sound cheerful, she knew as well as he that country lanes could meander for miles. She snuggled against him again and closed her eyes. She felt safe with this man. Her rescuer. Like a prince in a fairy tale.

Tristan paused for a moment, gazing down at the dainty figure in front of him. She trusted him to look after her. To keep her safe. He was at once shaken and flattered by her faith in him and prayed he would not fail her. His arms tightened around her and for a moment he did rest his cheek against her hair. A few white rosebuds still nestled among the curls, cool as silk against his skin, and he caught a hint of their fragrance. Or perhaps that was just his imagination.

Bah! You are turning into a romantic fool over this woman!

Sitting up straight in the saddle, Tristan urged the mare onwards into the darkness.

Chapter Eleven

The first pale streaks of dawn lined the horizon when they came to a crossroads. Ahead of them a wall built of smooth Ham stone stretched alongside the lane.

'This is promising,' Tristan remarked. 'There looks to be a park on the other side. Let us hope we find a gate lodge soon. Hold on.'

Natalya had been dozing but she clung tighter to Tristan as he put the horse to the trot. Although they did not come upon an elegant entrance, they discovered a wooden gate across a cart track winding through the trees. The gate was unlocked and a bare half-mile later they found themselves at the service quarters of a substantial country property.

Lights shone from a low building on one side of the yard. Natalya's sigh was a mixture of exhaustion and relief.

'The laundry, I suspect,' murmured Tristan, urging the mare towards the open doorway. 'They will be lighting the fires under the coppers to heat the water. Hello there!'

A startled maid appeared, wiping her hands on her apron.

'Can you take us to the housekeeper?' Tristan asked her. 'I fear it is a little early to be disturbing the master or mistress.'

The maid dropped a curtsy before setting off towards the back of the main house. When she disappeared inside, Tristan dismounted and reached up for Natalya.

'Come along.'

She slid down into his arms, but as her feet touched the ground, she realised that her limbs would not support her. Quickly she gripped his shoulders and Tristan's arms came around her.

'Steady now.'

She looked up to see him smiling at her. It was impossible not to smile back and when his arms tightened, her heart began to thud erratically. He was going to kiss her, she knew it, wanted it, most desperately, but she felt dizzy. There was a pain behind her eyes and darkness was pressing in. She could not see him clearly and, even as he lowered his head, everything went black.

Tristan had barely brushed her lips before he realised Natalya had fainted. He swept her up into his arms and was still looking down at her when the maid reappeared, followed by an elderly woman hastily securing the ties of a voluminous dressing gown around her ample person.

'Good morning, sir. I am Mrs Sturry, the housekeeper—' She broke off, her eyes widening at the sight of them.

Tristan realised how it must look, a lady in a tattered and besmirched white ballgown, lifeless in the arms of a hatless gentleman.

'There has been an accident...'

He trailed off, cursing the inadequacy of the words, but they were sufficient. The housekeeper clucked around them like a mother hen and begged him to bring his lady indoors. She sent the maid running ahead of her to carry the lamp and light the way. Tristan followed them up the stairs to a guest room where the housekeeper directed him to put his burden down upon the bed.

'Oh, dear, oh, my,' she muttered as she went around the room, lighting the candles. 'I did not expect this and Sir Toby and Lady Farnell gone to London, too! But they would not want me to shirk my duty as a Christian towards travellers in need, I am sure.'

Tristan sat on the edge of the bed, gently removing Natalya's white-kid slippers while the housekeeper babbled on. He only stopped her when she said she would send for the doctor to attend the young lady.

'Thank you, but that will not necessary. She has merely fainted from shock and fatigue.'

He took Natalya's hand, felt the steady pulse in her wrist, confirming his suspicion. Not for the world would he risk her health, but neither did he want to announce their presence to the wider world in case her abductors should hear of it.

'Ah, well then.' The housekeeper came closer and

stood, hands folded, looking down at Natalya. 'Poor dear needs rest. As do you, sir, I'll be bound. I'll send Maisie up with some soup for you and I will look out a couple of nightgowns for you and your wife.'

She bustled away, closing the door softly behind her. Tristan rebuked himself for not telling her they were not married. His senses were more disordered than he had realised. He glanced at Natalya, lying still and silent in her torn silk gown. Almost all the white rosebuds had disappeared now and her tangled curls were fanned out across the pillows like a dark storm cloud. A wry smile tugged at his mouth.

'Hell and damnation,' he murmured. 'Here's a pretty coil!'

Natalya stirred, fighting against the fog of a very deep sleep that had been plagued by disturbing dreams. Then she opened her eyes and realised she was not in her own bed. Nor was it her own nightshift she was wearing, for it was far too large and much thicker than the fine cotton shifts her aunt had purchased for her. So, it could not all have been a dream.

'You are awake.'

Turning her head, she saw Tristan sitting in a chair by the window. As memory came crashing back, she tried to stay calm and gather her thoughts.

'Where are we?'

'Farnell Hall, home to Sir Toby Farnell and his lady. They are in London at present, but fortunately for us their housekeeper, Mrs Sturry, is a good Christian and took us in when she learned of our predicament.'

Natalya put a hand to her cheek. 'What could you possibly have told her to account for our appearance last night?'

'I told her the truth, that you had been abducted and I rescued you.' He smiled. 'She thought it quite romantic.'

He had shed his coat and neckcloth, his shirt was open at the neck and the sunlight glinted on his hair, turning it a rich golden brown. With his handsome face and strong, athletic body, there was no denying he looked every inch a romantic hero. Natalya blushed furiously at the thought.

'You are probably wondering why I am here alone in the room with you,' he said, anticipating her next question. 'I am afraid our hostess thought we were man and wife. I was…er…not quick enough to refute the idea.'

'You s-slept here?' She shrank back against the pillows.

'In the chair,' he told her. 'It was not difficult; I was so tired I could have slept on a board.'

'Oh.'

He pushed himself to his feet. 'Would you like something to eat? I told Mrs Sturry I would go and find her when you were awake. She will bring something up for you to break your fast.'

'No, no,' she cried, distracted. 'I must get up. I must get back to Bath with all speed. Where are my clothes?'

She tried to throw back the bedding, but he stopped her.

'There is no hurry. Mrs Sturry has taken your gown away to clean it as best she can.'

'But I must get home!'

He said gently, 'It is well past noon now and too late to get you there today.'

'Nonsense. We cannot have come that far.'

'Far enough.' Tristan tucked the bedcovers back around her. 'I do not propose to ride into Bath with you across my saddle-bow. And on a Sunday, too. Think what a feast the gossipmongers would make of that!'

She fell back against the pillows. Despite her long sleep she felt too exhausted to argue. All she could do was whisper a faint, 'Thank you.'

He smiled and stepped back from the bed.

'We will need to hire a chaise. Our hostess tells me the nearest place to do that is Devizes. By the time I have returned here to collect you, we should not reach Bath before dark, and I want to make the journey in broad daylight, with plenty of traffic on the road.'

Natalya plucked nervously at the sheet.

'Do you think the men who abducted me might be watching out for us?'

'It is unlikely, but I will not take the risk of driving you home at night, when we would be most vulnerable to attack. Now, I will send Mrs Sturry up with your breakfast and I shall ride into Devizes and find a suitable vehicle to convey you back to Sydney Place tomorrow.' Without thinking she reached out her hand and he took it, smiling at her. 'Do not look so frightened, Natalya. You will be perfectly safe here while I am gone.'

'No, no, you misunderstand.' Her fingers clung to him. 'You must not go alone. I c-could not bear it if something happened to you.'

He sat down on the edge of the bed and regarded her for a moment, his grey eyes enigmatic.

'Nothing is going to happen to me, Natalya. I will be as quick as I can.' Giving her hand a final squeeze, he went to the door. 'Oh.' He turned. 'Just in case you were wondering. We are Mr and Mrs Quintrell. It is my family name, so not too far from the truth.'

With that he was gone. Natalya listened to his quick, firm tread on the boards fading away to nothing. She felt bereft. Not even his final smile could shake it. She allowed herself the indulgence of a few hot tears, which she dashed away when the door opened and the house-keeper came in with a heavily laden tray.

'There, there, dearie, there's nothing to weep about,' she exclaimed. 'You are safe enough here, you have my word on that. Now, you just eat up your breakfast, that will put some heart into you.' She put the tray across Natalya's lap and bustled about the room, plumping cushions and straightening ornaments. 'It is only ham and a little bread and butter, but I have brought you tea, as well, which Lady Farnell swears always perks her up.'

'That is very generous of you,' murmured Natalya, taking a sip.

'Nonsense, it's the least I can do, after the trouble you have been through. Your man was telling me how those horrid relatives of yours took against him when he married you and wanted to fetch you back. Shame-ful, I calls it, when anyone can see he is head over heels in love with you!'

'He—he is?' The teacup clattered in the saucer.

'Lord, yes! I've never seen a man more besotted, ma'am! And when he laid you down here, and you stirred and clutched at his hand, beggin' him not to leave you—well! It fair brought tears to my eyes to see the two of you. So don't you be afraid. If anyone comes here a-looking for you I shall send 'em to the rightabout.'

She was standing with her fists on her hips, looking so fierce that Natalya did not doubt her at all.

'Thank you, Mrs Sturry. You are too kind. Especially with your master and mistress away.'

'Aye, Sir Toby and his lady have gone to town, to see these foreign Emperors and Kings and the like who are coming to celebrate the fact that that French monster has been well and truly beaten and sent to Elba.' She snorted. 'To my mind he should be given the same treatment as his sort gave all those poor French aristos during the Revolution. They should cut off his head. But there, as a good Christian I suppose I shouldn't say so.'

Natalya did not know how to respond to this outburst so she concentrated on her breakfast. She found she was, after all, quite hungry and had soon eaten everything before her.

'I feel much better for that, Mrs Sturry, thank you.'

The housekeeper beamed as she bustled over to collect the empty tray.

'I knew you would. Now, I shall go and see if your gown is ready, then we can get you dressed before your husband comes back from Devizes.'

'Is it very far? That is, will he be long?'

'Ah, bless me, you are missing him already! He will

be back in two shakes of a lamb's tail, you mark my words, then you can have a cosy dinner in here, just the two of you. Your man thought you would prefer that to the formal dining room. I did tell him I was sure my mistress would not object to you using the family rooms, but he was adamant this would be better. It's my belief he does not want to impose on Sir Toby without express permission. Such a thoughtful gentleman, Mr Quintrell, is he not? And so handsome, too, if you don't mind my saying so.' She gave a fat chuckle. 'Ah, now I've made you blush. No need to colour up so, my dear, many a woman would give a lot to have such a man for a husband.'

She went out, still chuckling, leaving Natalya feeling more bereft than ever.

The housekeeper assigned one of the housemaids to help Natalya dress. Despite the best efforts of Mrs Sturry and her maids, the white gown looked shabby in the bright light of a summer's day. The satin was discoloured and the overdress showed signs of rough handling, with snags in the muslin and threads of the silver embroidery broken. Natalya sighed. It would have to do. At least there could be no doubting that she had been forcibly abducted, when she made her explanation to her aunt and uncle.

Once Natalya was dressed and had done her best to put her hair up into a knot, using the brush and comb Mrs Sturry supplied, she looked for some way to amuse herself until Tristan's return. It could be hours and she was grateful when the housekeeper brought her a pile of novels that her mistress had recently purchased. By a lucky chance, one was *The Absentee*, a novel by Mrs Edgeworth. Natalya's uncle had given her a copy as part of his study regime for her, so she had already started it. She quickly found her place in the story and continued to read, resolutely forcing herself to concentrate on the words.

Despite her best efforts, the time dragged and the summer sunshine was waning by the time Tristan returned. He came in, preceding his entrance with a brief knock and she jumped up, giving a sigh of relief when she saw him.

'You are safe!'

He was still wearing his riding jacket and she thought how well he looked in the blue coat and buckskins. Even his neckcloth looked crisp and white. It had obviously fared better from the laundry maid's ministrations than her poor gown.

'Quite safe.' His sober countenance was lightened with a brief smile. 'But I have bad news, I am afraid. There are no carriages available at any price.' He moved further into the room. 'There is some sort of gathering afoot. A boxing match, I suspect, although being a stranger, no one wanted to tell me too much, in case I informed the magistrates. There is not even a gig to be had tomorrow. I am sorry.'

'Oh.'

Strangely, Natalya was not as disappointed as she knew she should be. The idea of spending time here, with Tristan, was sinfully pleasing.

'However, I have the promise of a vehicle for Tuesday,' he continued. 'It is a rather shabby affair, but it was the best I could find and it will convey you back to Bath in relative comfort, I think.' He pulled a package from his coat and held it out to her. 'And I have this for you.'

She stared at the parcel.

'But it is Sunday. Nothing is allowed to be sold but milk and mackerel!'

'Then all I will say is that I did not steal it.' His sudden boyish grin made her heart skip a beat. 'I thought it might be useful.'

Natalya unfolded the brown paper to reveal a fine woollen shawl of the palest pink.

'Oh, it is just what I need.' She rose, shaking out the folds and throwing it about her shoulders. 'I shall not ask any more questions about how you procured it. I will just say that it is perfect and I thank you.'

She was tempted to put a hand on his shoulder and kiss his cheek, but she restrained herself, blushing slightly at the thought.

Tristan saw the gesture, the way her hand started to reach out towards him, then pulled back. An awkward silence stretched between them and he turned away, not wishing to embarrass her.

'Mrs Sturry told me she had served your dinner some time ago.'

'Yes. She said I should not wait. That you might be late.'

She sounded very subdued. No doubt she was reflecting on the delicacy of their situation.

'Yes, she said as much and that she has put aside a

meal for me.' He walked towards the door. 'I shall eat it downstairs, rather than disturb you.' When she did not reply, he continued, 'Having gone thus far, I am afraid we must continue with the pretence that we are man and wife. There will be gossip, but I hope we are sufficiently far from Bath for no one to guess the truth about you.'

He saw that Natalya was very pale. Her eyes were fixed on him, dark and anxious. He gave her what he hoped was a reassuring smile.

'If you are apprehensive about tonight, pray do not be. I have no intention of sharing your bed. I shall make do with the chair again. Or failing that,' he ended lightly, 'there is always the floor!'

She nodded, but as she turned away he caught a glimpse of unhappiness in her face and something more.

By heaven, he thought, shaken, was she *disappointed*?

His thoughts were in chaos. This was not the time or the place for a declaration. Their situation was far too delicate. And yet—

'Natalya, I mean you no harm, trust me.'

'Of course I trust you. I am an educated woman, a rational being and not some silly romantic ninny who thinks every man I meet will want to make love to me!'

She sounded quite calm, but she had her back to him and he could not be certain. He wanted to look into her face, to assure himself she was as rational as she professed herself to be.

Nonsense, you want to take her into your arms and tell her how desperately you want to make love to her!

It took him a supreme effort of will to keep his distance, but he succeeded, and after a moment she spoke again in a matter-of-fact fashion.

'I think I should write a note for the Pridhams, telling them I am well, but I wanted to wait until you had returned, in case you thought it unsafe to travel.'

'I do not think there is any danger, as long as you do not tell them our direction. Would you like me to undertake the task? I also want to send word to George Street, to apprise my valet of the situation.'

'Yes. Thank you, that would be very kind.'

'Very well. I shall seek out pen and paper and write the letters in the morning room after I have finished my dinner. That way I need not disturb you again.' Still she would not look at him. Tristan bit back a sigh. He said, 'You should go to bed, Natalya. I will ask the maid to come and help you undress. Goodnight, my dear.'

Natalya heard the soft click as he closed the door behind him and felt the emptiness of the room as the silence closed in around her. When he returned she would be tucked up between the sheets, the curtains pulled around the bed and he would sleep in the chair, keeping watch. Her chivalrous protector.

And knowing he would not disturb her made her want him even more.

Natalya slept soundly and did not wake until the maid came in with a cup of hot chocolate.

'It is nine o'clock, ma'am, and a lovely morning.' She continued to chatter as she fastened back the silk bed-hangings. 'Mr Quintrell came downstairs early to break his fast, 'cos he did not want to wake you.'

'Oh.'

Natalya sipped at her hot chocolate. She had barely moved in the night and one side of the bed was untouched, the pillows plump and pristine. A sigh welled up inside her. He had kept his word, he had not come to her bed and now she was not sure whether she was most glad or sorry.

However, it convinced her of one thing. He was not behind her abduction. This was no elaborate plot he had devised to seduce her. But if that was the case, he might be in danger.

She said as carelessly as she could, 'And where is Mr Quintrell now?'

'He's gone into Devizes with his letters. Said he didn't want to put Mrs Sturry to the trouble of sending a servant with them, which she was very happy to do, ma'am, but no, the gentleman says as how he would take them himself, even though it has been raining since dawn.' The maid finished bustling around and beamed at her. 'So, ma'am, would you like me to bring your breakfast on a tray now?'

Natalya held out the empty cup. 'I think I should like to wash and dress first, if there is any hot water?'

'Indeed there is, ma'am. I shall bring it up immediately!'

Natalya spent the morning in her room. The window overlooked the drive and she glanced out frequently, wondering just how long Tristan would be. She tried to concentrate upon Mrs Edgeworth's improving tale, but could not help looking up at regular intervals, wondering if he had returned. She missed him more than she could say.

It was a day of sunshine and showers and a short but violent downpour at about two o'clock rattled the windows. It also covered the sounds of approaching footsteps and Natalya gave a start when the door opened.

She could not prevent a smile of relief when Tristan came in.

'You are back! Did you get very wet? We have had rain, on and off, all day here.' She flushed at the banality of her greeting.

'It was the same in Devizes,' he told her. 'Fortunately, Mrs Sturry found me a greatcoat and hat to wear, which kept off the worst of the rain. The poor horse suffered more than I. You know, she really is an exceptional mare, far too good to be hired out to just anyone. When I get back to George Street I shall buy her before she can be ruined by some cow-handed novice. I shall send her down to my own stables at Dalmorren.'

She knew he was trying to put her ease and felt grateful, although she was barely attending, her thoughts fixed on the way his brown hair curled damply about his head.

She said, 'I thought you would be soaked to the skin.'

Suddenly she imagined herself helping him to strip off his sodden clothes, wielding a towel to rub dry the honed flesh she had felt beneath his shirt as they rode through the night. Natalya berated herself and tried hard to keep the thought from setting her cheeks on fire. Not only her cheeks, but her whole body. And she ached with longing. Oh, goodness, this must be the reason respectable women fell from grace! Or perhaps it was because she was the child of some wanton woman, who thought of nothing but earthly pleasures. To cover her confusion, she walked to the window.

'Thank heavens the rain has stopped now. I always think things look so much better when the sun is shining, do not you?'

'Natalya.'

She froze knowing he was standing close behind her.

'Natalya, you have no need to be nervous. I have told you, you have nothing to fear from me.'

'I know.' Her earlier garrulity had deserted her. It was difficult to speak, her voice felt strangled in her throat. 'I am being very foolish.'

'No, no, it is perfectly natural, given what has occurred, but I would not have you be afraid of me.'

'I am not afraid of you, Tristan.' She tried to laugh. 'We should blame my aunt and uncle. They have kept me so confined that I have no experience of being... being alone with a man.'

'That is how it should be for a gently bred young lady.' He put his hands on her shoulders and turned her towards him. 'However, if we are to be convincing as a married couple we must try to be at ease with one another, at least when the servants are present. Do you not agree?'

Her gaze was firmly fixed on his neckcloth, but she knew he was smiling. She could hear it in his voice. She knew if she dared to look into his grey eyes they would be smiling, too, and she would smile back and be lost.

I am lost now, she thought desperately. My heart is thudding so hard he must surely be able to hear it!

The wanton thoughts crept back. How would he react if she slipped her arms about his neck and kissed him? Would he be repulsed? If he rejected her, she would be devastated and it could only add to the constraint between them.

'Will you cry friends with me, Natalya?'

'Friends, yes.' One could talk to friends. Share secrets. One could joke and tease them. One was safe with friends. She managed a little nod. 'I should like that.'

'Good.' His fingers tightened momentarily on her shoulders before he released her. 'I recall you telling me you played chess regularly, did you not?'

'Chess?' She blinked. 'Why, yes.'

'There is a chessboard in the morning room. I noticed it when I was writing the letters yesterday. What do you say to my fetching it here?'

Friends.

She smiled. 'Why, yes, but I warn you, my lord, I have been well taught.'

'Even better.' He grinned at her. 'We shall enjoy a good battle!'

'Checkmate.'

Natalya uttered a very unladylike crow of triumph as she made her final move.

Tristan sat back. 'One game apiece. Shall we play again, a deciding game?'

Natalya nodded. She had enjoyed pitting her skill against Tristan. They were well matched and it had taken all her concentration to beat him.

'Yes, I should like that.'

He said, 'You play very well. Did you learn that at your exemplary school, too?'

'Yes. Then, when I came to Sydney Place, my uncle employed a chess master for twelve months to help me improve my game.'

'I cannot think of one lady of my acquaintance who plays as well as you. We have been thoroughly entertained for the past couple of hours, have we not?'

The dark thoughts that were never far away surfaced again. She turned her attention to the chessboard and began setting the pieces back in place. Is that what she was destined to be, an entertainment, a courtesan, designed for a rich man's pleasure rather than his duty? She had been given all the accomplishments of a lady, but the Pridhams were certainly not trying to marry her off.

Someone had gone to great lengths to prevent her forming an attachment. They had threatened Freddie and she believed the same person or persons had ordered her abduction. However, she could not believe it was the Pridhams. After four years living with them, she was convinced they would do nothing so out of character.

'You are missing a piece.' Tristan bent to scoop up one that had fallen to the floor. 'Here.' He smiled. 'You should never ignore the importance of a pawn.'

Their fingers brushed as she took the piece and a tremor ran through her.

Is that what I am? she wondered, fear gnawing at her insides. A pawn in someone's game?

Someone had plans for her and she was convinced they did not include a respectable marriage.

Tristan watched the play of emotion passing across Natalya's features. Had she, too, felt the frisson of excitement as their fingers touched? If so, it had frightened her and he did not want that. He wanted her to smile, to laugh. He wanted to protect her. To look after her for the rest of her life.

A knock at the door interrupted his line of thought and Mrs Sturry bustled in.

'I will have dinner ready for you in an hour, if it pleases you, sir, madam?'

Natalya looked blank for a moment. 'Why, yes. Yes, thank you.'

The housekeeper folded her arms over her apron and beamed, then she turned to address Tristan.

'It being such a fine evening I thought, sir, you and Mrs Quintrell might like to take the air in the gardens while I make everything ready. The roses are a picture at this time of year and you will be perfectly private there. You cannot be seen from the road and, in any case, there will be no one passing, for it leads nowhere but here. Now, what do you say?'

Tristan glanced at Natalya and was relieved to see that she was composed. She even looked amused by the housekeeper's good-natured efforts to get them out of the way while she tidied the room and prepared the table.

'Well, my dear, shall we agree to call it a draw and take a stroll in the gardens?'

'A walk before dinner is an excellent idea.' Her eyes twinkled shyly at him. 'It will give me the opportunity to wear the new shawl you brought me.'

He escorted her to the front door. Outside the sun had dried the paths and the clear blue sky offered the promise of a fine evening. The recently scythed lawns stretched away on either side of a winding drive and a path led them around the house to the rose garden, which was indeed secluded with tall hedges on all sides.

Tristan wanted to set her at her ease and he began with an innocuous comment about the gardens. She responded. They talked of plants, of houses and gradually she became more comfortable in his company. Soon they were conversing like old friends and he, too, relaxed, so much so that when she began to ask him questions, he responded readily. He told her of his family, of his sister and mother, both widows, both dependent upon him.

'Not for financial support,' he explained. 'My father provided well for Mama and he also secured an excellent marriage settlement for Katherine. Not that anyone could have foreseen that Erwin would break his neck in a hunting accident.'

'That was when you became Freddie's guardian?'

'Yes. Four years ago. Freddie was barely seventeen. It was a difficult time for him, but he has turned out very well, I think.'

'He is well regarded in Bath,' she told him.

'I am glad of it, but not surprised. He has a generous nature and makes friends easily. Katherine worries about him, but that is perfectly natural in a doting parent. My mother is just the same, only now she is growing older I worry about her, too!'

'You care a great deal for your family,' she remarked.

'You sound surprised.'

'No, not exactly. Envious, perhaps. I should like to feel more affection than I do for the Pridhams, but perhaps mine is a cold nature.'

'I doubt that.'

'No, I think it must be. I have very few friends in Bath, you see, and I have lived here for four years.'

'Do you have no friends from your schooldays?'

'No. They—*we* have all gone our separate ways.' She was silent, a slight shadow on her countenance as if her thoughts were not happy. He decided it was time to bring her back to the present.

'I hope you will not feel too uncomfortable,' he remarked, 'eating your meal in a bedchamber.'

'I am not unaccustomed to it,' she replied, giving him a slight smile. 'I always breakfast alone at Sydney Place.'

'What, always?' It was his turn to be surprised.

'Yes. The Pridhams do not like chatter at the breakfast table. In fact, my uncle can be very irritable in the mornings. I realised that almost as soon as I came to live with them and my aunt suggested I might prefer to break my fast in my bedchamber.'

'Are they kind to you, the Pridhams?'

'Why, yes. That is…' she hesitated '…they have no children of their own, you see. I think they find it difficult to show affection. Mr Pridham can be a little severe, if his will is crossed, but never cruel. He can be very dull, however, and I admit I find him quite irritating at times.'

'And are you often at outs with him?' he asked her.

She shook her head. 'I am very grateful to my aunt and uncle for taking me in. I appreciate all they have done for me and I do my best to please them. In fact, I like to please everyone, whenever I can.'

'Is that the reason you agreed to walk here today, to please me? Or perhaps it pleases *you* to step out with me?'

He was teasing her and she replied with spirit.

'Neither of those! I wanted to oblige Mrs Sturry. She clearly felt the need to make everything tidy and, after all her kindness to us, I did not wish to refuse.' She narrowed her eyes at him. 'I certainly did not wish to walk alone in the gardens with you.'

'Ah, I should have known that.' He gave an exaggerated sigh. 'After what happened when we arrived.'

Her mood changed to one of alarm. 'Our first night here?'

'When I helped you to dismount,' he explained, his sorrowful tone at variance with the wicked gleam in his eyes. 'You fainted off when I tried to kiss you. It was a most lowering experience. I have never had such an effect upon a woman before.'

Natalya could not help it. She giggled.

She quickly looked away and said, trying to sound

severe, 'Let that be a lesson to you, my lord. You are clearly in need of humbling.'

'Do you think me such a coxcomb, Natalya? Do you think I am beyond redemption?'

He had used her name! And his voice, suddenly so serious, but gentle, it wrapped around her like a velvet mantle. She felt out of her depth, her heart was fluttering like a bird, leaving her breathless and light headed. She struggled to bring her thoughts back to something more prosaic.

'Mrs Sturry was right,' she managed to say at last. 'The roses are indeed a picture.' She stopped beside one of the bushes. 'These blooms in particular are the exact shade of my new shawl.'

'Then I shall pick one for you.' Tristan took out his penknife and cut off a perfect bloom. He held it out for Natalya. 'They smell delightful after the rain, too.'

She closed her eyes as she breathed in.

'Quite heavenly,' she murmured.

As are you, Natalya.

Silently, Tristan tucked the rose behind her ear. She smiled up at him and he gently ran his fingers down her face, cupping her chin and turning it up that he might kiss her mouth. She did not resist him. Instead her hand crept up to his shoulder. He felt her fingers move over his collar and bury themselves in his hair. It was enough. He put his arms about her and pulled her close, deepening the kiss.

She gave a little mewl of pleasure, deep in her throat, and his arms tightened. He teased her lips apart, his tongue exploring her mouth while she clung to him, returning his kiss shyly at first, but with growing confidence. Their tongues danced together and the blood roared through his veins as she pressed her body against his.

When at last he raised his head, they were both breathless. She struggled in his arms and immediately he released her. Not completely, but enough that she might put her head back against his shoulder and gaze up at him, her eyes dark and luminous with desire. He kissed her again, then trailed his lips across her neck.

'I am falling in love with you, Natalya.'

'Is that wise?' She uttered the words like a sigh.

'Who knows?'

His lips sought hers again for another long, lingering kiss, but this time it was Natalya who broke away.

'We should continue our walk, my lord.'

There was a note of regret in her voice and that pleased him. He pulled her hand back on to his arm and they began to stroll again.

He said, 'You must know how much I would like to share your bed, but I shall not do so. I intend to see you safely returned to Bath, but then, madam, I shall court you as you deserve.'

He thought she would be pleased. Instead she averted her face.

Natalya blinked away the hot tears that threatened. He was too good, too kind. She had no idea what she deserved and neither did he. He seemed quite unconcerned about her shady past. Could he really wish to marry her?

Perhaps she had misunderstood. Perhaps he wanted to make her his mistress. She felt even more wretched. If that was her destiny, then she could think of no man she would prefer to be her lover, but recent events suggested the choice would not be hers. Or Tristan's.

She gave a little sob. 'I do not think you will be allowed to do that.'

'Natalya?' Tristan took her shoulders and turned her towards him. 'Are you weeping?' He cupped her face in his hands and gently smoothed his thumbs across her wet cheeks. 'Tell me what is upsetting you.'

'I am n-not upset as much as frightened.'

'Ah, my dear.' He pulled her close. 'I shall not let anything happen to you.'

'Not me.' She gave a tiny sigh and her fingers clung to the lapels of his coat. 'I am frightened for you, Tristan.'

'Me?' His arms tightened and for a moment he rested his head against her hair. 'There is no need for that, sweeting, I promise you. Come and sit down, then you shall tell me what it is you fear.'

He took her hands and led her to a nearby bench and waited in silence until, eventually, she began to speak.

'Freddie said he was approached by two men who warned him not to—to pursue me.'

'Young fool, I would rather he had not made you anxious with that tale!'

'No, he was right to tell me. And now, the attempt to abduct me. I believe the two events must be connected, but I have no idea why it should be. It frightens me, Tristan. I am afraid of what will happen to you if you are seen to be paying me too much attention when we return to Bath.'

'You should let me worry about that.'

She shook her head. 'I c-cannot. My uncle had promised to explain everything on my birthday, but then he said he *could* not yet tell me. As if he had received instructions on the matter.' She dropped her head. 'I very much fear my fate has already been decided.'

'Why should you think that?'

'Oh, little things that the Pridhams have said. My education, which was far in excess of what is considered necessary for most young ladies, or gentlemen, for that matter! And my aunt and uncle's insistence that I should continue to add to my accomplishments.' She tried to laugh. 'You will think I am being fanciful, perhaps. I just wish I knew about my history!'

'Then let me help. Tell me about your childhood,' he suggested. 'What can you remember?'

She considered for a moment.

'I was brought up by an elderly couple for the first seven years of my life, although I have no idea where we were living. Then I was sent away to school in Yorkshire until I was seventeen. Many of the girls were orphans or, like myself, knew nothing of their parents save that there were sufficient funds to pay the not inconsiderable fees. One or two of the girls knew that they had been born out of wedlock. One in particular I remember; she was the child of a notorious courtesan. Daughter of the demi-monde, some of the teachers called her, although they did not know we were aware of it! Her mother used to send her the most extravagant presents.'

She gave a little laugh. 'I remember once she was given a diamond tiara that had been presented to her mother by a visiting foreign prince. Is it any wonder that those of us who knew nothing of our parents should think we came from similar stock?'

'And what do you think now?' he asked her, smiling.

Natalya felt a blush coming. She should tell him what Mrs Ancrum had said, that she was most likely the baseborn daughter of a gentlewoman and that her father was not even an Englishman! She *should*, but the words would not come.

Instead, she said lightly, 'I do not doubt my history is far more commonplace. I am most likely an orphaned relative of the Pridhams. But I *do* feel as if I am being— being *prepared* for a role. At best, marriage. Or s-something less respectable.' She shivered, but covered it with another laugh. 'That is the drawback of being allowed to read extensively, I have the wildest fancies! I think the truth will turn out to be much more ordinary. Most likely I am destined to become a governess, or a lady's companion, or some such thing.'

He reached out and covered her hands in his own, saying roughly, 'I will marry you out of hand before I let that happen. Trust me.'

She nodded, but did not allow herself to consider the idea. Tristan might be willing to bestow upon her his hand and his name but if, as she suspected, she had been born out of wedlock, he would never be able to give her his heart. Why, only today she had read in Mrs Edgeworth's novel where the heroine was believed to

be illegitimate. Even such a good, brave hero as Lord
Colambre knew he could never love a bastard. How
much more difficult, then, for a respectable man of the
real world?

A shiver ran through Natalya. She gently disengaged
her hands and pulled the pink shawl a little tighter
around her.

'It grows cold,' she remarked. 'Perhaps we should
walk back to the house now.'

'Very well.'

They rose and Tristan once more offered his arm.
However, when she slipped her hand on to his sleeve he
did not move immediately and she glanced up to find
he was watching her.

'Well, my lord?'

'I am in earnest Natalya, I mean to marry you, if you
will have me. So, what do you say?'

Natalya felt the hot tears prickling her eyes again
and blinked them away.

'There is nothing I would like more,' she answered
him truthfully, 'but let us wait until I am safely returned
to Sydney Place.'

'Very well. I understand that you would like to have
your aunt and uncle's approval, but I shall marry you
without it, if necessary.'

Natalya said nothing. In Mrs Edgworth's novel, the
heroine discovered at the end she was neither illegitimate nor a pauper. Natalya thought the latter might not
prevent Tristan loving her, but if her birth was not respectable then that circumstance would choke his affection. If there was even the slightest doubt about her

birth, she could not marry him. It would cause a rift in his family and she knew how much he loved them. She also knew she loved *him* far too much to risk his happiness.

As they began to stroll back through the garden the warm air was redolent with the scent of roses. Natalya would associate their heavy perfume with Tristan's offer of marriage for ever. Only time would tell if she would think of it with satisfaction or regret.

Chapter Twelve

In the bedchamber, a small table had been placed close to one of the windows, to make the most of the evening light. Tristan and Natalya sat opposite one another, exchanging a smile as the servants carried in their dinner. Tristan had had the forethought to bring a full purse with him when he set out and he had given the housekeeper a generous amount to offset the expense of their residence at Farnell Hall. Now, he noted with satisfaction the number and array of dishes that filled the table.

Mrs Sturry had informed them that her master had taken the butler with him to their hired house in town, but he had clearly left behind the keys to the wine cellar, for the claret served for their delectation was excellent and he had no hesitation in recommending it to Natalya to accompany the tender slices of beef he carved for her.

They spoke little and on unexceptional topics, which was unsurprising, with servants bustling in and out of the room, but Tristan knew Natalya was preoccupied. She ate sparingly, taking only small amounts from the succulent dishes before her. He wondered if she was still shaken from her recent ordeal or merely tired.

When the covers were removed Tristan politely dismissed the housekeeper, telling her he would ring the bell when they needed her again. Then he sat back in his chair and smiled across the table at Natalya.

'That's better. I thought we should never have a moment to ourselves.' Her smile was perfunctory and he went on, 'Perhaps you would like to retire. Shall I ring for the maid to help you undress? You need not worry about propriety; I will take myself off somewhere for an hour.'

'No, I am not at all tired and I do not want you to leave.'

'I am very pleased to hear it. Shall we move to the more comfortable chairs?'

'Yes, please. And perhaps we might have a little more wine.'

He was surprised, but too pleased that she wanted his company to question her request. He went off to find Mrs Sturry and came back with another bottle of claret and a lighted taper with which to light the candles. Very soon the curtains had been drawn across the windows, shutting out the dusk, and they were sitting one on each side of the empty hearth within the golden glow of the candles. Tristan raised his glass to Natalya.

'Tomorrow you will be back in Bath. I shall speak to Pridham, suggest he takes on extra staff to guard you.'

'I am sure there is no need.'

'There is every need! If Pridham will not or cannot do it, I shall hire someone myself.'

'Really, my lord—'

'Tristan.' He liked the way she blushed when he corrected her, almost as much as he liked the sound of his name on her lips when she repeated it.

'That is better. After all, you are my future wife.'

She put up one hand. 'I have not yet given you my answer and I will not, until I know who I am. Please, Tristan, do not argue with me,' she pleaded with him. 'My mind is made up on this.'

His mind was equally made up, but he did not wish to quarrel and was very happy to talk of something else.

'Do you wish now that you had gone to London for the Peace celebrations?'

Natalya blinked in surprise. 'What an odd question.'

'I beg your pardon. I was casting about in my mind to find something to divert your thoughts away from your current predicament and I remembered there was to be the procession of royal dignitaries into London tomorrow.'

Natalya was touched by his concern, but she concealed it with a laugh.

'You have achieved your aim, then! Yes, I admit I would have preferred to be in London rather than to be abducted. How could it be otherwise? The Grishams offered to take me with them, you know, but Uncle Pridham would not allow it.'

'I should have thought he would have been eager for you to attend, as part of your education.'

She shook her head. 'There was never any question of our leaving Bath.' She paused, then said shyly, 'Perhaps *you* are wishing now that you were in the capital rather than becoming embroiled in my affairs.'

'I would not want to be anywhere but here, with you.'

His smiled warmed her and gave her the courage for her next words. Nervous excitement pooled deep inside. She took a breath.

'Then stay with me tonight.'

There, she had said it. Watching him closely, she saw the flash of desire in his eyes, quickly concealed but unmistakable.

'I intend to stay here,' he said lightly. 'We have already agreed I will be here to watch over you, Natalya.'

'Not sleeping in the chair.' Her mouth had gone dry. She ran her tongue over her parched lips. 'In my bed.'

It was as though the words had a physical presence. They hung in the air between them, almost visible. Tristan was watching her and Natalya held his gaze steadily, trying to convey how much she wanted him. After a long, long moment he rose, shaking his head.

'It is growing late and I think we have both had too much wine.' He gathered up the empty glasses. 'I will return these to the kitchens. Perhaps I should ask Mrs Sturry to let the maid sleep here tonight and make up another bed for me elsewhere.'

'No.' Natalya struggled not to sound desperate. It was all going wrong. She reached out and touched his arm. 'No, please, Tristan, do not leave me tonight.'

'I think it might be best, my dear.'

His gentle words were like a rebuke and she flinched.

Tristan moved towards the door. 'I will ask Mrs Sturry to send the maid up to help you undress.'

'But you will come back?' Her hands writhed together. 'You will come back to say goodnight?'

'I shall return.' He looked back at her. 'You have my word.'

Natalya collapsed on to the edge of the bed, shaking. From everything she had read, both in novels and her studies of history, she had thought it would be an easy matter to tempt him into her bed, but he had refused her. She closed her eyes. So much for her extensive education!

Frustration welled up and with it anger. What good was all her book learning now? Her uncle had said he expected it to yield a significant return. How could that be, except by marriage, or as mistress to a wealthy man?

In the dark reaches of the night, when her wildest flights of fancy seemed utterly plausible, she was convinced she would be sold to the highest bidder, or, indeed, that the deal was already done and she had been reared like some brood mare, pampered and groomed until she was claimed by her owner. Freddie had been warned off, she had been abducted. Whoever was behind this would not allow Tristan to thwart them for long.

This morning, with the daylight, her sensible, logical side had taken over. She had weighed up all the evidence and concluded that she was nothing more than someone's natural daughter. If so, her logical side reasoned that she could not allow Tristan to marry her and cause an irrevocable rift with his family and his friends.

Whichever scenario proved to be correct, Tristan was

out of her reach as a husband, but not as a lover. The future might be out of her control, but Natalya wanted to decide to whom she gave her virginity.

Tristan took the glasses downstairs and was on his way to the kitchens when he met Mrs Sturry, who took them from him, protesting that he should have left them for the servants to clear away.

'Lord love you, Mr Quintrell, you should not be troubling yourself with such things.'

'It was no trouble, Mrs Sturry. I was coming in search of you to say Mrs Quintrell is ready to retire, if you could send someone to attend her.'

At that point Tristan knew he should make his request for another bed to be made up, but he could not bring himself to do so. Natalya was clearly distraught from her ordeal and he could not bear the thought of her spending the night alone, of his not being near if she woke up in distress.

He therefore announced he was going out to enjoy a stroll in the moonlight. He took a turn about the lawns, but eventually he found himself among the roses. Their heady perfume was stronger at night. It reminded him of walking there with Natalya, of cutting a rose for her. Kissing her. He looked up at the moon, cursing softly.

'Confound it, man, don't dwell on that or you will never be able to keep away from her tonight!'

When he judged he had been out of the house for a good hour he made his way back to the bedchamber. He hoped that Natalya would be asleep with the curtains pulled closed around her bed. That way he would be able to avoid temptation. The night they had arrived at Farnell Hall he had kept a vigil, sitting at the bedside while she slept, smoothing the hair from her face, dropping a light, tender kiss upon her forehead and vowing to keep her from harm.

He knew now that he had loved her even then, but it was the kiss in the rose garden that had sealed his fate. When he had held her in his arms and she had responded so fervently, he had known without a doubt that he wanted her at his side for the rest of his life. He would marry her, but it must be done with propriety and not before she had had an opportunity to examine her own feelings. She had to be sure that it was what she wanted, too.

He entered the bedchamber to find the candles still alight. Natalya was sitting in bed, propped up against a bank of snowy pillows and wrapped in that ridiculously large nightgown the housekeeper had found for her. It buttoned high to the neck and her hair hung over one shoulder in a decorous plait. He breathed a sigh of relief. Nothing there to tempt a man.

His body contradicted the thought. He wanted her more than ever.

'You must get some sleep, Natalya. We have an early start tomorrow.'

'I know.' She was very pale and her dark eyes were fixed upon him. 'I wanted to say goodnight. And to thank you. For all you have done for me.'

'It was my pleasure.'

She reached out her hand and when he took it, she drew him closer.

'Will you kiss me goodnight?'

The words were low, her voice a little breathless, and the effect upon him was shattering, undermining his resolve to keep his distance. He leaned closer and brushed his mouth against hers. She responded immediately. He felt the tip of her tongue against his lips and it took every ounce of willpower to draw away.

'Be careful, Natalya, or I shall forget that I am a gentleman.' He kept his tone light, joking, but it was an effort when his whole being was screaming for him to take her in his arms. With a final squeeze of her fingers he released her and set about pulling the curtains around the bed. Her dark eyes followed him.

She said, 'You are a good man, Tristan Quintrell.'

His mouth twisted. 'You do not know how hard I am working to remain so! Sleep well, Natalya.'

Closing the final curtain, he blew out the candles until only one on the mantelshelf remained alight. Silently he stripped off his coat and waistcoat and sat down on the armchair to remove his boots. The room was warm, stuffy. He went over to the window and threw up the sash, leaving the curtains drawn back to allow the faint summer breeze to come in.

His body was still thrumming with desire. Even if he had been given the finest feather bed in England, he doubted he would sleep much tonight.

Tristan made himself comfortable in one armchair, resting his feet on the seat of the other, but he could not stop his thoughts wandering to the woman in the bed barely a few feet away. He squeezed his eyes closed and tried to drag his mind to something else, but the best he could do was to think of Natalya as he had seen her at her birthday party, dressed in that glittering white gown with her raven hair piled up on her head. In his mind he saw himself reach out and pull the pins from her hair. He watched the heavy locks cascade down over her shoulders like a black waterfall, enveloping him, drowning him...

He must have slept. When he opened his eyes, he realised he was staring at the hearth, a black square outlined by the pale marble surround. He heard his name. A soft whisper, barely more than a sigh. Sleepily he turned his head.

Natalya was standing beside his chair, her naked skin gleaming like ivory in the moonlight.

'What the devil!'

He scrambled to his feet. He was not dreaming. She was really there, in front of him. Her hair, black as pitch, was loose over her shoulders and a few dark locks hung down over her breasts. He clenched his hands at his sides to prevent himself from reaching out and pushing them aside.

'I cannot sleep.' Her voice was soft, but powerful as a siren song. She stepped closer. 'Take me to bed, Tristan.'

Another step and her naked breasts pressed against him. He could feel the warmth of them through his shirt and his breeches were suddenly too tight.

'Natalya—'

Her hands slipped around his neck, pulling his head closer.

'You intend to marry me, do you not?' she whispered the words against his mouth. 'Then why should we wait?'

It took a supreme effort of will for Tristan not to kiss her. He reached up and pulled her hands away. He held them against his chest and gazed down at her, trying to ignore the allure of her parted lips, the insistent demands of his own body.

'You are under my protection.' Dear heaven, he was so on fire he could barely speak. 'I have vowed to return you safely to your home.'

'Home!' She gave a ragged laugh. Even in the dim light of the moon he could see her eyes were swimming with tears. 'I have no home. Unless it is with you.'

Her voice trembled on a sob and it was too much. His iron will broke. With a groan he took her in his arms, crushing her to him. He kissed her, a hard kiss to which she responded eagerly.

He was on fire, the blood pounding through his body. He raised his head, dragging air into his lungs as he sought to control the raging desire. She lay back against his arm, looking up at him, her black eyes luminous in the moonlight and blazing with a desire to match his own. She was his, not in the eyes of the law, but that would follow. His spirit soared and he felt a primeval urge to throw back his head and howl in triumph.

'Tristan?'

He smiled down at her, suddenly humbled by her trust in him.

'Patience, love. This is too important a moment to be hurried.'

He swept her up into his arms and carried her to the bed where he placed her down gently on the covers. She lay very still, but he was aware that her gaze never left him as he undressed. Her sharp intake of breath when he joined her on the bed suggested she had never seen a naked man before. Her innocence was exciting, but it also sobered him. He must not rush this.

Natalya tensed as Tristan drew her into his arms. She was eager for his touch, but a little frightened, too. Then he kissed her and her fears melted away. She responded, her lips parting, and she relaxed as his mouth worked its magic. She sighed as his lips left hers and began to move over her cheeks, trailing kisses along her jaw. A moan of sheer pleasure escaped her when he nibbled gently at her ear.

His hand caressed her hip, then slowly brushed over her waist, smoothing gently over her skin until he was cupping her breast, his thumb circling the peak that was suddenly hard and aching. She was on fire, shifting restlessly against his touch. Such was the aching pleasure his fingers were wreaking she was only vaguely aware of his lips moving down her neck, placing butterfly kisses along her collarbone. They stopped briefly on the dip at the base of her throat, then moved on down to her breasts and she gasped at the double onslaught as his tongue caressed one hard nub while his thumb continued to pleasure the other.

She sighed and arched her body, offering herself up

to him, no longer afraid, but revelling in the sensations he was arousing. Her own tentative caresses became more certain, she ran her hands over his flesh, exploring the firm sculpted muscles of his back. He shifted slightly, his mouth sought hers again and he kissed her with renewed intensity.

She was almost swooning with delight as his hand roamed over her skin, down across her stomach, and she lifted her hips, inviting him to go on. Her bones had melted. She had never felt more alive, receptive to his every caress. His fingers slid between her thighs and she felt herself opening, moving restlessly against his hand as ripples of excitement began to build inside. Her own hands slid down his back. She tried to pull him on to her. He resisted, murmuring softly against lips.

'Hush, my darling. Trust me.'

'But I want you, Tristan. I want to be yours, completely. Oh!'

She gasped, her ability to speak suspended as his fingers drove the tide of pleasure even higher. She dug her nails into his shoulders, her body pushing hard against his hand, quite beyond her control. She bucked wildly and was distantly aware of crying out as she tipped over the edge of reason and tumbled into dizzying oblivion.

Dawn was breaking when Natalya awoke. Through the window she could see the pale grey clouds streaked with pink. She stretched and ran her hands over her naked body. She had thought by giving way to the strong desire she felt for Tristan that the yearning would disappear, but when she turned her head to look at the man sleeping beside her, the longing for him was stronger than ever.

He had brought her body alive, teasing her senses, drawing out responses she had not thought possible. And yet he had not entered her. He had held her shuddering frame until the ecstatic spasms had ceased and dried her tears when she had wept with guilt because he had put her pleasure above his own.

'There will be time for that when we are married,' he had told her, holding her close. 'I will not tempt fate and risk giving you a child until you have the protection of my name and my fortune.'

She wanted him to hold her again, to bring her once more to the peak of elation, where her body was singing and she thought she might die of sheer pleasure.

Tears stung her eyes. This was not what she intended. She had believed one night with him would suffice, hoped that when she sent him away, refusing to allow him to sacrifice himself by marrying beneath him, she would have the pleasant memory of a night spent in his arms.

Now she knew that one night was not enough. A lifetime would not be enough.

Tristan stirred. He reached out for her, murmuring her name. Natalya summoned up a smile, but she was not quick enough. His gaze sharpened and he searched her face.

'What is it love, what has upset you?'

'Nothing, mere foolish fancies.'

She burrowed close, breathing in the musky scent

of his skin, trying to memorise the faint trace of citrus spicy fragrance. She would discover the name of that perfume and buy a small bottle. A reminder of Tristan. He hugged her to him.

'Are you regretting what we have done?'

'Oh, no, no!' She gave a little sob and clung tighter.

'You are worried for the future, then? You must not be. I shall marry you as soon as it can be arranged, you have my word on that.'

When she did not reply he held her away a little. 'Did I frighten you, is that it? You did not enjoy it—'

'No, no, you are quite wrong,' she told him, blushing. 'I—I enjoyed it a great deal. It was so much more than I had expected.'

'I am very glad about that.' He drew her close and kissed her. 'Perhaps we should do it again, just to make sure.'

Her insides curled with pleasure as his hands began to roam over her body. She returned his embrace eagerly, pushing aside her fears for the future and abandoning herself to the present, until his caresses drove all coherent thoughts from her mind.

Chapter Thirteen

When they sat down to breakfast together, Natalya struggled to smile as Tristan outlined his plans for their future. She would not have been surprised if he had been reluctant to marry her, after she had thrown herself at him so wantonly. Even if her behaviour had not repulsed him, once he learned the truth about her birth he would realise she was not a fit wife for him. And if he did not see it immediately, his friends and family would soon make the matter plain.

He was sitting opposite her and she watched him closely, devouring the sight of his lean, handsome face. He was smiling and looking more relaxed than she had ever known him.

He thinks he loves me, she thought sadly. He is still caught up in the passion of what has happened, but that cannot last. Eventually it will fade and he will see me for what I am, a baseborn impostor whom he cannot respect. Then his passion for me will die and I could not bear to see that.

Tristan was refilling their coffee cups. He said, 'I shall speak to Pridham today, as soon as we return, to assure him I mean to make an honest woman of you.' He reached across the table and took her hand. 'Where do you wish to be married, in Bath? Or there is a pretty little church near Dalmorren Manor, my house in Sussex.' He laughed. 'We might even be married in London, if you wish to cut a dash!'

'Ah, stop. Please, stop!' She forced out the words before her voice was choked with tears.

In an instant he was at her side, pulling her up out of her chair and into his arms.

'Natalya, my love, what is it?'

She clung to him, her face buried in his shoulder. 'My aunt and uncle might not consent.'

He stroked her hair, a gesture that she thought might break her heart. No one had ever shown her such tenderness before.

'You are of age now,' he murmured. 'What can they say? And after what has occurred here, I do not think they have any choice.'

She looked up, saying earnestly, 'Tristan, I do not wish the Pridhams to know we posed as man and wife. At least, not yet. I would like to talk to them alone, first.'

'Very well,' he said, kissing her nose. 'But if they raise any objections to my marrying you, then we must tell them everything. I will not allow anything to stand in our way.' He held her away from him, his brows coming together in a frown. 'Now what is it? Natalya, tell me.'

He was so good, so kind, she could not allow him false hope. She bowed her head and took a breath.

'Tristan, I did not want to speak of it until I was quite sure but… I have reason to believe, *good* reason, that I w-was born out of wedlock. If that is the case, I c-cannot marry you.'

A heartbeat's silence.

'And why is that?' Tristan's voice, calm, polite. Was he trying to be gallant or did he really not understand?

'Because of the scandal. We would not be accepted.'

'You have been accepted in Bath.'

'There are already rumours. If it were not for Mrs Ancrum's patronage, people would not be so kind to me, I know that.'

'The lady is one of the highest sticklers in Bath. If she has befriended you, she must believe your birth is respectable.'

'No. Quite the opposite,' she said unhappily. 'She thinks I might be the natural daughter of someone she used to know. She has been afraid to look into it too closely in case she finds irrefutable proof.' Natalya raised her tearstained face to look at him. 'Tristan, until I know who I am I c-cannot agree to marry you. You see that, do you not?'

For a long moment Tristan looked at her, his eyes searching her face, then he nodded.

'I understand your scruples, Natalya, but it does not matter to me who you are. I will marry you whatever your history.'

His response made her feel more wretched than ever.

'You deserve a wife with a spotless bloodline. If

mine turns out to be tainted, then it would not only reflect badly on you, but on everyone connected with you:
Freddie, your sister, your friends—even your mother.
I will not be the cause of a rift between you and those
you hold most dear.'

'Natalya—'

When he went to take her back in his arms she
jumped away.

'No.' She put up a hand, as if warding off a blow.
'No, Tristan, I cannot marry you until I am sure I will
not bring disgrace upon you or your name.'

'You could never shame me, my love, but I understand your fears. I will take you back to Sydney Place
and we will demand the truth from the Pridhams.'

'No! Not today!' she begged him. She dragged out
her handkerchief to wipe her eyes. 'I pray you, Tristan,
I do not want to discuss it any further today.'

'Poor love,' said Tristan, reaching out to touch her
cheek. 'This ordeal has shaken you more than you will
admit.'

'Yes,' she agreed, clutching at the excuse he offered
her. 'I think I need a little time to recover from…from
everything that has happened.'

'Of course.' He pulled her into his arms again. 'But
not too long, my dear, I am impatient now to make love
to you properly. As my wife.'

She clung to him, closing her eyes and trying to fix
in her memory the sound of his voice, the feel of his
heart beating against her cheek. The familiar scent of
his skin. If her fears were realised, she would never
have the chance to do this again.

* * *

They arrived back at Sydney Place shortly after noon, Natalya travelling in the hired carriage while Tristan rode alongside as escort. They were shown directly into the drawing room, where Mrs Pridham fell on Natalya's neck and hugged her in a display of uncharacteristic emotion.

'My dear child, we have been so anxious for you! Until we received Lord Dalmorren's message, telling us you were safe, I was in an agony of apprehension, wondering what could have happened! What a shocking ordeal, to be stolen away like that and with only the clothes you stood up in.' Her eyes fell to the pink shawl around Natalya's shoulders. 'I suppose the kind people who took you in found that for you. But let me look at you.' She held Natalya away from her. 'You are not hurt. Not at all? You are sure of it?'

Her aunt's eyes darted to Tristan before coming back to Natalya and searching her face.

'I am perfectly well, Aunt,' she replied calmly. 'I was rendered unconscious by my abductors with some drug, which gave me a slight headache, but Lord Dalmorren rescued me before any real harm befell me.'

'You have been away from your home for *three nights*,' put in Mr Pridham, his tone one of outraged disapproval. 'It would have been better if His Lordship had brought you back to us immediately.'

Natalya blushed at the implication, but Tristan answered him.

'Miss Fairchild was extremely shaken when I found her.' A trace of hauteur had crept into his voice. 'She was in no state to travel further that night and I considered her welfare to be of greater import than your reassurance.'

'Quite, quite, but nevertheless—'

'We found refuge in a gentleman's house, sir, perfectly respectable,' Tristan continued, ignoring the interruption. 'One of the maids accompanied Miss Fairchild here and is even now returning in the hired coach.'

Giving you no opportunity to question her, Natalya added, silently.

Mr Pridham looked reluctant to let the matter drop, but after an inward struggle he said stiffly, 'We must thank you, my lord, for taking such good care of our niece.'

'It was an honour, sir. But I should like to know how such an abduction could have taken place. From your garden, I understand. How did these men gain entry?'

There was an awkward pause.

'They were admitted by a treacherous groom,' said her uncle at last. 'He and his cronies thought they might make a little money by holding our niece to ransom.'

'I see. Then you will be able to apprehend the villains.'

'Yes, yes, it is all in hand.' He walked over to tug at the bell pull. 'We will not detain you any longer, my lord. I am sure you must wish to get back to George Street.'

'Not at all. I have no desire to leave here until I am assured of Miss Fairchild's safety.'

Mr Pridham drew himself up. 'Natalya's welfare is our prime concern, Lord Dalmorren. We shall take the greatest care of her. Now, my lord, allow me to ring for the servant to show you out. I think it best if my niece is allowed to retire to her room and rest.'

Tristan hesitated and Natalya quickly stepped forward.

'Let me add my thanks to those of my aunt and uncle, sir.' She held out her hand to him. 'A few days' rest and I shall be quite restored.'

She squeezed his fingers, silently begging him to understand.

'As you wish, Miss Fairchild. I shall send a messenger in the morning to enquire after your health.' He added, his eyes teasing, 'And every morning until you are well enough to see me.'

He bowed over her fingers and was gone. Was it her imagination or did her aunt and uncle exchange a look of relief with his departure?

Mrs Pridham was eager to carry her off to her room, but Natalya held back.

'I did not recognise my abductors, Uncle. Which of the stable hands let them in?'

'A new man, recently engaged,' he replied dismissively. 'You would not know him and you must not make yourself anxious over it. The matter has been dealt with. Perhaps, Mrs Pridham, you will take Natalya upstairs now?'

'Oh, yes, yes, of course. Come along, my dear. I instructed a bath to be prepared for you and we must get you out of those clothes. They are quite ruined, alas. Aggie shall throw everything out.'

Natalya clutched the pink shawl closer. She would

allow her maid to dispose of everything else, but not that. It was Tristan's gift to her and, along with her memories, it was all she would have of him.

Tristan made his way back to George Street, a frown furrowing his brow. He felt uneasy about leaving Natalya at Sydney Place. If she had been willing, he would have preferred to take her into his own family until he could marry her, but she was insistent that she should return to Sydney Place. He could understand that, for she was anxious to question her aunt and uncle about her origins.

It was not that he thought the Pridhams were behind the abduction. Their relief at her safe return had been genuine enough, but it irked him that they had been more interested in the time he and Natalya had spent at Farnell Hall than her abduction. Pridham's explanation about the rogue stable hand was a little strained, too.

Perhaps he was being unfair. It was possible the man was embarrassed that his niece could have been taken from under his nose. Well, that would not happen again. He would set someone to watch the house. He would not run the risk of her being spirited away a second time.

Tristan was still deciding which of his staff he would set to this task when he entered his house and was informed that Mr Denham was waiting for him in the drawing room.

'Charles!' He closed the door and crossed the room. 'When did you get here?'

His secretary put down the newspaper and rose to his feet.

'Last night.' He gripped Tristan's outstretched hand. 'Your valet was telling me about your little adventure. Have you seen him yet? He will be in a stew until he knows you are safe.'

'The servants will tell Hurley I am returned.' He waved Charles back to his seat. 'What news?'

'I have been making enquiries about Miss Fairchild, as you instructed. I think I have found something.'

Aggie was helping Natalya into her dressing gown when there was a scratching at the door and Mrs Pridham came in.

'Ah, you have finished bathing, my dear, good.' She flicked one hand to dismiss the maid. 'I thought I should come and see you, to talk to you.'

Natalya had never heard her aunt sound so conciliatory and she was immediately on her guard.

'Very well, ma'am.' She sat down at the dressing table and began to pull the pins from her hair. 'What would you like to talk about?'

'You have had a terrifying ordeal, Natalya.'

'Not so terrifying. Lord Dalmorren rescued me within hours of my being carried off.'

Natalya watched in the mirror as her aunt paced to and fro, her fingers twisting restlessly together.

'Yes. Quite. Lord Dalmorren is indeed to be praised for his swift action.' She came to a halt behind Natalya. 'He must appear a veritable hero to you, my dear. Such a handsome man, too. No one would blame you if you were to think yourself a little bit in love with him. And being alone with him like that, I am sure he could be very…persuasive.'

So that was it. By a supreme effort of will, Natalya did not blush. She met her aunt's eyes in the mirror.

'Lord Dalmorren did not seduce me, Aunt, if that is what you wish to know.'

'Oh, good heavens, no one is suggesting anything of the sort! I would never—'

Natalya swung round on the stool. 'My uncle asked you to come here, did he not?' Her aunt's little shake of the head was not convincing. 'He wishes to know if I am still a virgin.' She added bitterly, 'If your *investment* has been devalued.'

Mrs Pridham looked distressed. 'Really, Natalya, it is not like that at all. We are naturally concerned for you. We thought perhaps we might ask a doctor to visit you. To…to reassure us that you are unharmed.'

'Indeed?' Natalya kept her head up, her whole demeanour challenging. Not by the flicker of an eyelid would she give herself away. 'Yes, by all means let us invite Dr Caldwell to visit me. You wish him to confirm that I am still a maid, do you not? I will be sure to tell him all about the abduction and how Lord Dalmorren rescued me. And I will explain to him the reason for my uncle's concerns, that he doubts Lord Dalmorren's word and that you do not trust me to tell you the truth!'

'No, no, there is no question—that is, we will not ask the good doctor to call, if you do not wish it,' her aunt replied hastily. 'Mr Pridham is naturally anxious. He merely wants to make sure…'

She trailed off miserably and for a moment Natalya

almost felt sorry for her. Uncle Pridham was too embarrassed to ask such intimate questions himself, so he had bullied his wife into it. Natalya chose her next words carefully.

'You may reassure my uncle, ma'am, that Lord Dalmorren did not steal my virginity. I will swear an oath on it, if you wish, but I trust my word will suffice?'

'You may be sure I shall tell him what you have said, Natalya.' Her aunt looked a little shocked at this blunt language. 'I am sure Mr Pridham did not mean—that is, it is because he cares for you, my dear.'

'But he does not care enough to tell me who I am.'

'Alas, our hands are tied on that.' Mrs Pridham stopped and clamped her restless hands to her mouth. 'I can say no more on that head, my dear, pray do not ask me.' She drew in a breath, composing herself before continuing in a much more normal voice. 'Pray believe that we only want what is best for you, my dear. And on that subject, we think it would be best if you kept to your room for a while. We have let it be known that you are indisposed. We did not want anyone in Bath to know what has happened to you. Only think of the gossip!'

'And we must avoid scandal at all costs, must we not?' retorted Natalya, her lip curling.

'Yes, indeed we must. I am glad you understand, my dear. I will have your dinner sent up to you.'

She went out and as the door closed behind her, Natalya's shoulders slumped. Why had she come back? Tristan had offered to take her to his family and now she almost wished she had agreed, but the idea of explaining her uncertain origins to Lady Dalmorren was too shameful to contemplate. Although a doting mother would be only too willing to support her if she refused to marry Tristan. But what would she do, where could she go? It was best she stayed here until her aunt and uncle told her the truth about her parents. Whatever that might be.

Chapter Fourteen

'Lord Dalmorren, ma'am.

Mrs Ancrum looked up from her book. 'It is a little late in the day for a morning call. I was about to go in to dinner.'

'I beg your pardon ma'am, this cannot wait,' he said bluntly. 'It concerns Miss Fairchild.'

'Natalya?' She was suddenly alert, her gaze piercing. 'What has happened to her? The Pridhams were not at church on Sunday and when I called at Sydney Place to enquire, they told me she was unwell.'

'She was abducted, ma'am. On the night of her birthday.'

'Mercy me!'

Briefly Tristan explained what had happened.

'I returned her to Sydney Place earlier today and she is safe enough, for the moment, but I need you to tell me everything you know about her.'

Those shrewd old eyes regarded him in silence for a moment longer. Then, 'Have you dined?'

'Not yet.'

'Very well. Eat with me and we can talk over dinner.' She rang the bell. 'I will have another place set.'

Tristan glanced down at his travel-stained coat. 'I am not dressed for dinner, ma'am, and I would rather talk now.'

'Nonsense, you need to eat and it won't take a moment to arrange. Your dress don't worry me—besides, it is better than having my food spoiled by the delay.'

Tristan ground his teeth with impatience, but the old lady was right. Barely five minutes later they were seated at the dining table with the first of the dishes before them.

'Now...' Mrs Ancrum waved the servants away '...before I tell you about Natalya, you must tell me why you are interested in her.'

'Good God, madam, she was abducted. Is that not reason enough?'

She gave him a hard look from beneath her brows. 'I thought perhaps you were interested in her for more... personal reasons.'

'I intend to marry her, if that is what you mean.'

The frown vanished and the old lady cackled in triumph.

'I knew it!'

'But that is for the future. I do not believe the abduction was a random attempt to extort money from the Pridhams, which is the tale they gave to me. I think it has something to do with Natalya's history and I want to know why that should be.' He waited while Mrs Ancrum chewed her way through a few choice slices of chicken before asking bluntly, 'Who *are* her parents, ma'am?'

Another pause while the lady picked up a crumb and popped it in her mouth.

'Very well, my lord, I will tell you what I *believe* is the truth.'

Mrs Ancrum pushed her plate away and Tristan listened intently as she related her story.

'A common enough tale,' she ended. 'A young woman cast off in disgrace and abandoned by her lover. My only regret is that I did not make more effort to find Elizabeth earlier. I might then have been able to help her.'

'But you did make enquiries at the time?'

'I did indeed, but I could not find her, nor could I discover that a marriage had taken place. I admit I was hampered because I did not know the identity of her lover. All I could discover from Elizabeth's family was that she had died in childbirth. There was no word of the babe and I thought it most likely she had perished, too. Until I saw Natalya in Bath.'

'You befriended her.'

'Yes. I had no proof she was Elizabeth's daughter, but the more I saw, the more I was convinced of it. I made up my mind that if I saw any sign that Natalya was ill treated, I would step in.' She spread her hands. 'But how could I? She was given every luxury and, as far as I could tell, she had wanted for nothing during her childhood. I had always thought the Faringdons abandoned the child, but they must have thought better of it, placed her with the Pridhams and paid for her upbringing.'

'And you have never said a word of this to Natalya?'

'Not until her birthday. She came to me, distressed that the Pridhams had again refused to give her any information about her parents. I told her what I have just told you, but I explained that I could not be sure, that I had no proof.' She sat forward. 'Surely, my lord, you do not think the family could be behind the abduction? What purpose would it serve?'

'That is what I have been asking myself. Are you in touch with the Faringdons, Mrs Ancrum?'

'No, and nor do I wish to be, after the way they treated Elizabeth. The scandal had been forgotten by the time they brought out her stepsisters and they managed to find husbands for them both. They all live in deepest Lincolnshire now.' The old lady's mouth turned down. 'The embodiment of genteel respectability. I cannot think they would wish for any connection with Natalya, especially after all this time.'

Tristan asked several more questions, but there was nothing more to be learned here.

As soon as they had finished their meal, he took his leave.

'What you have told me is very useful, ma'am,' he told her, bowing over her hand. 'Added to what my secretary has gleaned.'

'And is she Elizabeth's daughter?' He said nothing and her thin, beringed fingers clung to him. 'Damn you, Tristan, you know something more and you will not tell me!'

He smiled. 'Alas, ma'am, I will not, because at present it is nothing more than conjecture. I must leave for town at dawn, where I hope I shall now be able to solve the mystery.'

'And you will tell me? You owe me that, I think.'

He nodded. 'If Miss Fairchild permits. She is my first consideration. I shall be leaving too early in the morning to see Natalya before I go, so I will leave a note for her. However, I am sure she would appreciate a visit from you, ma'am. To remind her that she has friends here.'

He walked to the door, but as he opened it she called him back.

'Whatever Natalya's origins may be, I have made her my heir, although she does not yet know it.'

'Are you telling me that to make her a more attractive proposition?' He smiled. 'Tell her she is an heiress, by all means, but I pray you will also make it plain that I will marry her whatever her birth and even if she comes to me without a rag to her back!'

Natalya had no objection to keeping to her room. She needed time to think. She also wanted to give Tristan time to reflect upon his rash proposal before she saw him again. She whiled away the days with her sketchpad and her books, or with the newspapers that Aggie brought up, once Mr Pridham had finished reading them.

However, by Saturday she was so tired of her own

company that she begged she might join her aunt and uncle for dinner, where a chance comment from her aunt caught Natalya's attention.

'Lord Dalmorren has left Bath?'

'Yes.' There was no mistaking the angry look Mr Pridham threw at his wife. 'He sent me a note on Wednesday, advising me of the fact.'

Wednesday! Natalya's brain reeled. The day after returning her to Sydney Place.

'Never mind that,' put in Mrs Pridham, trying to redeem the situation. 'Mrs Ancrum has called almost every day to ask after you. She sends her regards and is so sorry you are not well enough to see her.'

Natalya frowned. 'I did not know she had called or I would have come downstairs.'

'We thought it best you were thoroughly rested before having any visitors,' said her uncle.

'And as a matter of fact, it is quite fortunate you did not see her,' Mrs Pridham chattered on. 'I saw Colonel Yatton in Milsom Street this morning and he told me the poor lady has succumbed to a slight chill. But I am sure she will call again when she is better.'

'That is very kind of her.'

Natalya answered mechanically, her spirits faltering as she thought of Tristan. While she had believed him to be in Bath she had felt strong. Now, suddenly, she felt very much alone. Perhaps he had been lured to London after all. The newspapers were full of reports of all the entertainments arranged for the Allied Sovereigns, including, at the end of this week, a visit to

Ascot, for the racing. As a sportsman, surely Tristan would not wish to miss that.

Natalya thought of the Grishams and hoped they were enjoying their visit. They might not be invited to attend the grand reception at Carlton House or Tsar Alexander's levee at the Duke of Cumberland's residence, but there were plenty of other diversions to be enjoyed throughout the summer: balls, routs and even fireworks in Hyde Park. No, she could not blame Tristan if he had been lured away to town, although it was dispiriting to think he could forget her so easily.

She turned back to her uncle. 'Did Lord Dalmorren leave no message for me?'

'None.'

'And does he mean to return?'

'He did not say.'

'He promised to send someone every day, to enquire after me. Do they come?'

Perhaps Tristan's servant could convey a message from her.

'You would do well to forget him, Natalya. He is not for you.'

His dismissive tone flicked her on the raw. She put up her chin. 'And why should he not be? Am I so unsuitable?'

Mrs Pridham disclaimed in a fluttering voice, only to be interrupted by her husband.

'It would be a most ineligible match!'

'Oh, why?' He did not respond and Natalya's hands clutched at her napkin. She said boldly, 'I demand you tell me what you mean.'

'Natalya, my dear!'

Mr Pridham waved his hand to silence his wife. He glared at Natalya.

'You *demand*? Ungrateful girl! We have given you every indulgence, every advantage and this is how you repay us?'

'I wish only to know who I am. Who are my parents?'

She kept her head up, her eyes on his face, determined not to give in.

'Mr Pridham?' Her aunt whispered the name. 'Perhaps we should tell her.'

'I am awaiting a letter,' he replied, goaded.

'A letter?' Natalya echoed. 'From whom?'

He ignored her question.

'It should arrive any day now, with instructions on how we proceed. You must be patient a little longer, Natalya. I hope I shall be able to answer all your questions very soon.'

'But I do not see why you cannot tell me now!' She pushed back her chair and rose. 'I am one-and-twenty. You cannot keep me here. If you will not tell me, then I shall have no choice but to leave this house.'

'You are quite free to leave whenever you wish, but where will you go? You have no money, save the pin money we allow you. Will you throw yourself on the mercy of your friends? Mrs Ancrum, perhaps?' His brows rose and he said coldly, 'What will you tell her— that we have abused you, treated you harshly? No one would believe you and think how it would look! All will be revealed shortly, I promise you.'

Mrs Pridham touched her hand. 'My dear, pray do not be too hasty. Believe me, it will be very much to your advantage to be patient a little longer.'

She wavered.

Her uncle said, more gently, 'Your aunt is right, Natalya. We know what is best. Pray bear with us. You will thank us, once you know everything.'

Natalya looked at him suspiciously. 'And when you have told me everything, will I still be free to leave here?'

'Your future will be out of my hands.'

'But will it be in *mine*?'

'What nonsense is this?' exclaimed Mrs Pridham. 'No one wishes you to be unhappy, Natalya. Now, if you have finished eating, shall we withdraw? Perhaps you would like to play for me, while Mr Pridham enjoys a glass of port here.'

'No, thank you.' Natalya struggled to keep calm. 'I think I will retire, if you will excuse me.'

When Aggie had helped her into bed, Natalya begged her to leave the curtains pulled back and she lay alone in the darkness, wondering what she would do. Her uncle had said she was free to leave, if she so wished, but where would she go? The thought of leaving the only home, the only family she had ever known was quite terrifying and even Tristan was no longer in Bath to support her. She might fly to Mrs Ancrum, seek refuge with her, but her uncle was right, that would only give rise to the worst sort of speculation, and what had

Mr and Mrs Pridham done to deserve the ignominy of being the subject of such gossip?

There were no physical walls to her cage, but she was trapped, all the same.

By morning Natalya was no closer to finding a solution to her problems, but after a good night's sleep her fears and anxieties seemed foolish. After all, they were not living in the Dark Ages. Perhaps, after all, there was a reasonable explanation to everything.

She was just finishing her breakfast when Mrs Pridham came into her bedchamber to invite her to join her at the Abbey for the morning service.

'I should be delighted to attend,' replied Natalya, suddenly feeling more cheerful at the prospect of leaving the house. 'I will need time to change my gown.'

'Excellent!' Mrs Pridham beamed at her. 'I will meet you in the hall in, say, half an hour. And bring a wrap, my dear. You know the sermons can be very long and I wouldn't have you get chilled.' She bustled away.

Thirty minutes later Natalya was almost ready to go out. She went to the linen press to fetch a shawl. A colourful array of woollen and silk wraps were folded and stacked on the shelf. Her fingers hovered over the pink shawl which Aggie had washed and placed on the top of the pile, then she pulled out the plain green cashmere beneath it. She did not want to think of Tristan today. He had left and she must not rely upon his returning.

* * *

Once they were settled in the carriage for the short drive to the Abbey, Natalya said, 'Perhaps, afterwards, we might call upon Mrs Ancrum. I should so like to enquire after her, as she has done for me this past week.'

'I think not, my dear. Your uncle does not want you to overexert yourself. We shall return directly to the house.'

Natalya hesitated, wondering if she should argue, but in the end she decided against it. If her elderly friend was not well, she needed to rest.

'Very well. Perhaps I can take Aggie with me in the morning and I will leave a note for her.'

'Yes. Perhaps. Now, Natalya, when we reach the Abbey we shall go inside directly,' said Mrs Pridham. 'There is a chill wind today and dawdling out of doors could well set back your recovery.

Natalya laughed at that. 'It is not as though I have really been unwell, Aunt!'

'Pray guard your tongue, Natalya,' she muttered. 'We have been most careful to keep your disappearance a secret from everyone. We must depend upon Lord Dalmorren's discretion, but he is a gentleman, and as long as he stays silent, no one need know the true facts.'

Natalya stared at her. 'But when you found I was not in the house, surely you made some enquiries of our neighbours and friends?'

Mrs Pridham looked flustered.

'It…it was not necessary. Your uncle suspected from the start that a ransom would be demanded for your safe return.'

'So you did nothing.'

'We…um…we sent an express to—to Bow Street.'

'Bow Street? *London!*' Natalya was shocked. 'Good heavens, I could have been spirited out of the country before help came from that quarter!'

Mrs Pridham cried out at that, her distress so uncharacteristic that it only added to the wild speculation that raced through Natalya's mind and would not be silenced. She continued to dwell upon it throughout the service and even afterwards, when they left the Abbey and she greeted acquaintances with calm complaisance and assured them that she was quite recovered from her malady.

Aunt Pridham refused to say anything more, even in the privacy of the carriage, but Natalya was not to be deterred. When she saw her uncle at dinner that night, she asked him about engaging a Bow Street Runner, only for him to deny it and claim his wife had quite mistook the matter.

'I would have taken measures, only Lord Dalmorren's note arrived, telling me you were safe.'

'But that would have been some time after I was taken,' Natalya argued. 'You mean you did *nothing* to find me?'

He said shortly, 'I contacted those I thought might know.'

'Oh? Who might that be?'

'Everything will be made clear to you very soon.'

'But you cannot tell me now.'

'I cannot.' He glared across the table at her. 'Eat your dinner, madam, and pray ask me no more.'

'But, sir—'

With an oath he tore his napkin from his neck and threw it down.

'Damnation, madam, *will you be quiet*? If you cannot desist from these interminable questions, you can go to your room and I will have your meal sent up. I will not be hounded like this at my own dinner table!'

'Very well.' Natalya rose. 'But you need not send anything up to me, I am not hungry.'

She was shaking with fury but she managed to walk out of the dining room and up the stairs to her bedchamber, where she collapsed on to the bed in tears of rage and frustration.

Natalya tossed and turned in her bed, her mind shifting between Tristan's sudden departure from Bath and the Pridhams' strange behaviour regarding her abduction.

Her uncle had said previously he was waiting for instructions before he could disclose anything about her birth, but from whom and why? Was it the same person he thought might know about her abduction?

At school, a passion for Gothic romances had fuelled Natalya's imagination and the idea of being the baseborn child of a rich and unscrupulous villain had been exciting. Now that she suspected she might indeed have such a parent, it was more than a little alarming.

'Oh, you are being ridiculously fanciful!' she scolded herself, turning her pillow and thumping it back into shape. 'There is probably nothing more sinister than a legal complication to do with wills and inheritance that has to be resolved.'

Yet her thoughts refused to behave and she continued to conjure ever more outrageous scenarios for her fate until at last she fell into a sleep of sheer exhaustion.

'Wake up, Miss Fairchild. Wake up now.'

Natalya shrugged off the maid's hand on her shoulder and opened one bleary eye. Outside her window, the sky was the clear grey of a very early dawn.

'What is the matter, Aggie? It cannot be time to get up yet.'

'No, miss, but the master has told me to have you dressed and downstairs as soon as possible!'

This time there was no mistaking the urgency in the maid's voice. Natalya shook off her sleepiness and quickly jumped out of bed.

Twenty minutes later she entered the drawing room. Mrs Pridham, a silk wrap fastened over her nightgown, was sitting on the sofa and looking very tired. Her husband stood before the fireplace in his banyan, slippered feet apart and hands behind his back. His countenance was as grave as ever.

'Come in, Natalya, and shut the door.'

'Good heavens, sir,' she exclaimed, regarding them in alarm. 'What has happened, what is the matter?'

'I told you yesterday I was awaiting a letter regarding you,' he said. 'It arrived yesterday afternoon, but I thought it best not to apprise you of it then. I deemed it better to let you get a good night's rest.'

'As it happens, sir, I slept very badly,' she retorted. 'From whom is the letter?'

'A person most nearly concerned with your welfare.'

'M-my father?' she stammered. 'Or even, perhaps… could it be that my m-mother is alive?'

'I am afraid not,' her uncle replied, his tone clipped. 'Neither of your parents is alive.'

Natalya knew that. Of course she did. No one had ever told her anything different, yet she realised that she had always nurtured a tiny flame of hope. Now that flame flickered and died. Grief ripped through her, tearing at her heart. She wanted to be alone, to collapse in tears, to wail and cry and mourn for the parents she had never known.

Her uncle was speaking again, saying in a matter-of-fact voice, 'You are to be ready to leave at six o'clock. Mrs Pridham has instructed breakfast to be served in the dining room immediately and I have already instructed your maid to pack a trunk—'

'Leave? I am going out of Bath?' She glanced down at her skirts. Suddenly the relevance of Aggie selecting her dove-blue walking dress was clear.

'What if I refuse?' She ran her tongue over her lips. 'I am of age now, sir, you cannot make me go.'

'We would never force you to do anything you did not wish to do, Natalya, but our responsibility for you ends today. When you leave this house you have a choice: go your own way in the world, or you travel to meet your benefactor.'

Mrs Pridham rose and stood beside her husband. 'You have always wanted to know your history, Natalya, this letter comes from someone in a position to answer your questions.'

'Perhaps it is the same person who had me abducted!'

'For heaven's sake, girl. This is the man who has provided so generously for your upbringing all these years. Without him you would most likely have ended in the Foundling Hospital!'

His words hit Natalya like a blow.

'You were *paid* to look after me. I was a…a *commission*.'

'You must not think that we have not enjoyed having you with us these past four years,' said Mrs Pridham, twisting her hands together. 'We could not have hoped for a better behaved or more biddable charge.'

The shock was receding. Natalya said bitterly, 'You were appointed to complete my education, I suppose. To see to it that I attained all the accomplishments necessary. Will you receive a dividend for the satisfactory completion of the contract?'

Mr Pridham regarded her coldly. 'We have always done our best for you, Natalya. I hope you believe that.'

'Your best!' She shook her head. 'I thought perhaps there was some family link, or at least that you had known one or other of my parents and were doing this for their sake, if not for mine. That, at least, was how I explained your lack of affection. I thought you would not tell me about my past because it was too painful.'

Mrs Pridham bit back a little cry. 'We were expressly forbidden to do so.'

'Leaving me to think the very worst.'

Natalya gathered her thoughts and her pride, coming

to terms with the fact that she had no parents. No relations at all, not even the two people standing before her. For four years she had lived with the Pridhams. They had been her guardians, she had looked up to them, been guided by them. She had forgiven their coldness, believing they had always had her best interests at heart. Now they seemed diminished, somehow.

She said, 'I am obliged to you, then, for looking after me. For giving me every advantage money can buy. Now, if you will excuse me, I shall go and see if Aggie has finished packing my things.'

'Will you not take breakfast with me?' asked Mrs Pridham, surprised. 'You will need something to eat before your journey.'

Natalya was already walking to the door, but she stopped. She was tempted to reply that in all her time at Sydney Place she had never been invited to take breakfast with them, but that seemed petty.

She said, 'It is already gone five and I must prepare for my journey. I will send Aggie to fetch up a little bread and butter for me to eat as I pack.'

The hall clock was chiming the hour when Natalya walked out to the waiting carriage. She was reassured by the fact that Aggie was to accompany her. The maid was in a dither of excitement, but Natalya felt remarkably calm. In truth, there had been no time for grief or histrionics.

She had no expectation of returning to Sydney Place, or of seeing the Pridhams again. Apart from the clothes which Aggie had already packed, Natalya had had to decide very quickly which of her belongings she would take with her into her unknown future. It had not been difficult. A few treasured keepsakes from her school-days, her presents from Mrs Ancrum and her mother's pearls. And the pale rose-pink shawl that she threw around her shoulders.

The travelling chaise looked new and expensive with liveried postilions and four glossy horses to pull it. A footman was sitting on the leather bench at the back, while a second stood by the open door, waiting to hand Natalya into the sumptuous interior.

It is not too late, Natalya. Refuse to go. Throw yourself on Mrs Ancrum's mercy until you can contact Tristan.

She glanced back to where Mr and Mrs Pridham were standing on the steps. There had been no exchange of kisses, no warm hugs and words of regret expressed at her leaving, but they had done their duty and looked after her for the past four years with kindness, if not love. She could not believe they wished her harm.

And Tristan? Her heart contracted. It was almost a week since she had seen him and there had been no word, but she was convinced he had not abandoned her. It was a misunderstanding, something that she might be able to resolve at some later date. But until she knew about her past, she could not make promises for the future.

Resolutely, she stepped into the carriage.

Chapter Fifteen

'Damn it all, Hurley, I told you not to wake me!'

Tristan raked a hand through his hair. He had driven through the night from London and fallen into bed shortly before dawn. His eyes felt gritty and his temper was definitely uncertain.

'I beg your pardon, my lord, but Simon wishes to speak with you.'

Tristan recalled Simon was one of the men he had set to watch the Pridhams' house. He rolled out of bed and thrust his feet into his slippers.

'Send him in.'

By the time the man entered his bedchamber, Tristan was wrapped in a silk-brocade banyan and had sent Hurley to fetch up water for washing.

'My apologies for disturbing you, my lord, and it might be nothing.' Simon stood before him, nervously turning his hat between his hands.

'Tell me.'

'Miss Fairchild left Sydney Place this morning, my

lord. She was accompanied by her maid and looked to be perfectly at ease. There was no sign of anyone forcing her into the carriage, but I thought you should know.'

'The devil,' muttered Tristan, frowning. 'What time was this?'

'Six o'clock, my lord, on the hour. I know because I heard a clock chiming from one of the houses, it being a warm night and the windows was open, you see.'

He stopped when Hurley came in with a jug of hot water.

'Go on,' barked Tristan. 'Tell me everything you observed while I wash and dress.'

'It was a travelling chariot, my lord, newly painted.' Simon told him. 'Yellow and black, with two postilions for the team of four bays and two servants in the hind boot. I could see the body was lined in blue silk, too. Fringed. No hired hack, I reckon. Looked like the equipage of a gentleman and a rich one at that.'

'And the passengers? Was Miss Fairchild alone?'

'Her maid went with her, sir, no one else. I saw them loading two trunks and a portmanteau.'

'You did very well, Simon. With your description of the chaise it should not be difficult to discover which road they took out of Bath, although I have a pretty good notion of where they are going.' Tristan was already tying his neckcloth while Hurley was shaking out his riding jacket. 'Take a couple of fellows with you to report back and in the meantime have John make sure my chaise is ready with all speed!'

* * *

It was a long journey and the weather was inclement. Sunshine and showers. Natalya knew they were travelling east, but other than that she had little idea where they were going. They changed horses frequently, and at each stop coffee and a little food was brought out to the carriage by one of the footmen. Whenever Natalya or Aggie stepped out of the carriage to use the necessary at the posting houses, one of the servants escorted them. They were civil, but uncommunicative, and Natalya wondered uneasily what would happen if she should ask to be taken back to Bath.

Aggie, however, had no such concerns. She thought the journey an exciting adventure and looked out eagerly at the passing landscape.

'Are you not the least bit anxious about the future?' Natalya asked her, as they drove across a particularly bleak expanse of heath.

'Oh, no, miss,' came the cheerful reply. 'Mrs Pridham told me that if I was a good girl and did as I was told it was very likely I would be allowed to remain as your lady's maid. If you was agreeable, that is,' she added hastily.

A small comfort, thought Natalya, reasoning that if she was to keep her maid then the Pridhams did not expect her to become a governess, or a companion.

She tried to calculate how far they travelled and, by the time the carriage slowed and turned into a gated drive, she thought it must be close on a hundred miles. They should be near London, although she had no sense of it, for the last part of their journey had been off the main coaching road and through thick woods.

She sat upright and stared out of the window as the carriage rattled its way through a landscaped park. Eventually they emerged from the trees and she saw that the drive ended at a pretty manor house. Its steeply pitched roof was studded with windows and topped with tall chimney stacks. Below, there were regularly spaced windows on two floors and a rusticated basement level. A set of shallow stone steps swept up from the drive to the main entrance, which was crowned by a shell-like pediment. Everything was neat and well maintained. It spoke of affluence, as did the comfortable equipage that had carried her from Bath in such luxury. Should she be reassured by that?

The carriage swept around the curving drive and came to a stand. As Natalya alighted a man in a black coat hurried down the steps and bowed to her.

'Miss Fairchild. You are expected, ma'am.'

The servants were unloading her trunks. Natalya swallowed, cast a quick glance to make sure Aggie was at her shoulder and followed the man into the house.

A woman in a black gown and snowy apron and cap was waiting in the hall. Her rosy cheeks and cheerful countenance were reassuring.

'I am Mrs Noakes, the housekeeper.' She dropped a curtsy. 'Your rooms have been prepared, if you and your maid would care to follow me. I am sure you would like to wash and change your gown before anything else.'

Natalya would have preferred to be taken directly to meet her mysterious benefactor, but after a journey of eleven hours she suspected she looked quite dishevelled. She and Aggie followed the housekeeper up the stairs to a comfortably appointed bedchamber with a dressing room, where Mrs Noakes pointed out that a truckle bed had been prepared for her maid.

'Now, ma'am, when you are ready, you just ring the bell and I will come and fetch you.'

Natalya interrupted her. 'Mrs Noakes, who am I to meet here, what is his name?'

The housekeeper shook her head. 'I am afraid I cannot tell you that. As a matter of fact, I am not sure of his name myself. I have instructions merely to look after you until he arrives.'

'You do not *know*?' Natalya stared at her. 'Is this not his house, then?'

'Goodness me, no! The master has given the gentleman the use of the Lodge for a few days.'

'And who *is* the master?'

'Ah, now, that is a delicate matter and not one I can discuss.'

Natalya gave a little cry. 'I do not understand any of this!'

Mrs Noakes regarded her sympathetically. 'No, ma'am, but I am sure it will all be explained in due course.'

'That is all anyone ever says to me!' Natalya bit her lip. 'And if I wish to leave?'

The housekeeper looked a little shocked at that.

'Leave? But you have only just arrived! However, if that is what you wish, then I am sure we can arrange for the chaise to be brought back to the door for you very quickly.'

'You were not given orders to keep me here?'

'Lord love you, no, Miss Fairchild! I am sure no one wishes to do that.'

The housekeeper was smiling at her, no hint of guile in her homely countenance. Natalya sighed. She had been travelling all day and the thought of quitting this place and travelling through the night to return to Bath did not appeal to her.

She sank down on the stool in front of the dressing table.

'Very well, I will stay. For now.'

The housekeeper beamed at her and dropped another curtsy. 'Thank you, ma'am, I will call back for you presently.'

Mrs Noakes hurried away, her black skirts rustling, and Natalya was left alone with her maid. For a moment she felt dazed and not a little frightened, then she squared her shoulders. She had decided to stay, so she had best prepare herself.

'Very well, Aggie, you should unpack a clean gown for me.'

A clock somewhere was striking six when Mrs Noakes escorted Natalya to the drawing room. It was exactly twelve hours since she had left Bath. She was on edge and she had to screw up her courage even tighter when she realised that the housekeeper was not coming in with her.

The drawing room was empty. Natalya felt almost

weak with relief and it was a few moments before she could take in her surroundings. The room was furnished in comfortable elegance. The pictures on the walls were mainly of horses, with a few hunting scenes and one of game birds that she thought might be by Hondecoeter. Most likely this was a hunting lodge, then. Remote, secluded. She shivered suddenly and rubbed her arms. She felt as trapped and hunted as any of the poor creatures in the paintings. Too late to go back now. The best she could hope for was that the mystery would soon be explained.

She heard the door open and looked round expectantly, but it was only a liveried servant bringing in refreshments, a selection of wines and a jug of fresh lemonade, together with a plate of little cakes. Natalya took a glass of lemonade, deciding she needed to keep a clear head for whatever was to come.

Chapter Sixteen

Natalya had eaten one of the cakes and finished her lemonade when an elderly man came into the room. She hastily rose from her chair and studied him carefully.

He was tall and lean, his short black hair streaked with silver. He carried an ebony cane in one hand, but he barely used it for support. His bearing was upright and on the breast of his dark evening coat was a large jewelled order of merit.

He bowed to her. 'Have I the honour of addressing Miss Natalya Fairchild?'

She curtsied. 'You have, sir.'

He raised his quizzing glass to observe her. Natalya put up her chin and gave him a challenging look in return. He smiled slightly and lowered the glass.

'Forgive me, my dear. It is impolite of me to stare.' His voice was soft and heavily accented. 'Allow me to introduce myself. I am Prince Ilya Mikhailovich Borkusov.'

Prince!

She swallowed. Hard. 'You are a Russian prince?'

He inclined his head.

'*You* are my benefactor?'

'Alas, no. That privilege belonged to your father.'

He had used the past tense. She clutched the back of a chair.

'He is dead, then.'

'He is. I am so sorry.'

He was only confirming what the Pridhams had told her, but it did not prevent her feeling another sharp stab of grief. The Prince gestured with one white hand. 'Shall we sit down?'

Natalya was very glad to do so. She folded her hands in her lap and waited until the old man had lowered himself on to a chair opposite. There was probably some protocol that decreed she should wait for him to address her, but she was far too impatient for that.

'Do you know my history?' she asked him. 'Can you tell me?' He was silent for a moment and she added, *'On peut parler en français, si vous préférez?'*

A faint smile curved his thin lips. 'I see that the money your father put aside for your education was not wasted. But we shall continue in English, your native tongue.' He steepled his fingers and stared at them for a long moment. 'Your father came to England in 1792, to join the entourage of the Russian Ambassador, Count Semyon Vonotsov. Your mother, he met in London. She was the daughter of a wealthy English gentleman. They fell in love, but were forbidden to marry.'

Natalya's chin went up. 'She was not noble enough for him, was that it?'

'That was not the reason, my dear. You see, his bride had already been chosen for him, a young relative of his mother. His parents were unyielding, they insisted the match must go ahead. But young love, it is very strong. It was an *affaire de coeur* and the lady's family, they cast her off when they learned she was with child.'

Natalya interrupted him. 'I beg your pardon, sir— your Highness—the lady you mention, would that be Miss Elizabeth Faringdon?'

'The same.'

She nodded. Mrs Ancrum's suspicions had been correct.

The Prince frowned. 'You are familiar with the story? It was my understanding that nothing was to be divulged to you. Your father's instructions were explicit on that matter.'

'I learned of Miss Elizabeth Faringdon from an acquaintance who saw a likeness between us. But it was conjecture, sir. There was no proof and the Pridhams have told me nothing.'

'They do not know the whole and they had orders not to inform you of your parentage.'

'You should be pleased, then,' she retorted bitterly. 'They have followed those orders, to the letter.'

'You have my sympathy, my dear. From everything I have learned since coming to England, your guardians have proved themselves scrupulously honest, if unimaginative, in their dealings with you.'

'Perhaps it would have been better if they had not been quite so meticulous.'

'Perhaps. However, what is done is done. Now we can move on.'

'But not before you have told me everything you know about my parents.' She stopped, conscious that this was not the way one should address a prince. 'I beg your pardon, your Highness, I do not mean to be impolite, but I have waited so long to learn the truth.'

He inclined his head. 'Your curiosity is understandable, my dear.'

Another pause. Natalya curbed her impatience. Only her hands, clasped so tightly that the knuckles gleamed white, showed the extent of her anxiety.

'The lady, your mother, died soon after your birth. Mikhail Nikolayevich, your father, was distraught. He had been summoned back to Russia, ordered to return and marry the woman chosen for him.' The old man stopped, his mouth turning down a little. 'The letters he received from his parents and from his fiancée were so full of anger that he was afraid to take the child with him. His family refused to acknowledge his daughter and he feared she would be put away, an embarrassment to be forgotten.'

'No. How cruel.'

The Prince's eyes flickered over her.

'Such things are not unknown, even in your country. Mikhail left his child in England. His Russian friends here helped him to set up a generous fund to provide for her. She was to be cared for and given every advantage money could buy.'

She felt the press of tears against her eyes.

'He did not quite abandon me.'

The old man's face softened. 'No, Natalya, he never intended to abandon you.'

'What happened to him, after he returned to Russia?'

'The arranged marriage went ahead. Alas, after a series of miscarriages, the wife died of a fever without providing Borkusov with a child. That was six years ago. In 1808.'

She realised he was waiting for her to comment.

'Our two countries were at war by then.'

'Precisely. Your father wanted to return to England and claim you, but at that time it was impossible. He sent word to his contacts here and told them you were to be brought up as an English lady. The Pridhams were employed to oversee your education and to take you in, when your school had taught you everything it could. They were to instruct you in the ways of polite society. To instil in you the accomplishments demanded of every young lady and to look after you until you reached one-and-twenty.'

'And did *looking after me* include threatening my friends?'

'You mean the young gentleman who was paying you so much attention? That, I regret, was a mistake. As was your abduction.'

'You knew about that!'

'I learned of it when I reached England. When it was seen that their heavy-handed attempt to discourage Mr Erwin had failed, your father's envoys here were afraid you would marry him before I arrived to tell you the truth about your family. They did not trust the Pridhams to keep you from marrying Mr Erwin and…er…took matters into their own hands.'

'What did they plan to do with me?'

'They were going to carry you to London and hold you at the Embassy until my arrival. I shudder to think what Count Lieven would have said to that! Bah, such incompetence! Believe me, my dear, I am sincerely relieved you came to no harm through their deplorable actions. I hope you will forgive them. Undoubtedly, they are fools, but they acted with the best of intentions.'

She said, with careful restraint, 'May I suggest, your Highness, that the whole sorry matter could have been avoided if I had been told the truth at the outset?'

'Your father's instructions were clear: everything was to be explained to you when you came of age, not before.'

'But the Pridhams did *not* tell me.'

'When I knew I would be accompanying his Imperial Majesty to London, I sent word that I wanted to tell you myself and my orders were passed on to your guardians. I very much regret I was not able to meet with you on your birthday.'

She felt her anger welling up. How insensitive of them all, to keep her in ignorance. Did they not realise that she would think the worst, that she would dread the future?

No. It was hardly their fault that she had allowed her vivid imagination to run away with her. Now it seemed that her story was nothing more than the sad and commonplace tale that was all too familiar. She had been born out of wedlock, her mother had died giving birth to her and her father had done his best to provide for her. She swallowed back her anger.

'Will you tell me, your Highness, what became of my father?'

A shadow passed over the lined face.

'Borkusov joined the army. He distinguished himself in battle, but, unfortunately, he was killed in battle in 1812.'

'Borodino,' she whispered.

'Yes.'

Natalya put one hand to her mouth. Mr Pridham had insisted she learn about the Russian battles although she hated the stories of violence and bloodshed. Had he known her father had died there? She recalled reading of heavy losses on both sides. The Russians lost one third of their army and withdrew. The French invaded Moscow mid-September, only to be defeated when they retreated from Moscow a month later. She bowed her head, mourning the father she had never known.

'Mikhail Nikolayevich died a hero, Natalya.'

There was a commotion in the hall. The Prince rose from his seat as the door burst open.

'Tristan!' She flew across the room and hurled herself against him.

'Natalya.' His arms closed around her. 'Thank heaven. Are you hurt?'

'No. I am quite well. Now you are here.' She closed her eyes and hugged him, overwhelmed by a profound feeling of relief. 'How did you find me?'

He smiled. 'I learned this house is leased by Count

Lieven, the Russian Ambassador. He uses it to entertain his guests when they attend Ascot.'

'And the Allied Sovereigns were here to attend the races on Friday,' she exclaimed. 'It all makes sense now.'

She became aware of an incomprehensible stream of words coming from the servant who had followed Tristan into the room, a loud and voluble flow that was only stemmed when the Prince commanded him to be silent and added, with quiet dignity,

'We speak in English, Piotr, as we agreed.'

The servant bowed low. 'Your Serene Highness. A thousand apologies. I told Lord Dalmorren you were engaged, but he would not be denied. I could not hold him.'

The Prince waved him away and turned back to Tristan.

'Dalmorren?' he murmured, as if trying to place the name.

Natalya gently released herself from the safety of Tristan's arms and turned to face her host.

'Yes, your Highness. May I present to you the Nineteenth Baron Dalmorren.'

'Indeed?' The Prince's cold glance swept over them both. 'Charmed, I am sure, my lord. But now you have ascertained that the lady is unharmed, perhaps you would be kind enough to withdraw while we finish our conversation.'

Natalya reached for Tristan's hand. 'I would like him to stay. Lord Dalmorren rescued me from my abductors. I have no secrets from him.'

'Thank you, my love.' His smile warmed her. He kissed her fingers and pulled her hand on to his arm before turning back to the Prince. 'I believe, your Serene Highness, that, as her grandfather, I must apply to you for Natalya's hand in marriage.'

'My grandfather!'

The Prince inclined his head. 'It is true, Natalya. I was about to explain when Lord Dalmorren burst in so unceremoniously. Prince Mikhail Nikolayevich Borkusov was my son.'

Natalya turned to stare up at Tristan.

'You discovered this? But how?'

'My secretary was waiting in George Street for me, the day I brought you back to Bath. I had asked him to look into a possible link with the Russian Embassy. I remembered Mrs Grisham saying that Mrs Pridham had a relative working in one of the Embassies. It was a slim chance, but it made sense, when I considered your name and the fact that Pridham insisted you should take an interest in Russian events. Denham turned up several possibilities, young diplomats working in London at the time of your birth. I went to see Mrs Ancrum. What she told me sent me to London to confirm the details with Welbeck Street.'

'The Russian Embassy,' said the Prince.

Tristan shook his head. 'No. I visited the Russian church. There I was shown the records.' He looked at her. 'I found evidence of your birth, Natalya, as well as the record of your mother's death. And, more importantly for you, perhaps, your father's name. From the entry concerning their marriage.'

'M-marriage?' She gripped his arm tighter as his face swam before her eyes, then she blinked the tears away and saw he was smiling down at her.

'Yes, my darling. Elizabeth married her lover, months before you were born.'

'Then I am not...' She swallowed and turned to look at the Prince. 'I am not...'

'No, Natalya, you are my son's lawful child. My grandchild.' He stepped closer and held out one white hand. 'I have no other surviving children. You are the last of my bloodline, Natalya. I have come to take you back to Russia with me, to take your rightful place. Princess Natalya Mikhailovna Borkusova.'

Natalya is a princess!

A chill ran down Tristan's spine. The announcement should not have come as a surprise. He knew Natalya's lineage, which was how he had known where to find her, but the reality of it did not hit him until the Prince took Natalya's nerveless hand and lifted it to his lips. Only then did he understand the implications of her status.

The Prince had stepped back and was regarding them both.

'Perhaps we should all sit down and take a glass of wine.'

He rang the bell and Tristan escorted Natalya to a chair. He stood beside her, as if on guard, while a liveried servant entered, carrying a tray. When wine had been served, and the servant withdrew, he and the Prince sat down.

'Perhaps, your Serene Highness, you will tell us what your plans are for Miss—for the Princess?'

'Princess Natalya will assume her rightful place as my granddaughter and my heir with immediate effect. The Allied Sovereigns leave England for the Continent on the twenty-second of this month and we shall be in their party.'

'And what of the Pridhams?' Natalya asked him.

'You need consider them no longer.' The Prince dismissed them with a casual wave of one white hand. 'Their tenure as your guardians ended when you came of age.'

'I understand that, but the proprieties,' she pressed. 'I will need a chaperon, will I not, if I am to go into society?'

'Undoubtedly you will enter society. I have arranged it all. While we remain in England, you will join the entourage of the Grand Duchess of Oldenberg.'

Tristan's brows snapped together. 'Tsar Alexander's sister?'

'Her Imperial Highness has many ladies among her retinue. I have already appointed one who shall act as chaperon and she will accompany the Princess on our tour of Europe and afterwards back to St Petersburg.' The Prince turned to Natalya and his thin smile appeared. 'When I said you would take your rightful place, I meant it, my dear. You are beautiful, educated and accomplished, just as your father decreed you should be. I have no doubt you will be fêted at all the courts of Europe. The world will be at your feet.'

The cold icy hand squeezed even tighter around

Tristan's heart. Natalya was staring at him, her face pale. He had to stamp down the urge to cross the room and pull her up into his arms. She was beyond his reach now. As the Prince had said, she had the whole world at her feet. He forced his frozen lips into a smile and raised his glass in salute.

'Do you hear that, my dear? All your fears about your origins are unfounded. I could not be happier for you. My felicitations, madam. You have a glittering future ahead of you.'

Natalya blinked. She had never heard Tristan sound so uncaring. It shocked her. It was as if he had cut away the ground beneath her feet and she had fallen from a great height. She could not speak, could barely breathe.

The Prince continued to outline all the treats in store for her.

'We shall visit the capitals of Europe,' he announced. 'Undoubtedly, your education has been very good, but there will be omissions and these must now be addressed. I shall show you the greatest treasures and works of art Europe has to offer. You will be presented at all the royal courts and meet princes and emperors. Then I shall escort you to your new home. You must become acquainted with your country, Natalya, with your family. In St Petersburg, there will be balls in your honour. The Tsar has already expressed his wish to meet the daughter of a hero of Borodino.'

With a sob she put up her hand to stop him.

'Wait, wait. What if I do not *wish* to go to Russia?'

There was a half-beat of hesitation before the Prince

replied, 'Then you need not go. We are not savages, you will not be coerced. You are free to make your own decision.'

She looked at Tristan, but he avoided her gaze as he jumped up and walked away across the room. Silently she begged him to turn around, but he stared resolutely out of the window.

'There is no question. You must go.' He threw the words over his shoulder. 'What is there here for you? I know how much you want to travel, to see the world. You have your wish, then.'

He was speaking harshly, his voice cold, like a stranger, yet only moments earlier he had been about to ask the Prince for permission to marry her. Natalya put a hand to her head. Something was wrong.

'Your Serene Highness,' she addressed the Prince as she had heard others do. 'Would you—that is, may I have a few moments alone with Lord Dalmorren, if you please?'

'No.' Tristan turned. 'It would be most improper. Besides, there is nothing to say that Prince Borkusov cannot hear.'

'Very well.' She dug her nails into her palms until they hurt in an effort to speak calmly. 'I thought, my lord, that you wished to marry me.'

'That was when I believed you had no other option. Everything has changed. You are a princess. You have the world at your command.'

With the window behind him, she could not read his expression. But his voice was hard, devoid of all emotion.

'I do not *want* the world.'

The Prince pushed himself out of his chair and gave a small tut of displeasure. 'Now that, Natalya, is a most foolish statement. How can you know what you want until you have tried it?'

'His Serene Highness speaks the truth,' said Tristan. 'You have the opportunity to live a life of untold luxury and privilege. Your every wish will be granted.'

'No, it won't!'

She flung the words at him. Suddenly she was fighting for her life. She jumped up, frustrated by the evening sunlight that kept his face in shadow. She took a step closer.

'I thought you loved me.'

'I felt sorry for you.'

His words hit her like cold water. She stopped, throwing out an arm to grip the chair-back and steady herself.

'I d-do not believe you.'

'Oh, I think you should, my dear,' said the Prince, coming towards her. 'I understand Lord Dalmorren's dilemma. Here is a young woman, frightened, alone. Without parents or family. She is in need of protection. Any man of honour would feel the same. But now he understands that is not the case. You are not alone. You have a family and the opportunity to make a great match.' He touched her arm and said gently, 'Think of it, Princess Natalya Mikhailovna. I will take you to your homeland, you will resume your rightful place in an ancient and much-respected Romanov family. Would you reject such an honour in order to remain in England and marry a mere baron?'

Natalya looked at Tristan. He neither moved nor spoke. She tried to smile.

'Would that be so very bad?' she murmured.

'As your grandfather I could not agree to it,' the Prince announced coldly. 'My lands, my fortune, can only pass to you if you return with me to Russia and live with your family. And if you marry anyone below your own rank, then you lose the right to call yourself Princess.'

'And now I know you have family,' added Tristan, 'I cannot in honour marry you against their wishes.'

'Thank you, Lord Dalmorren.' The Prince bowed to him. 'I am relieved to hear you say so. I can now die content, knowing the Borkusov fortune will pass through my direct line. I will take the Princess to Russia with me and she will become a much-loved and respected member of my household. My own dear wife died a few years ago and it will make me happy to see my granddaughter take her place as mistress of my properties. She may have charge of it all, if she so wishes.'

'I can think of no woman more suited to take on that task, your Serene Highness.' At last Tristan came away from the window. Natalya saw how pale he was, noted the tense line of his jaw. When he turned his gaze upon her, his eyes were as cold and hard as slate. 'So. Everything is decided.'

A sudden wave of anger flared in Natalya.

'How dare you!' Her furious glare moved from one

man to the other. 'Do you think I will allow the two of you to organise my life? How dare you be so presumptuous as to think you will decide what I should do. I shall make my own choice!'

'You would be foolish beyond belief not to go with the Prince,' said Tristan harshly. 'There is nothing for you here, madam. There *is* no choice.'

Natalya looked at the two men facing her, Tristan pale and implacable, the Prince coldly confident of the outcome. Her ragged breathing steadied. She had one final card to play. She knew it might cost her everything, but suddenly she felt quite calm.

She said quietly, 'Oh, but there is a choice, my lord. I can leave England with the Prince, or I can remain here. A ruined woman.'

'I beg your pardon?' The Prince stared at her.

'Confound it, woman, say nothing more!'

She ignored Tristan's angry command and turned to her grandfather, meeting his startled gaze quite steadily.

'You may be aware, your Highness, that when Lord Dalmorren rescued me, we were obliged to stay at Farnell Hall, some miles east of Devizes.'

'Natalya, be quiet!'

'For three nights, we slept in the same room. In the same bed.'

The Prince shook his head. 'But this cannot be. My son's instructions for your upbringing were quite explicit. You were to remain unmarried, a maid, until you could be restored to your rightful station, when you would be a fitting bride for any prince in Russia.' He scowled. 'This Pridham, he wrote to me a long letter.

He assured me nothing had occurred during your absence from his house!'

'Mr Pridham wanted to engage a doctor to examine me—'

Tristan's statue-like demeanour shattered. He let out a roar.

'He did what?'

'I refused,' Natalya kept her eyes fixed on the Prince. 'I persuaded him it was not necessary. You may ask the servants at Farnell Hall if you wish. They will tell you we were Mr and Mrs Quintrell, man and wife, while we were there.' She raised her chin. 'I am no longer a maid. I gave myself to Lord Dalmorren out of love. I do not wish to marry anyone else and I doubt they will want to marry me, once they know the truth.'

The Prince turned his outraged gaze upon Tristan. 'Is this true, Lord Dalmorren?'

'We shared a room, yes.'

'And we shared a bed,' added Natalya, meeting his eyes and daring him to contradict her.

There followed a long, tense silence before Tristan exhaled sharply.

'She would hardly make up such a story...' his lips twitched '...just to marry a mere baron.'

Only then did Natalya realise she had been holding her breath.

'But you are the *Nineteenth* Baron Dalmorren,' she reminded him, smiling.

The look that passed between them was not lost on the Prince. He shook his head.

'You are more like your father than I had thought,

Natalya,' he told her, a hint of petulance in his voice. 'You will let your heart be ruled by love.'

'I will. If love will have me.' She held her hands out to Tristan. 'You see, I do not want to be a princess. I want to be a lover, a companion, to face life's challenges side by side with my mate.'

The Prince closed his eyes and gave a little shudder.

Tristan came over to her, smiling. 'Such language, my love, you are embarrassing his Serene Highness.'

'Which shows you just how far beyond redemption I am sunk!' She took his hands and held them against her breast. 'I love you, Tristan, and I will marry you, if you will have me. But if you have doubts, if you are not perfectly sure, I pray you will tell me. I am not quite destitute; I shall throw myself on Mrs Ancrum's mercy. I am sure she will take me on as her companion.'

'No need for that.' He smiled down at her, his eyes warm. 'I quite forgot to tell you, she informed me before I left that she has made you her heir.'

'There you are, then, I am not at all to be pitied and you need not feel obliged to offer for me.'

'I do not feel in the least obliged,' he muttered, pulling her close. 'I love you to distraction, my heart's darling, and I want to marry you. More than anything in this whole damned world.'

He kissed her then and for a long, long moment she forgot everything but the comfort of his embrace.

Until a cough from his Serene Highness reminded them of their surroundings.

'*Da, da*, you have convinced me that you will have

one another and I shall not stand in your way. But there are practicalities we must discuss.'

Tristan dragged his thoughts away from kissing Natalya and reluctantly raised his head. 'Practicalities? You need not concern yourself, Prince Borkusov, I will deal with everything.'

'You are marrying my granddaughter, Baron Dalmorren. It must be done correctly.'

Natalya twisted out of Tristan's arms and turned to the Prince.

'Oh, I thought you had quite cast me off.'

'My lands and fortune must remain in Russian hands. If you will not come to Russia, then I cannot make you my heir. However, you remain my granddaughter and I shall do what I can for you while I am in England.' He paused. 'Let me see. By your English calendar it is the thirteenth today. If the marriage can take place before I leave on the twenty-second I will attend and give you my blessing.'

Natalya shook her head. 'It takes three weeks for the banns to be called.'

'We might obtain a special licence,' suggested Tristan. The Prince raised an enquiring brow and he explained, 'The Archbishop of Canterbury will grant a special licence and a couple may be married wherever and whenever they wish.'

'Ah. Then you may leave that to me. I shall attend to it.'

Tristan coughed. 'I think you might find, your Highness, that I need to visit the Archbishop in person.'

The Prince waved this away with an imperious hand.

'My aide-de-camp shall arrange the whole. Natalya will be married at the embassy, as befits her rank as my granddaughter. It is not impossible that one or two of the Allied Sovereigns, perhaps even your Prince Regent, might attend. If they are not engaged elsewhere.'

'Wait, wait, I pray you,' Natalya objected. 'I have not agreed to any of this!'

The Prince looked at her, one brow raised. 'But you are desperate to marry your Baron, are you not?'

'I am *determined* to marry him,' she said. 'But—'

'Then it shall be as I say. I deplore your decision to marry beneath you, but I am a generous prince. I am a benevolent grandfather. I shall bestow upon you a handsome wedding settlement.' He glanced at the clock. 'Now. It is very late. We must have a room prepared for Lord Dalmorren tonight.' He reached for the bell, then stopped. 'No. I shall go and find Piotr myself.'

When he had left the room, Natalya and Tristan remained at a distance, looking warily at one another. Tristan was the first to break the uneasy silence.

'I never expected his Serene Highness to show so much tact.'

'Nor did I. But...'

'But what, my darling?'

She looked at him. 'Oh, Tristan, have I coerced you most dreadfully into this marriage? I never meant to do that.'

He laughed and closed the gap between them in a couple of strides.

'I love you so desperately that I would marry you

under any circumstances.' He caught her hands. 'The Russian Embassy is not where I expected to become leg-shackled, but it will do admirably. However, if you would prefer to marry in Bath, with all your friends, you must say.'

She stopped him. 'I have very few real friends, Tristan. I hope we can persuade Mrs Ancrum to travel here. There is just time for it to be arranged. But what of your family?'

'Mama is currently with my sister and—!' He broke off and raked a hand through his hair. 'Good God, Freddie! How am I going to explain to him that I have stolen you for myself?'

A little gurgle of laughter escaped her.

'You have not *stolen* me at all, my lord. Freddie was well on the way to falling out of love with me before I was abducted.' She twinkled up at him. 'The Grishams are already in town and I think, if we can persuade them to come to the wedding and to bring Jane, you will see that your nephew's affections are already turning elsewhere.'

'Truly? Then I am very relieved to hear it! As I was saying, Mama, Katherine and Freddie are currently at Frimley, which is barely thirty miles from London so they will most definitely attend.' He hesitated. 'And what of the Pridhams?'

Natalya's smile slipped a little.

'As my guardians for so many years they should be invited, although I find it hard to forgive them for telling me nothing about my origins!'

'Ah, but if Pridham had defied his instructions, I

might not have thought it necessary to come to Bath and see Freddie's mysterious Miss Fairchild.'

She looked up at him, her eyes wide with horror. 'We might never have met! Oh, Tris, it doesn't bear thinking of.'

'Then don't,' he told her, pulling her into his arms. 'Stop thinking and kiss me.'

* * * * *

*If you enjoyed this story, why not check
out these other great reads
by Sarah Mallory*

Pursued for the Viscount's Vengeance
His Countess for a Week

*And be sure to read her
Saved from Disgrace miniseries*

The Ton's Most Notorious Rake
Beauty and the Brooding Lord
The Highborn Housekeeper